The demon kissed her.

And he was still kissing her.

Tamatha backed up against the brick wall and wobbled in her pink leather heels, but he caught her about the waist with a sure and guiding hand—not breaking the incredible, shockingly hot kiss.

This man kissed her like he knew her. Had tasted her lips before. His mouth was firm and demanding, intent. Nothing about him being a demon repelled her. Everything about him made her want to get closer, dive deeper. To study him for more reasons than that he was demon. If she could run her hands over his skin, she would. She must.

She pushed her hands over his shoulders and teased the short, dark hair at the back of his neck. And then she glided up the back of his scalp and forward. Her forefingers glanced over the adamant growths at his temples she suspected were horns. Interesting. And he answered her greedy coax by dashing his tongue against hers and daring her to meet him as he deepened the kiss. Which she did.

CAPTIVATING THE WITCH

MICHELE HAUF

First Published in Great Britain 2016
By Mills & Boon, an imprint of HarperCollins*Publishers*
1 London Bridge Street, London, SE1 9GF

© 2016 Michele Hauf

ISBN: 978-0-263-92159-5

89-0116

Our policy is to use papers that are natural, renewable and recyclable products and made from wood grown in sustainable forests. The logging and manufacturing processes conform to the legal environmental regulations of the country of origin.

Printed and bound in Spain
by CPI, Barcelona

Michele Hauf has been writing romance, action-adventure and fantasy stories for more than twenty years. France, musketeers, vampires and faeries usually populate her stories. And if Michele followed the adage "write what you know," all her stories would have snow in them. Fortunately, she steps beyond her comfort zone and writes about countries and creatures she has never seen. Find her on Facebook, Twitter and at www.michelehauf.com.

Chapter 1

The evening hours in the Council's archives were indeterminable from the daylight because the vast archives were located two stories below Parisian ground and formed a labyrinth of rooms, cubbies and hallways over many acres. It was like something out of a fantasy movie with the secret passageways and mysterious decor that might suddenly open to a dark chasm so cold your breath would fog, or a dimly lit library whose ceiling soared many stories high, or instead a small Regency-styled tearoom smelling of lilacs.

And sometimes after the witching hour things started moving.

Nestled in a room filled to the industrial iron-beam rafters with dusty old tomes and spiderwebs, Tamatha Bellerose noticed the thoroughly modern fluorescent lighting flickered. Someone was either accessing a security camera or one of the biometric-scan doors. Probably her boss, Certainly Jones, was on his way to remind her—as he did at least once a week—she didn't have to work so late.

Tamatha didn't mind. Since being hired to work in the Archives three months ago, she had been in a witch's information heaven. While she had been hired for general filing and straightening, it was approved that she would spend time studying as she had mentioned that was her reason for seeking the job. Not a problem for her boss. And when Certainly had suggested she choose one of the messier storage rooms—the one housing all demonic artifacts, texts and accoutrements—she'd been thrilled.

Diabology fascinated her. Her grandmother Lysia (whom she had not the pleasure to know) had been a diabolotrist. The tales told by Tamatha's mother, Petrina Bellerose, had been enough to stir Tamatha's curiosity. She wanted to learn everything she could about demons because they were such varied and interesting creatures. And they weren't all bad, as most people assumed. Their species and assorted breeds were as numerous and diverse as the humans who walked the earth.

She'd decided to start with the demons who inhabited the mortal realm, and after she'd learned all that was available, she'd move on to those occupying Daemonia, the Place of All Demons, and then Faery, and then perhaps even Beneath. Many years of work ahead of her to master diabology. She hoped Certainly wouldn't mind if this cleanup project carried on awhile.

There wasn't much else to do in the Archives beyond dusting and looking up things when her boss requested the assistance. The Archives housed the largest collection of paranormal ephemera in the known universe. All spells and grimoires, a copy of the *Book of All Spells*, potions, objects of magical nature and even creatures of mysterious origins. Some were preserved through taxidermy or in creepy glass receptacles. Some were even stored *live*.

Beyond the label of assistant archivist, Tamatha considered herself a keeper of books and historical material that told stories about the paranormal species and shaped their origins and evolution. And that was pretty cool.

Sighing, she leaned over the centuries-old grimoire of *Basic Demonic Bindings* and took a moment to consider how lucky she was to have scored this job. It paid the bills and she got to learn. A witch couldn't ask for much more than that.

Not that she needed the money. She was quite well-off, thanks to nearly a century of wise investments. And she never got so deeply into a relationship with a man that they considered marriage, and thus, joining incomes. That way lay poverty, Tamatha believed. Her last lover, a cat shape-shifter, had been quick to suggest marriage, a combining of their lives. The familiar had been too charming, too suave. And she had fallen for his seductive spell like a cat to nip. Only, she had suddenly remembered one day, while in the midst of a sensual reverie, how much she didn't like cats. And then the family curse had seen to preventing any rash decisions she may have made regarding making the relationship permanent.

The Bellerose curse ensured the females in her family for the past three generations had bad luck with love and lovers. Relationships never lasted. Most lovers went mad. Literally. The occasional unlucky lover ended up dead.

The familiar had been run over by a car a month after suggesting he and Tamatha start a family together.

Over the decades, a few other lovers had died, but maudlin grief wasn't her style. She'd written such expected deaths off as the Bellerose curse and had moved forward. It was something she knew how to do. It was all Tamatha had ever known, for she had watched many of her mother's lovers die, as well.

"But I am hopeful," she whispered.

She was determined to never give up on love. Someday it might stick. And she strove to follow the family motto: Love Often. Yet what was generally whispered after that declaration of love was "because they never last long." Not so much a family joke as the truth.

Why she was musing over the fate of the Bellerose women's lovers was beyond her. Though her mind did tend to wander after hours bent over a book. Not that there was anything at all wrong with that. Tamatha's favorite thing in the world was to lose herself in a book. And to try out new spells.

"I want to test this binding spell," she said and tapped the handwritten text before her. "I think I've got it down. Just say the right words—*scatura, demonicus, vold*—and voilà!" Bound demon.

From there, she could ask the demon questions and study it while not having to worry it might harm her. Because the best way to learn was from the source. She preferred live studies as opposed to dusty tomes. But she had no demon friends, and none of her witch friends had close demonic contacts, either. Which was a good thing. She didn't run with witches who summoned demons to do their bidding. That was cruel.

She wondered how difficult it would be to locate a demon willing to let her bind it. She had lived in Paris only a little over a year, after moving here from Belgrade, where—well, yes, that shapeshifter affair. Her "friends" list was slowly growing, listing mostly witches, because that was who she generally trusted and understood. But there were a couple vampires and the werewolf/vampire half-breed Rhys Hawkes whom she considered her friends.

Her boss, Certainly Jones—or CJ, as he asked her to call him—was a dark witch who practiced the dark arts.

Didn't make him evil or wrong. The dark was necessary to balance the light, which was what Tamatha practiced.

Though adding diabology to her oeuvre would darken her talents. She didn't mind shadowing her aura. She aimed to be well-rounded in all magical arts, and knowledge of all aspects of witchcraft would help her to understand and relate to others much better. And as long as she avoided malefic magic, she was good with the balancing act the light and dark would work on her soul.

"Tamatha?"

She spun around from the grimoire she'd been perusing to spy CJ's dark sweep of long hair. He stuck his head between the opened door and wall. The tattoo on his neck was a ward against vampires. CJ sported dozens of tattoos and most were spells or wards.

Tamatha found a tattooed man incredibly sexy. Something about creating art on his skin to share with the world. But she would keep it professional with CJ. His wife would appreciate that.

"I'll leave soon, boss. It is after hours, and I wanted to do some studying. I found something interesting."

"It's after midnight."

"Really?" Wow, time had flown this evening. She eyed the teapot on the table, which was empty—five cups ago. "Right. I suppose I should be heading out." Not that she ever slept more than a few hours a night. "I'll be back in the morning, bright and early."

"Tomorrow is Saturday," CJ said as she gathered her purse and stepped into her high-heeled shoes, which she always slipped off when she tucked up her legs in the plush gray velvet easy chair. "I don't want to see you in here until Monday. Got that?"

She saluted him. He winked and left her to straighten the work area and turn out the lights. While her OCD magic generally took care of things in her immediate range, snapping unarranged items into order as she walked by, it worked only in close range. Mostly, humans didn't notice, and those who did, she quickly did a hands-on straighten to make it look as though she'd physically touched the object.

Swiping her hand over a sprinkling of dust on the top of a stack of books, she had to restrain herself from grabbing the feather duster. And then she couldn't resist a quick touch-up. Tapping her littlest fingers together, which activated her air magic, she blew gently over a row of books. The dust swirled and lifted and dispersed into nothing.

With a satisfied nod, she said, "Always better than manual labor. So! Midnight. And a full moon tonight. This night promises a new beginning."

Or so it had said in her horoscope that she'd read on the back of a stranger's newspaper while taking the Métro to work this morning.

"Ha! Horoscopes," she said with a laugh as she strolled down the dimly lit hallway to the elevator, her heels clicking brightly on the bare concrete floor. "I'll take real astrology any day. And that says the full moon brings family and challenge to my life."

Her only living family—her mother, Petrina—lived in Greece with her current lover. Petrina and Tamatha talked once a month. They had a great relationship. Unfortunately—or fortunately, depending on the degree of attachment—Petrina's lover was dying. Again, the curse. Her mother wasn't upset over it. Though she had mentioned something about perhaps giving him some belladonna to help him along so he didn't have to suffer.

As for the challenge the horoscope had promised… "I like a good adventure." But she wouldn't admit that adventure was hard to come by with her nose stuck in a book all day. Her life was exciting. Mostly.

Maybe.

"Hardly."

So she put a lot of focus and energy into her studies. She had mastered earth, air, water and even fire magic. The sigils tattooed on her fingers representing each of the four elements allowed for easy access to a specific elemental spell. She also practiced ornithomancy (divination by birds), alomancy (divination by salt) and pyromancy (fire divination). And her venture into diabology would eventually add demonomancy to that list. As far as witches went, Tamatha was quite powerful. But never powerful enough when the world offered so many opportunities to learn and expand her knowledge.

She stepped into the elevator and tugged at her gray pencil skirt with fingers beringed in lapis lazuli (for truth), amethyst (for grounding and balance) and bloodstone (for healing). The elevator moved laboriously up two floors. She'd left her reading glasses on, and she now tucked them into her purse. They were fabulous cat's-eye frames bespangled with rhinestones at the corners of each eye. She was into the rockabilly look and was pleased it was actually making a style comeback with the humans. Easier to fit in when she resembled others.

On the other hand, she never wanted to conform. That was for uninteresting people who didn't know themselves.

Once out of the elevator, she nodded goodbye to the hirsute night guard, who she suspected was a werewolf, but he never seemed to want to converse, barely looking up from his handheld television as she passed and never offering a vocal "*au revoir*" or even a confirming nod.

Ah well, she couldn't befriend them all. And he was a shapeshifter, so yeah, nix that.

Located on the Right Bank in the 11th arrondissement, the Council headquarters opened into a dreary alleyway that was far from parking or any Métro station. Out of the way and unassuming. Tamatha could do without the ten-minute walk to the closest subway. She lived across the river in the 6th, near the Luxembourg Gardens. It was a fine walk on a sunny day, when she remembered to bring along walking flats. Not tonight, though, with the promise of rain thickening the air.

Muttering the words to the demon binding spell, she delighted in how easily she remembered things like Latin spells or even long ingredient lists for poultices and charms. If only her luck with men could be so simple and long lasting.

The curious thing about the family curse was that no one was really sure how it had originated, nor had anyone tried to vanquish it. Sure, the Bellerose women were independent and much preferred lovers to a more permanent husband. But Tamatha had already had her share of lost lovers since she'd started dating in her late teens in the 1930s. She was ready for some permanence. For a good old-fashioned love affair that might result in something more promising than death to the male party.

Warm summer raindrops spattered her cheek and she picked up into a sort-of run. The fastest she could manage in four-inch heels and with a tight skirt was a penguin waddle.

Touching her middle fingers together to ask for a rain-parting spell, she dodged left into a cobblestoned alleyway she knew was sheltered with close-spaced roof ledges—and she ran right into a man. He had been walking swiftly as well, and when they collided he let out an "ouff" and gripped her by the shoulders.

The first thing Tamatha noticed in the moon-shielded darkness was the glint of something shiny and black at his temples, beneath the hairline, and the barest scent of sulfur. Demon? A brief red glow ignited in his eyes.

She reacted. *"Scatura, demonicus, vold!"*

"Wait—"

It was too late for his protest. The man dropped her, his arms slapping to his sides and his body going rigid. He wore half gloves on his hands, and his exposed fingers crooked into ridged claws. His feet stiffened within his boots and he teetered, falling backward, his shoulders and head hitting the brick wall of the building but a foot behind him.

His eyes glowed red and he growled at her through tight jaws. "Witch!"

Chapter 2

Edamite Thrash had been minding his own business, racing against the rain to get home, when he collided with a deliciously scented female with skin like ivory, hair the color of silvered snow and wide green eyes. It was as if entering another realm when he'd touched her and she had surrounded him with citrus, sensuality and softness, and then—

Damn it. He couldn't move his limbs. And his veins felt as if ice flowed through them. The chill was moving down his thighs and toward his calves. Every muscle strung tightly. The witch had bound him.

"Get this…off me," he hissed, thankful he could still speak. Though he clenched his jaw tighter. And his body leaned against the wall. How soon before his boots would slide on the wet pavement and he toppled? "Damn you! Witch!"

"Oh my goddess, it really worked!" she said with more enthusiasm than he thought appropriate.

The witch peered into his eyes as if looking for something she'd lost. Even in the darkness her giddy thrill showed in the gemstone gleam of her gaze. Stepping back, she looked him up and down. From the top of his slicked-back black hair, down his black suit and trousers, to his leather boots. Ed had never felt more humiliated. So inadequate. If he could lift a hand he would make her regret it. In his trouser pocket he felt his mobile phone vibrate. No one would call him at his private number unless it was important.

"I've always wanted to bind a demon," she offered with a gleeful clasp of hands before her. Many crystal rings flashed in the moonlight and he noted the small tattoos on the midjoints of each of her fingers. Sigils of some sort. Nasty witch business, no doubt. "And I did it!"

"Against my will," he snarled. "Take this binding… off me, or…" To make the sounds leave his mouth was a monumental task. "I will kill you, witch!"

Her happiness flattened to curious concern as she tilted her head and tapped her lower lip. A plump pink lip that looked all too tempting even in his bound, defenseless state.

What was he thinking? Witches were disgusting.

"You actually think that threatening to kill me will convince me to release you?" she prompted.

Probably not. But he'd been speaking reactively not rationally.

"Fine. Please, witch—" Oh, how he hated to condescend to her sort.

"My name is Tamatha." She offered her hand to shake, and when he could but look at it, a pitiful statue tilted against the wall, she dropped her hand. "Sorry. My bad. I learned the demon binding spell this evening. Must be the full moon. It's magical, isn't it?"

Ed inhaled a deep breath to calm his anger. He had to do something if he was going to talk his way out of this one. "How about I promise not to harm a hair on your witchy head if you remove the binding? I mean, what are you going to do with a stiff demon anyway?"

Her lips curled to an expectant smirk, and her eyes brightened as they strolled down the front of his torso to *just there*.

And Ed realized what he'd said. Really? Her mind went *there*? Well, he could entertain a few lascivious thoughts about those lips— No! This situation was embarrassing and ridiculous. And never would he entertain anything with a witch. Been there, done that. Learned his lesson well.

"Please, Tamatha?" Right, appeal to her personally. Befriend the enemy.

"Before I release the binding, tell me your name," she entreated, "and what breed of demon you are. I'm studying diabology. I'm very interested in your species."

Yikes. The woman was some kind of fangirl. That creeped him out. Just his luck with women, though. They either wanted to marvel over his oddities or run screaming from them.

"If I give you my name, you've control over me," he said tightly. His jaw muscles felt like stretched iron. "Not going to happen."

"Oh, but I— Oh, yes, I see what you mean. Witches can control demons with their full names. Could you maybe tell me what kind of demon you are? I'll release you then. Cross my heart."

The gesture of crossing her heart disturbed Ed. He would have flinched if he wasn't bound. He'd once been told about the witch's crossed heart but couldn't recall what it meant. A wicked gesture with malefic intent?

He didn't want to give her anything, but her knowing his breed wasn't going to hurt him any more than this wicked chill icing his veins. "Corax demon," he said. And then, to keep it light and perhaps her mood light as well, he offered, "Such fortune that I run into a witch who is practicing her spells this ugly moonlit night."

"Oh, it's not ugly out. You think it is? Rain is cleansing and it washes away the icky city smells."

"What I think is that we are done conversing. The cold." It took all his effort to curl his fingers upward into an ineffectual claw. "It's icing in my veins."

"Oh! Really? That must be a side effect of the spell. Yes, I think I recall the binding, if left on too long, will paralyze. There was also the side effect of chilblains, headaches and possible extended, er—" Her eyes dropped to his crotch again.

Ed gritted his jaws. Really? His cock *was* hard, now he noticed. Even more humiliation. Gorgeous as she was, this chick was one wacky witch. Who smelled like something he wanted to bury his nose in and suck down whole— damn it!

"*Vold, demonicis, scaratus,*" she recited.

With but a sweep of her hand before his chest, the chill exited Ed's veins downward, seeming to sluice out the soles of his boots. His shoulders relaxed, as did his legs. He started to go down. The witch reached to help him, and in her sudden panic, she grabbed him by the head. Her palms slapped warmly against his temples. The horn nubs that jutted up but millimeters through his hair heated and glowed beneath her touch.

He never let anyone touch his horns. Mercy, but that felt too good. The contact provided enough energy transfer to allow him to straighten his legs and catch himself before sprawling on the ground.

Coming upright before her, he matched her height, which was a surprise, but then he decided she must have been wearing high heels. Excellent. That would make it difficult for her to run when he strangled her.

Ed gripped her by the neck, squeezing as hard as his anger would allow him to squeeze, and—

The demon kissed her.

When Tamatha had expected him to hit her, to bruise her with his terrible clutch about her neck in retaliation for the binding she'd put on him, he instead…kissed her.

And he was still kissing her.

Her pink leather shoe heels backed up against the brick wall and she wobbled, but he caught her about the waist with a sure and guiding hand, not breaking the incredible, shockingly hot kiss.

This kiss was the furthest thing from retaliation. So she surrendered to the weird moment and even forgot about the rain spell, reveling in the spill of warm summer rain down her neck and cheeks.

This man kissed her as if he knew her. Had tasted her lips before. His mouth was firm and demanding, intent. Nothing about him being a demon repelled her. Everything about him made her want to get closer, dive deeper and seek his insides. To study him for more reason than that he was demon. If she could run her hands over his skin, she would. She must.

She dropped her shoulder bag and pushed her hands over his shoulders and teased the short, dark hair at the back of his neck, gripping it to hold him at her mouth. And then she glided up the back of his scalp and forward. Her forefingers glanced over the adamant growths at his temples she suspected were horns. Interesting. And he answered her greedy coax by dashing his tongue against hers and daring her to meet him as he deepened the kiss. Which she did.

The sulfur she'd originally scented was no longer noticeable. The crisp, cool tang of his aftershave filled her senses with ice and cedar. She would never forget this man's scent.

What *was* his name? Sure, she could control him with his name, but she wouldn't. Maybe. The binding had been an unintended reaction. But what joy that it had worked! Of course, then he had called her a witch with such vitriol she had tasted his hatred for her as if it were acid on her tongue.

If he would stop kissing her she could step back and be wary.

On the other hand, right now, lack of wariness suited her fine.

He muttered an appreciative moan against her mouth, and then as suddenly as he'd kissed her, he pulled away and wiped his lips. "Wha—?" He winced and shook his head. "What the hell? Why did I...? I did not just kiss a witch."

"Uh, yes, you did. And it was awesome."

"Not awesome. No! Witches are...vile." Again he wiped his lips, and Tamatha cringed. He admonished her with a wagging finger before her face. "You made me do that."

"No, I—"

He snapped his fingers, abruptly cutting her off as if she were a child being scolded by a rude teacher. "If you want to keep breathing, stay away from me, witch."

And he stalked off, glancing over his shoulder at her once. He slapped his hand against a thigh, tugging a phone out of his pocket, and stomped away.

Tamatha offered a wave. Silly. And stupid. He'd been offended by kissing her? She hadn't made him do a thing. He'd wanted to kiss her.

Vile?

"Not so pleased about kissing you, either," she muttered.

But she couldn't quite bring herself to wipe off his kiss. Instead, she tapped her mouth and decided to stick with the good memory of his demanding and sensual lips against hers.

"I kissed a demon," she said in wonder. And for as much as he had been repulsed, she could not summon a tendril of disgust. A smile curled her rain-sprinkled lips. "And I liked it."

He clicked to answer the ringing cell phone as he stalked away from the repulsive witch. She had tasted—well, not vile, but rather sweet. Though he'd not admit that out loud.

"Thrash! You gotta help. They're getting closer. I can't get out of here!"

It was his friend Laurent LaVolliere, a fellow demon whom he considered family, for their grand-relations had once formed the Libre denizen centuries earlier here in the very heart of Paris. Laurent sounded out of breath and frightened. The man was a strife demon; it took a lot to frighten him.

"Tell me where you are, Laurent."

"The Montparnasse!"

"Where in…the cemetery?"

"Their skin… Ed, it's falling from their faces. And… stuff is oozing from their mouths. There's so many of them. I can feel their dark magic. So…powerful. I can't move!"

The terror in his friend's voice sent a shiver down his spine. "I'll be right there. Hold on."

Ed shoved the phone into his pocket. Yet something compelled him to glance over his shoulder. The witch was nowhere to be seen. Talk about tormenting demons under the full moon.

But he couldn't bother with a silly witch and that ridiculously hot kiss. Laurent was in trouble.

He spread back his arms and tilted back his head. The sensation of feathered barbs piercing his flesh always hurt like a mother. The price he had to pay for shifting. His molecules rearranged and did their own thing and his form separated into dozens of soot-winged ravens. As one entity the conspiracy of ravens swooped upward and soared in the direction of the cemetery. Beyond a vast city garden, the graveyard marked a dark blot amid the roofed and pavement-tangled city.

When he came to human form with a shiver of his body to gather in his energy and shake off a feather or two, he stood in a dark graveyard packed with tombstones, mausoleums, crumbling stone crosses and moss-frosted angels. Fully clothed, a phenomenon beyond his explanation, he wore no trace of his previous form. He could smell the anomaly immediately and felt its presence as a tightening in his horn nubs. And the witch ward on his forearm burned as it had not previously in the alley.

When his eyes landed on the band of growling creatures—who were wrapped in shredded linens, some of their hair gone and skin indeed falling away from some of their bones—he heard his friend's scream. And witnessed his destruction.

Laurent let out one agonizing shout at sight of Ed: *"Les Douze!"* Then his body was torn away at shoulders, hips and head. His remains did not immediately ash as with most demon deaths.

One of the hideous creatures sighted Ed. He reactively sent a stream of energy mined from his vita, his very life force, toward it, which manifested as black smoke, enforced with demonic magic. The force should knock it from its feet and slam it into the nearby tombstone, breaking its body and killing it. The current of black energy coiled about the creature. Instead of succumbing to defeat, the zombielike thing merely swayed as if an annoying breeze had washed over its decrepit structure.

The rest of the creatures spied Ed. The one next to the thing that had taken his energy zap as if a mosquito sting dropped Laurent's disembodied arm and growled at him. One opened its mouth and the lower jaw unhinged.

"Didn't think zombies existed," he hissed.

Zombies were not tops on his list. He never watched the popular television show because they were so unbelievable. The dead did not come back to life. Right?

The group of things—whatever they were—groaned and stalked toward him.

Ed knew when he was overwhelmed, and he was going to count his lacking ability to put the one off its feet to lingering remnants of the sexy witch's binding spell.

"Find your rest, Laurent!" he shouted, then shifted to a conspiracy and flew out of there and back to his home, where he landed on the rooftop, fell to his knees and caught his palms on the concrete surface.

It was raining harder, and he prayed no lightning snapped the sky. Lightning worked like an electrical jolt to his bones, no matter how distant the occurrence.

Shifting into and out of his humanlike demon form took a lot out of him. He rarely utilized the skill because he could generally get where he needed to go by car or on foot. He'd be exhausted for hours now. But he was safe at home. Safe from...

"What the hell killed my friend?"

Chapter 3

Les Douze was French for The Twelve. And something about that moniker rang a bell in Ed's memory. Perhaps he and Laurent had discussed it once? But why, and what did it mean?

After searching for hours through the database his office maintained—hacked from Hawkes Associates—Ed learned The Twelve had been a coven of witches from the eighteenth century who had been accused of witchcraft by the locals and burned to death in the Place de Grève, which was now the Place de l'Hôtel de Ville, or city hall. A remarkable and grisly event that the human Parisians had talked about for decades and the real witches would never forget.

That verified what Ed suspected. He rubbed the small, solid black circle sigil on his forearm that had burned when he'd first landed in the cemetery. Indeed, those creatures had been witches. But what sort? Witches were generally *alive*. Not even generally, but rather, exclusively.

Those things after Laurent had been remarkably zombie-like. With skin falling from their limbs, their only audible sounds had been grunts and groans. Strange, metallic gray stuff had oozed from their mouths. But really? Had *dead* witches killed Laurent?

"But *Les Douze* were burned," he muttered, closing his laptop and leaning back in his office chair. "They were reduced to ashes. Things don't come back from the dead. Not usually."

He'd heard the rumor about a tribe of revenant vampires who had been resurrected from the dead. And sure, he guessed dark magic could bring anything back to life. A dark witch or warlock could conjure such a monstrosity. But it would be a real zombie. Zombies were shambling bone sacks. Their brains had to be degraded or completely gone. A revenant could not feasibly survive for long.

As far as he knew.

Ed wasn't up on zombies and dead things. He didn't want to be, either. But he had watched his friend get torn, literally, limb from limb. He couldn't ignore that horrific incident. And no doubt, Laurent had tried to communicate something about *Les Douze*.

The office was quiet and vast. Black marble stretched the floor and up all the walls. It was peaceful here six floors above the big bustling city. Sometimes too peaceful. But then again, something always happened to shake him to the core and exercise his diplomacy and survival skills. Like impossible zombie witches killing his friend.

Thinking about witches made Ed shudder. Demons and witches had a strange and volatile relationship. Most witches could not control a demon unless they had originally summoned that demon. Likewise, demons hadn't much control over witches. But the most powerful witches could control demons and use them for nefarious means.

Every demon child was told scary tales at bedtime, and Ed's mother had loved to frighten him with tales of wicked witches.

There's nothing you can do to outrun them. He recalled the creepy, dramatic voice of his mother, Sophie, as she'd lean over the bed and speak to the sheet he'd pulled over his head in fright. *If you ever see a witch, Edamite, run!*

Of course, then his mother would laugh and leave him shivering in bed, wishing his father were actually married to his mother and living with them so he could run to him for a sympathetic hug. It hadn't been that his mother was vindictive. Ed guessed she simply never realized how those tales had freaked out her son.

Unfortunately, such childhood frights had not completely warned him off witches. He'd dated two. Two too many.

The first had been flighty and fascinated by his demonic nature, yet had only lasted so long as he could endure her silly human propensity to gossip, shop and text, text and text some more. The second had tried to enslave him and had come so close that he'd felt her power strip him of his innate magical defenses. It had been three days of relentless torture he would never forget.

But he was a grown man now. He was a high-ranked demon in the city of Paris, thanks to his not showing fear in the face of challenge and his tendency to take charge and get things done. He was respected and revered by his kind. And witches should walk a wide circle around him.

Not kiss him.

You were the one who kissed her.

Funny thing, that. She must have used magic to get him to lock lips with her. Why she would do that was beyond him. Must have been a distraction so he wouldn't strangle her in retaliation for the binding. Weird way to go about shifting the balance of power. And how had she, a witch, controlled him when she had not summoned him?

"She must have great power," he muttered.

But did it matter? He should not give another moment's consideration to a pretty witch with wide green eyes and soft lips, whose derriere had wiggled teasingly in her tight skirt. He'd learned his lesson. Witches could never be trusted.

There were more important things on the table now.

Some very powerful magic had been present in that cemetery. It had torn Laurent apart. As well, he'd felt the air crackle with the unseen magic. A force greater than the creatures he'd witnessed, perhaps? He wielded demonic magic, but if the tales of demon/witch relations were accurate, it was never effective against witches for long. And he suspected his ability to use magic against witches had irrevocably weakened, thanks to his ill-fated romance with Witch Number Two.

Yet, if it were witches, he was going to need some powerful magic to figure this out. At the very least, provide him with answers, perhaps some suggestions as to how to approach the creatures he had seen.

Had Laurent's death been a bizarre but singular event? Did he have to kill them? How to kill them? Only another witch's magic might serve the killing blow.

Could he lower himself to work with a witch? There must be someone else who could tell him about witch magic. The werewolves and vampires Ed called allies likely wouldn't know much. He considered contacting John Malcolm, the exorcist he kept on his payroll. The man was more versed in demons and ghosts. Though he had begun dabbling in witch finding. It was a medieval, yet very necessary, practice that few specialized in nowadays.

Ah hell. He'd give it a go and contact a witch. For Laurent's sake. The man had been a good friend; he deserved the investigation, if not downright vengeance. And Ed would rather jump into a situation with a knowledgeable enemy than wait for a less informed ally to wander along and half ass the situation.

He pulled out his phone and dialed Inego, one of his field assistants. "I need you to find the most powerful witch in Paris," he said. "Bring John Malcolm along."

"The nutty one with the crazy eyes? Isn't he an exorcist?" Inego asked.

"Yes, but he's added witch finding to his oeuvre. He should be able to track one for you."

Tamatha had encountered a corax demon. She wrote the term in her purple-glitter-covered notebook and underlined it. The breed was related, somehow, to the *Corvus corax* species of ravens. Perhaps the demon could shift to raven form? Many demons possessed shifting abilities. She'd have to look it up when she got to work on Monday.

What she did know was that the breed could be very grumpy following a kiss. And not at all friendly. She wasn't going to write about the kiss in her notes, though.

She set the notebook aside and it automatically straightened on the bench to align with the painted brown wood. She pulled out from her purse a pair of black rhinestone-bespangled sunglasses. The high sun warmed the Luxembourg Gardens today. The air smelled green and alive. A nearby pear tree scented the air sweetly. Yet she wished she were inside, two stories belowground, sorting through dusty pages in the archives.

But she would follow her boss's suggestion that she not return to work until Monday. Perhaps a relaxing weekend was needed. So to put herself in the vacation mood, she had given herself a mani/pedi this morning. The gray, sparkly polish glinted in the sunlight and went well with the silver rings she wore and her hair. She'd got her silver hair from her mother, whose shade had been slightly darker and tinted blue. Petrina had told her Grandma Lysia's had been blue-black.

The park wasn't as crowded as she'd expect on a sunny day. It was early yet and most were probably at home eating breakfast, save for a few mothers and their children scattered around the pond tracking sailboats.

Tamatha worshipped nature and was pleased she'd found a place to live so close to this lush garden escape. The few people who did wander about also soaked in the sunshine. When had the Parisian men started wearing such tight, brightly colored pants? Not at all garish, the style showed off some nice thighs and well-shaped derrieres. Had she really been away from the dating scene for so long? She preferred a stylish, gentlemanly look, groomed hair and maybe some stubble and a mustache.

"And tattoos," she said with a smile.

She had many. Some were spell tattoos; others were personal, such as the Bellerose family crest she wore on her right biceps. It featured a bell-shaped pink rose surrounded by black and gray shaded arabesques, and the family motto Love Often was inked in Latin—*Amor Modum Saepe*.

She recalled the corax demon had tattoos on his neck. A vampire ward similar to the one she wore in white ink (more discreet). And the backs of his hands had been virtually blackened with ink, though maybe that had been the black leather half gloves creating the effect; she'd looked so quickly. That was the only body art she had noticed because he'd worn a suit and buttoned-up gray dress shirt, which had given him a *GQ*-with-an-edge look. And his black hair and brows had drawn her focus to his pale gray eyes.

Eyes that had briefly glowed red. She wondered now

if the glow was something that happened without his volition. Was it controlled by emotion? Anger? Reaction to
surroundings? Instinct? Was he aware when they turned
red? All of the above?

So many questions and so many books to read to learn
the answers. The prospect of research thrilled her.

She smoothed a hand over the volume on European
demon breeds she'd taken from the Archives, thinking
reading was pleasurable, but an afternoon sitting across
a café table from a sexy demon, asking him anything and
everything she wanted to know, would prove more desir-
able. Gazing into his eyes. Drawing in that interesting icy
cedar scent…

Tamatha straightened abruptly and slammed the book
shut. "You do not have a thing for him," she admonished.
"He called you vile."

The guy must harbor the age-old hang-up most demons
had toward witches. She thought it silly. But some habits
died hard. And she knew more than many witches who still
avoided vampires because the longtooths possessed the
ability to steal a witch's power through bloodsexmagic—
biting, and draining them of magic while they had sex.
Ugh. Nothing sexy about that scenario whatsoever.

She had never dated a vampire and generally preferred
human men. They were easy enough to figure out. Though
she never got too serious. The family curse and all. While
she'd never been directly responsible for a death, there
had been that time she'd mixed magics and a windstorm
had uprooted a tree and sent a branch straight through her
lover's heart. He'd hit her once, and she'd feared him every
time he'd walked through her door. Had he got what he deserved? It wasn't for her to judge, but certainly she hadn't
cried over his death.

What she wanted was a challenge, someone to seduce and stimulate not only her mind, but her body, as well.

"I don't even know his name," she whispered, then sighed again. Chasing the mysteriously sexy demon out of her head was proving impossible. Ah well, a little daydreaming never hurt anyone.

Nearby the octagon pond, Tamatha heard a splash. She saw two feet upend over the edge of the pond and a sailboat bobbled frantically. A child had fallen?

Heartbeats thundering, she reactively touched her middle fingers together to activate her water magic and whispered a controlling spell. A *whoosh* like a tidal wave curved toward the pond shore, spitting the kid back onto the pebbled ground. A mother shrieked and rushed for her soaked child.

And Tamatha exhaled with relief. "Whew."

Chapter 4

Ed looked up from his laptop to see Inego and Glitch forcing a squirming, struggling—bound—woman into his office. A plastic grocery sack hung over her head, though the long silver-white hair that he recognized so well spilled out beyond her shoulders.

"What the—?" He marched up and pulled the bag from her head.

"You?" she gasped. Lifting her bound hands, the fingers of which having been completely wrapped up with thin white cording, she asked, "What in all the moons?"

"What is the meaning of this?" he asked Inego (of the twosome, the one who he suspected had more brains). "I asked you to bring me the most powerful witch in Paris."

"She's it, boss. We saw her save a boy in the park. Didn't even have to twitch her nose to do it, either."

"Did John verify it?"

"Yep. He picked her out before that happened. Said his

witchy radar was going off the scale and told us to check her out."

Ed stepped back from the witch and noticed she looked as surprised as he. Though that could have something to do with the ropes and the rough treatment she must have received when brought here. If John Malcolm had verified her power, then it was possible. He'd had no idea she was so powerful.

On the other hand, she had bound him with nothing more than a few words.

Well, well. This could get interesting. If not…uncomfortable.

"What are you up to?" she asked. "I thought you hated witches. Called us vile."

Indeed he had. Not the best way to start a working relationship, but he could manage. "I needed to speak to you," he said. Could he really do this? *Did* he need a witch? Especially one so distracting as this one?

"So you—you kidnapped me?"

"This is not a kidnapping."

Though when she shook her bound hands between them and gave him an incredulous gape, he couldn't deny it did look nefarious, if not downright cruel.

"Now you know what it feels like," he said reactively. "To be bound."

Her jaw dropped, stupefied. He couldn't help a vainglorious smile. So he wasn't keen on condescending to her sympathies. The witch had bound him. And it had hurt like hell.

To his men he said, "I didn't tell you to tie her up. I just asked you to bring her to me."

"She's a witch, boss. We had to tie her up or she'd put a spell on us. Malcolm told us the marks on her fingers cast spells if she can use her hands."

Ed considered that one and conceded with a nod. "True. Good call, men."

"Oh, I am so out of here." The witch backed away, bound hands beating the air with her words. "Most powerful? Maybe. Most pissed off? You better believe it."

Glitch rushed to grab her by the arm and she struggled, kicking her high-heeled shoe and landing the pointed toe on his thigh. Yikes. That had to hurt. Glitch yowled and hobbled off, clutching his wound. Inego grabbed her other arm.

"Enough!" The minions glanced to Ed.

The witch pleaded with her thrust-up hands. "I can still throw magic with my hands bound. But I'll be much more compelled to listen if you treat me with respect."

Indeed. But could he trust her? She'd once already used witchcraft to soften his anger and make him kiss her. Her mouth was a pretty pale pink today. And those eyes. Had he ever gazed into such vivid green eyes? There were things in them. Mystery. Adventures. Worlds.

Hell. No. He wasn't gazing.

"I'll count to three," the witch threatened. "Then I'm bringing out the big magic."

"Boss?" Glitch asked on a worried wobble.

"What kind of minions are you?" Ed said to them. "You're frightened of one little witch? You managed to get her here without taking harm."

"I'm going to have a bruise," Glitch whined and clutched his thigh.

"Where did I find you two?" Ed muttered, pacing before the threesome.

Right. He'd rescued the dastardly duo from exile to Daemonia after both had been caught with their proverbial fingers in the cookie jar. Working a V-hub and selling vampire blood to their fellow demons. They were two stupid lunks who had needed direction and a purpose. Which he was trying to give them.

And the best way to lead was by example.

Ed thrust out some minor magic in a black curl of smoke that melted the ropes bound about the witch's hands. "My men should not have been so cruel. I apologize."

"Yeah? Too little, too late, buster. This is nuts!" She turned and marched out of his office, the tight skirt she wore luring his gaze to the sensual wiggle beneath the pale green fabric. Yeah, so gazing was good. Real good.

Inego and Glitch cast him wondering stares, which blew his gaze off course.

"Idiots," Ed hissed. He strode after the pissed-off witch. What was her name? "Tamatha!"

Instead of turning right to go down the hallway to the elevator, she'd unknowingly taken a left and now stood like a captive doe before the wall where his secretary normally sat. At least the secretary was spared this scene, though. She was out having a baby demon that could very likely be born with scales, thanks to her affair with a dragon shifter.

"I'm so sorry." Ed walked up to her and tried to put his hands on her shoulders to calm her, but she slapped at his wrists and hands. "Tamatha, please, I want to talk to you."

"They put a freakin' plastic bag over my head!"

He managed to pin one of her shoulders against the wall and worked to wrangle her opposite wrist, to calm her, to make her listen to him. And to be prepared should she try to fling more magic his way.

"I could have suffocated!"

Indeed, he had best give more detailed instructions next time he sent his men after such a pretty, delicate creature who— "Ouch!"

Pressing his forehead to the wall beside her head, he rode out the pain of a direct hit from her pointy-toed shoe to his shin. Damn, those things were sharp! He was probably bleeding. He didn't want to risk looking because he still had her in a loose but compliant hold.

"Sorry," she said softly. "I didn't mean to hurt you. I'm not cruel. But you bring up my defensive instincts."

When her hand stroked over his cheek and temple, a wave of strange desire shivered through his system.

"Tamatha," he gasped. A lush tide of delicious warmth overtook his muscles and his body melted against hers. He could not…resist. "Oh, goodness and light."

Bracketing her face with his hands, he kissed her like he'd never kissed a woman before. Sweetly. Reverently. With such a longing that it must have shown all over his skin in the shivers he felt riding the tattooed surface. Her breath spilled over his lips and entered his pores. Her aura of lemon perfume surrounded him with a sticky sweet allure.

He was falling, succumbing, slipping into a strange kind of submission…

Realizing he was once again kissing the witch, Ed abruptly broke the connection. "Ah hell." He looked at his hands, still gently bracketing her face. And there, on her face, the glint in her eye as the curve of a smile tickled onto her perfect lips. "What did you do to me?"

"Me? You're the one who keeps kissing me. I didn't do a thing but get kidnapped and roughed up by your henchmen. And then you pressed me up against the wall and had your way with me." She cast her glance aside. "Not that there was anything wrong with your way. Which is why I haven't wielded magic against you. Yet."

"I believe I should be thankful for that. Why is it every time I see you I want to…to…?"

"Hurt me?"

"I don't hurt women. I just want to—" he made a mo-tion to shove but curved his fingers away from touching her "—push you away. Witches are vile."

"So you've said. Repeatedly. Great way to kill the mood, buddy." She shoved his chest, but he didn't step away from her.

"Yes, but if you are so repulsive, then why do I end up kissing you every time we meet?"

She tilted her head and tapped a finger on her lips. Those luscious, sweet, soft lips demanded more thorough attention. And so he would see to it they had it.

Ed again kissed her, this time pushing his hands through her hair and caressing the softness that spilled over her shoulders in waves of unnatural silver. Goddess hair, he thought. Not of this realm. He pressed his body along hers. To feel her, to take her all in…

"Ahem," she muttered against his mouth, and he sensed her need to push him away, when all he wanted to do was get closer than close. Inside her. Intimately. Her gaze veered over his shoulder and to the door of his office.

Ed glanced around behind him. Glitch stood in the doorway, observing with a smirk and dancing gaze. The idiot didn't need to say a thing.

What luck that the most powerful witch in Paris was also one who attracted him like no other and promised to give him dreams that would keep any sane man begging for more. She was a witch, but she wasn't one of those nasty witches his mother had warned him about. She couldn't be.

But then, that was the same thing he'd thought about Witch Number Two before she'd tried to enslave him.

Ed gripped Tamatha by the wrist and pulled her toward the office, but she planted her feet and tugged.

"We need to talk," he said hastily.

"I'm not going in there with those creeps leering at me. A plastic bag," she reiterated. "Seriously!"

Releasing his hold on the stubborn witch, Ed gestured toward the idiots. "Leave. Go do...that thing I needed you to do."

"What thing, boss—?"

Inego shoved his partner out of the doorway. "You know, that *thing*. Sure, boss. We're out of here."

"There is no thing," Glitch argued as they strolled down the hallway.

Exasperated by his employees' incompetence, Ed pushed his hands over his hair, and then remembering his guest, he took a moment to vacillate on what he was about to do. Make nice. With a witch. Because he needed one.

First, he had to determine if he could trust her.

He gestured to Tamatha that she enter his office. "Please?"

With an impertinent lift of her chin, she strode through the doors, quickening her pace as she passed him and walking to the center of the black marble floor that stretched far too long to his desk. This office was too large and ostentatious, but he'd got the rental for a steal because a mass murder had taken place in it a few years ago. He had sensed the malefic vibrations in the air—and still did on occasion—and he'd had it smudged more than a few times, but that never seemed to clear the negative energies.

"I don't know your name," she said. "You know mine. Tamatha Bellerose."

"Bellerose," he repeated, but didn't recognize the surname. "Pretty, like its owner. My name is Edamite. You can call me Ed."

"Edamite? I've never heard that form of the name before. I would say 'glad to meet you, Ed,' but I'm not terribly thrilled about this situation." She cast her gaze about the room, briefly noting the few items displayed on the wall. "Generally my dates are a bit less...kidnappy."

She shivered and embraced herself. The blouse she wore

was a sheer, filmy black thing that showed a glimpse of the black lace bra beneath. And on her arms, beneath the sheer black, he made out a tattoo, but couldn't remark its design. Smaller symbols had been inked on the midsection of each of her fingers. Spell tats, no doubt. And there at her neck was a white ink symbol he recognized. A vampire ward. Smart witch.

He rubbed his forearm where beneath the shirt was the witch ward. It usually tingled when a witch was near. And it did now. But why hadn't it when he'd run into her the other night?

"Cold?" He passed her by and walked to his desk, intent on maintaining his calm and not rushing over to steal her into his embrace and devour her again. What was up with that? He was not lusting over a witch. That way lay trouble.

"Something awful happened in this room," she said, her gaze still taking the area in. "Have you smudged the place?"

"Half a dozen times. Never seems to chase away whatever morbid stuff remains. I've given up on trying."

"I could do it for you and it would work. Whoever has smudged it previously wasn't bleeding into the very pores of the stone beneath our feet. Earth magic is required. Murders," she said suddenly and with knowing. "I don't want to stay in this room much longer."

"Okay, fine, Tamatha, but give me two minutes, please?"

"If that's how long it will take for you to explain why you had me kidnapped, then…go."

"It wasn't a—" Ed surrendered the argument with an exhalation. "My men are assholes. I apologize for their ineptitude. To get to the point…" He spread out his hands before him. "I need a witch."

He didn't know if he could trust her yet. What was he

saying? Why hadn't he a plan? Damn, she was so gorgeous. He'd say anything to have another kiss.

Really?

"Well, well." She lifted her chin and assumed a haughty pose, which was made all the more attractive by the tight skirt and slender gams and that curly goddess hair that Ed could still feel crushed between his fingers.

"Well, well, what?" he asked.

"I'm studying diabology and demonomancy. It so happens I need a demon."

"You mean to study? To put under a microscope and observe?"

"Oh, not like that. Maybe a little. Textbooks and dusty old grimoires are excellent resources for learning, but I'm more of a hands-on kind of girl. I would love to have a demon to talk to and ask questions. Learn things."

He smoothed a palm over his hair. She was annoying and she was appealing. And he wasn't sure which side was going to win out, but she was the only witch he had right now. And apparently a powerful one. He wanted to play her carefully, lest he became one of those demons from his mother's faery tales. They had never survived to the end of the story.

"I don't do the bug-under-the-microscope thing," he offered.

"You want a powerful witch? You gotta bargain, buddy."

So that was the way of it? The magic he'd felt filling the atmosphere in the Montparnasse cemetery had been incredible. Immense. He needed dark magic to fight it, but more likely, light magic to win against it. And Tamatha looked like a witch of the Light.

"*Are* you a witch of the Light?"

She nodded. "Mostly."

Well, she was honest. And her hair spilled like liquid

silver over her shoulders. It was gorgeous— Ah! He had to focus.

"You said you are studying demonomancy? That's controlling demons. How do I know you won't try to control me? Er...*again*."

"I'd never do such a thing. I've never summoned a demon, either. It's wrong to exert your control over others."

He lifted a brow at that one.

She shrugged. "Well, you know, I have to practice my spells. The binding was a reaction."

"So you said. But it was an exertion of control."

"Guilty. I do have a thing for keeping things orderly, which I've been told is also a means of control." She glanced around the room. "I'd show you my OCD magic, but this place is spotless. Too cold."

Yes, yes, so he didn't do the decorating thing beyond the few magical items on the wall he displayed from the stash he'd acquired over the years.

"I don't think I can trust you, witch."

"You pronounce 'witch' as if it's an oath or curse word."

Now it was his turn to offer a shrug. "Your kind and mine have never been friends."

"I promise you I won't try to control you again, Ed."

"Witch's honor?"

She drew a cross over her heart, which gave him a shiver.

"You know what it means when I cross my heart?" she asked.

He shook his head. "Something bad, I'm sure."

"When we witches cross our heart, it is the truest and most sealing bond to our word."

That didn't sound so awful. Rather noble, even. Hmm...

"It would mean a lot to me," she said, "if you would agree to answer some questions and let me, well..."

"Study me?"

"Not under a microscope."

Mercy, he didn't want this alliance. All his rational instincts screamed—*stay away from the witch!* Yet the louder voice moaned in anticipation for one more kiss. Could he control her with seduction? Because he had to keep her under thumb to keep his risk low.

But, oh, the things on her he'd like to feel gliding beneath his thumbs.

"Fine," he said. "So you agree to be the witch I need, if I agree to be the demon you need?"

She nodded. Her high-voltage smile beamed to match those world-filled eyes.

"You don't even know why I need a witch," he countered.

"I assume it's to cast a spell. Do you need me to clean this office?"

"Uh…" He strolled the floor, walking slower as he passed beside her. She smelled like lemons hanging fresh in the tree, sweet yet spiked with a bite of sour that a man desired to lick purely for the tangy thrill of it.

How to ask for the magic he needed without sending her running? What witch would agree to work against her kind? He hadn't enough information on *Les Douze* to know if she would be open to his needs. What *were* his needs, beyond to destroy some dead witches? If they really were witches.

He had to work up to that slowly. Convince her that she wanted to stop those witches, and not because a demon had asked her to. How to do that?

She tilted her head. A lift of her brow not only took him in, but also teased. And a crook of her finger and a lick of her lips delivered the coup de grâce. Yeah, seduction. The woman was a master at it. And she hadn't to do anything more than quirk one of those luscious brows. He could kiss her again. Right now. Pull her to him by curling his hand around the back of her neck and bruising her mouth with his until she gasped for freedom.

The most powerful witch in Paris? He'd expected some-one more...dark. And haggish, actually. Older, too. Al-though, he shouldn't judge by appearance. Paranormals who lived centuries had a tendency to age so slowly one could never know if the sexy young vixen eyeing him was in her third or fourth decade, or perhaps her third or fourth century.

But he'd never get anywhere if all he did was make out with the woman. The way he could get her to help him was to keep it businesslike. Professional. And he had to check out her skills, make sure she was up to par.

"Right, the murders," he muttered, grabbing the oppor-tunity. "Can you cleanse this office?"

"That's the reason you kidnapped me? To ask me to clean your office?"

He nodded. No sense arguing the kidnapping. It had gone down that way, and he wasn't proud of it. "Like I said, my men can be indelicate."

"Seems a rather dramatic effort for something so anti-climactic."

He could give her a climax if that was what she wanted—Ah! No. He had to stay on point. *Business, Ed, business.*

"I do like to clean rooms," she said. "But I'm not sure. It seems a little suspicious."

Because it was. Kidnapping a witch just to wave around a smudging stick and chant a spell?

"Why such a powerful witch to do a cleansing?" she asked. "I mean, the room is tainted, but any witch could do this."

"You yourself noted the previous efforts have been

worthless. You must understand my need for someone with a bit more skill?"

She bristled proudly, tugging at the ends of her lush hair. On the side of her littlest finger was another tattoo. Words. Probably a spell. Ed didn't try to read them. One never knew what horrors reciting an unknown spell could unleash upon his head.

"Ask me something," he volleyed.

"What do you mean?"

"Something you want to know about demons. It's a trade for your trust."

"Oh." She wiggled her shoulders. The excitement that she exuded was like a natural pheromone, so effortless and addictive. He breathed her in as if he were the lucky observer of an exotic flower who only put off her scent a few minutes a day before closing up. "Okay. Let's see… I know you're a corax demon. Can you shift to a raven form?"

"I shift to a conspiracy of ravens."

"Oooo." When she made that sound, she pursed her lips deliciously. Ed squeezed his hands together behind his back. "Can I see your horns?"

"No!"

"But those nubs at your temples. That's where they come out?"

He nodded. They grew to full length when he was angry. Or sometimes when he was aroused. He couldn't control the anger horns, but the other time, when he was having sex, was an option he employed if he wanted to heighten the experience. Because to have his horns touched? Oh, baby. Yet, sadly, he'd attempted it only once before. She'd run screaming. He'd learned his lesson about what to reveal about himself when having sex with a human woman.

She pointed to his gloved hands. "Why do you wear those? More horns?"

Actually, thorns. The thorns on his knuckles grew when he got angry, and they were deadly sharp, leaving a poison in his victim's cuts that could kill. The half gloves were a safety precaution because he didn't like to kill people. Not unless they deserved it.

"Forget it," she said suddenly. "I have to leave this room. I'm not properly warded and this malefic aura is creeping me out."

"Fine. Can you return later to cleanse it?"

"I can," she said, walking backward toward the door. "If you promise we'll talk afterward."

"Research and a cleansing? It's a date."

"It is?"

"Uh, er…a business date. I mean, you know. Why else would I have you brought here?"

"Did you request me specifically or did those idiots grab any witch off the street?"

They had grabbed a witch John Malcolm had deemed most powerful. Lucky for him it had been the one witch he wouldn't mind spending some time with.

"Does it matter? I've stated my need. You've agreed to meet that need, as I in turn will meet yours by answering your questions. We are in accord."

"Sure." She nodded and gestured toward the door behind her. "Can I leave now?"

"Of course. You're not my prisoner."

"Will I run into your henchmen on the way out?"

"No. I promise. And again, I apologize."

"I'm not one to hold a grudge. I forgive you for your odd means to hiring a witch to clean this office. Thank you, Ed. I'll return later. Ten?"

"Sounds fine. I'll be here. Alone."

She raised a curious brow.

"No henchman," he reassured her.

With a nod and wink, she left him standing there, watching her retreat. That sexy swing of hips and the brush of her long hair across her elbows was like poetry. A raunchy poem with a lascivious plot.

When she had turned the corner toward the elevator, Ed let out a low whistle. "Now to win her trust," he muttered. "And destroy some dead witches."

Chapter 5

Tamatha fixed her hair in the mirror and touched up with a little pencil to her right brow. Her hair was naturally white with silver tones, but she liked to soften her darker brows with gray pencil. A smooth of powder across her forehead and a touch of pale pink rouge to her cheeks. She never wore lipstick. Just a little lip balm. Because what man wanted to kiss a woman with greasy red lips?

And she'd already got two—no, three—kisses from Ed. A man who fascinated her as much as he disturbed her. Because he had sent minions to kidnap her! But then he'd kissed her. And then he'd acted nervous and kind of shy, so she could hardly blame him for the rough stuff. She could certainly blame the minions. But not Ed. Right?

She, the most powerful witch in Paris? Hardly. Certainly there were many witches more powerful. While she had mastered all four elements, she was sadly lacking in the various -mancys and study of specific magics. Perhaps only a warlock or thousand-year-old witch might be so powerful. But if she had copped to the truth, he would have tossed her out in search of the real deal. And by all means, she wanted to work with him.

To learn about demons, of course.

It wouldn't be because she found him handsome and was intrigued by his many tattoos and didn't want to end what his hot kisses had only begun.

Maybe a little.

"I have a date with a demon," she said as she spun into the bedroom to check her closet for an appropriate dress. Something sexy and yet it was a business date, so no lace and nothing too low cut. But always body-hugging.

"A date with a demon who kidnapped me," she corrected herself, her enthusiasm wilting as her fingers slid over the red silk wiggle dress. "What are you doing, Tamatha?"

"I should ask the same." Amberlee, a fellow witch friend, had stopped by an hour ago with some fresh rue and mega-bytes. Amberlee practiced tech magic. She wandered into the bedroom and plopped onto the end of the queen-size bed. Her bright red bob contrasted with her severely arched black brows, but both matched her red-and-black-striped dress. "You're talking to yourself, *mon amie*. Or are you working a spell? Am I interrupting?"

"No. Did you get the memory installed on my laptop?"

"Yes. Now you have ten times as much space to ignore on that tech device that always has dust on it."

"I'm not much for technology. I prefer paper and pen."

"Then why the upgrade?"

"I do like to store the photos I take with my phone. The laptop serves as an excellent photo album. I'd like to photo-graph my grimoire someday and keep that safe."

"Let me know when you do that. Tech magic tends to dis-tort grimoire text. The two magics clash. You won't know it until it's too late and your valued grimoire has been completely erased. You'll need a spell to properly store any information."

"Good to know."

Tamatha pulled out the purple velvet dress and held it before her. The fitted fabric would hug her slender frame and accentuate her cleavage with a sweetheart neckline. The black lace collar had skulls worked into the intricate stitching.

"I adore that one," Amberlee said. "Sensual with a touch of goth. So you've seduction in mind?"

"You think it's too sexy?"

"I'd do you wearing that dress."

"Yes, well, you'd do me, him and it, so I won't take that one personally. Who, or what, is your date tonight?"

"A werewolf from pack Conquerier. Sweet guy. Intense sexual appetite. He likes to howl."

"Nummy."

"Yeah, I like to howl right along with him. Especially when he hits the sweet spot with his fingers. What about your date?"

"It's not really a date. I'm going to cleanse an office for a guy. A demon, actually." She caught her friend's nod of approval.

"Demons do it devilishly," Amberlee said. "Or wait. Is this to do with your venture into diabology? Please tell me you don't intend to simply study this guy."

"Yes, study is exactly what I had in mind." She pulled the dress off the hanger. "I have already performed a binding spell on him, and he didn't hold that against me. Not too much. Maybe a little? I certainly won't hold the kidnapping against him."

"The—what? Slow down, Tamatha. I seem to be missing something here. Some demon kidnapped you? And now you're going on a date with him?"

"Suffice, we had an interesting meeting. And tonight…" She slipped into some high black Louboutin heels with purple tulle bows on the toes. "After the business of cleansing murdered spirits is completed, I want to talk to him. Learn about him. This date is strictly for the purpose of furthering my demonic research."

Amberlee put up a palm as she shook her head miserably. "You're killing me, Smalls. You and your work ethic. Please say when such research is concluded then the dress will come off. Maybe show the demon a few of your tattoos?"

"Don't be silly. I never have sex with a man on the first date. That's just gauche."

"What about Love Often?"

"I do. But you don't expect me to love him after one rather curious meeting, do you?"

"I suppose not."

"Besides, I don't know anything about him beyond that he's a corax demon—that means he can shift to ravens—and he's an excellent kisser. And he did have me brought to him, so I can only assume he's got no hang-ups about the demon-witch thing. Although he does seem to say the word *witch* with more vitriol than anyone should. Hmm…"

Amberlee rolled her eyes. "You and your adventurous heart. Be careful, Tamatha. And don't forget your white light before you go."

"Good call. I wasn't wearing it when his henchmen kidnapped me this afternoon. Best to go prepared."

"Henchmen?" Amberlee thrust up her palm. "I won't ask. I know it's wild, adventurous and your kind of weirdness. I'm headed home to pack. The wolf is bringing me to the Rhône Valley for the weekend. He owns a castle. If

I'm lucky I'll get to have sex with him fully shifted. Fur
and fangs, baby!"

Tamatha did not disguise a shiver as her friend pranced
out, en route for some kinky werewolf sex. Getting naked
with a man shifted into animal shape was so not her scene.
She'd never thought about sex with the familiar in his cat
form. But she did like her men interesting.

"And, apparently, with horns," she said to her reflection.

Unzipping the dress, she stepped into it and pulled it up.
Purple velvet seduction? So maybe a little flirting could
be allowed. After the business.

The air held the dry, sweet scent of sage and lavender
long after Tamatha had finished the cleansing. She'd focused her energy toward the marble floor and walls where
the vibrations of whatever vile act had occurred in this
room lingered. Lives had been stolen. More than one. In
hideous manner. She didn't want to know the details. It
wasn't important. The spell captured those remnants, and
with the use of her air magic, she sent them through the
window and into the ether to dissipate.

Barefoot, she stood up from her kneeling position on
the floor in the middle of the salt circle she'd poured earlier. Eyes still closed, she swept her hands over her head
and down her body to clear away any negative energy that
may have latched on to her. And then, drawing her hands
up her body from toes to crown of head, she replaced that
sensitive open aura with a white light.

When she opened her eyes, the demon stood three feet
away from the line of salt, hands shoved in his black trouser pockets. This evening he wore a gray-striped business
shirt without a tie, and the open collar revealed tattoos
or sigils that climbed his neck. Sleeves were rolled to his
elbows, revealing yet more black ink in various designs.

Gave him a bit of a gangster vibe. Add to that the dark hair parted neatly at his right temple, slicked back with a bit of pomade, and his gray eyes that held a hopeful curiosity, and he took her breath away.

Oh, what another kiss might lure her to do. Like unbuttoning that shirt and running her palms over his chest, which was nicely muscled, because the shirt stretched over some well-honed pectorals.

Of course, that meant he was strong, and she still didn't know him at all. Would he harm her? She had a tendency to overlook danger. She preferred to see the best in most; the worst only after they'd proved their lacking worth. She *had* slapped the binding spell on him, so he could still hold some residual anger.

Tamatha shivered, but the sudden rise of insecurity reminded her she'd been in the office alone with him for over an hour and he hadn't harmed her. And she did wear the white light.

"It's good," she said.

"Cleansed?" he asked incredulously, his body leaning forward in expectation.

"Of course. Can't you feel it?"

Straightening, he spread out his palms, half-covered by the gloves, and looked about the candlelit office. Tamatha had requested only the six white candles provide the lighting while she smudged. Unnatural light would have decreased the spell's efficacy. "I don't feel anything."

"Exactly." She stepped out of the circle and slid her feet into the pumps.

In the circle remained the extinguished candle, a calcite wand, which aided in clearing negative energy, and her amethyst-hilted athame. She'd collect them before she left. They needed time to rest, and if any residual dark energy remained, the salt would leach it out.

"You'll have to vacuum the salt later. Give it at least eight hours to allow any remaining dark energies to dissipate."

"Me and salt…" He mocked a shudder.

"Ah, yes, demons and salt."

"Not so pretty."

Well, she wasn't a maid, but she couldn't stand for things to be out of order. But she also didn't intend to stick around all night. He'd have to deal with cleanup duty on his own. "So is that wine for drinking?"

Ed grabbed the bottle from a marble-topped vanity by the wall and from the cupboard underneath pulled out two goblets. "It is. Thought I'd bring out my best Beaujolais if you managed to work your magic."

"Thanks, but I'll take information for the cleansing." She accepted the goblet he handed her. She quickly sipped and averted her eyes from the dark tattoo that crept up under his ear. "No remaining evil in this room now. Unless, of course…"

"Unless I create the evil myself?" he volleyed at her. His eyes had a means of dancing with hers in a challenging yet sensual manner. A defiant smolder. Such a look stirred in her core and tightened her nipples.

She shrugged and resisted falling into that appealing challenge by taking another sip of wine.

"You know, not all demons are evil. We get a bad reputation from media and silly movies."

"Oh, I know that. Your species is vast and varied. Though, the majority can tend to be nefarious and malefic. I sense you straddle the line between good and evil."

He didn't respond, and she followed him to the black leather tufted couch. She sat first, in the middle, and he moved over and sat three feet away from her. Humph. Yes, well, it wasn't a date. Maybe?

"The same goes for we witches," she said in an attempt to defend whatever it was about her he wasn't willing to sit close to. "We're not all vile. Very few of us are."

"I've grown up listening to faery tales of your sort. You must allow me my ingrained childhood fears."

"Really? A big strong demon like you feels faint around a little ole witch like me?"

"No one said anything about fainting. I just like to stay on alert when in the presence of…your sort."

"Yikes. What does it take to win you over? I've cleansed your office. I've kissed back as good as you've given."

He put up an inquisitive finger. "About those kisses."

"What about them?" Pressing a palm into the black leather, she leaned a little closer. "Want to try it again?"

"I, uh…" He actually cringed from her, which gave her pause. She sat up straight and tugged at her skirt hem. Really? Those faery tales he'd been told as a child must have been some doozies. Probably featured the classic hag. Oh, how inaccurate they could be. Most of the time.

"You said you wanted to ask me things," he offered as if tossing the suggestion out to deflect her sudden sway toward romance. "Ask away."

"Awesome," she said with little of the enthusiasm she should have.

The man had the weirdest ability to attract her while repelling at the same time. She shouldn't take it personally. But when one was kissed so well and thoroughly, it was hard to not want more.

Perhaps since they were in his office he assumed a work attitude. Though it was late, she had no idea if a secretary lingered in an office down the hall or even if his henchmen were on the premises. Business it was, then.

Kicking off her shoes, she pulled up her legs and leaned an elbow on the back of the couch so she faced him. On the floor, her shoes righted and snapped into an orderly side-by-side position.

"What the hell?" the demon asked.

"My OCD magic. I like order."

"And control, as you've mentioned. But really?"

"I can't control it. I used to control it, but eventually the urge to straighten got so strong it took on a life of its own. It works in about a five-foot range."

"So things snap into order as you walk by?"

She nodded.

"Weird."

"Really?" Toggling the fragrant wine goblet in her hand, she asked, "Says the corax demon who can shift to raven form."

"More than one raven—an entire conspiracy. And that's not weird. It's genetic."

"It's still weird. Does it hurt? How is it controlled?"

"It stings like a mother for two seconds and then I don't feel anything but the freedom of flight. Multiple times over. When I'm in that form, all the ravens fly in sync and are controlled as one by me. But if I need one part of me to do something, I can break off and fly solo. It's complicated. Of course, shifting takes a lot out of me. I don't do it often. Driving usually gets me wherever I need to go."

"Is that feather on your neck related to ravens?"

He stroked the tattoo, which appeared as soft as a feather and seemed to undulate under his finger as if touched by a breeze. "It is. It's not a tattoo but a demonic sigil. Unlike a tattoo, the sigils simply appear on my skin. It's not ink but darker pigmented skin cells. This feather is the top of the complete sigil that stretches the length of my spine. All corax demons sport something similar."

"That's fascinating." She leaned forward but cautioned herself from reaching to touch him. Much as she wanted to nuzzle her nose against his neck and breathe him in, she would not go there. Not when she could sense his need to lean back as she neared him. "Were you born here in the mortal realm or did you come from Daemonia?"

"Mortal realm, born and bred. I have a certain distrust and dislike for those from Daemonia."

"Why?"

"My opinions are not important to your research, are they? Let's stick to facts and avoid the personal." He tilted back the rest of his wine and got up to refill, and then he returned to the couch with the bottle and topped off hers. He remained a good distance from her. Which annoyed her. "Next question."

Nothing personal? He was protective of himself. Perhaps she'd read too much into his incredible kisses. Way to anticipate a fabulous date night. Not.

Oh, who was she kidding? She wanted details more than she wanted kisses.

Yeah? Tell yourself another lie, Tamatha.

Shaking off the nuisance inner voice, she allowed her eyes to glide about the office to the marble walls and across the windows. The desk and wine cupboard were topped with the same black marble streaked through with silver mica. Above the vanity sat three objects on separate shelves, which had been lit by halogen beams before she'd requested only candlelight.

"Is that an alicorn?" she asked of the object on the center shelf. "If so, I'm stunned."

"I buy and sell objects of magical nature. And yes, the three items are a genie in a bottle, an alicorn and a bit of angel dust on the third shelf."

Wow. A genie in a bottle? He'd better not let that loose or he'd be responsible for a world of hurt. The angel dust intrigued. It was terribly expensive to buy at the Witch

Bazaar, and she'd never the interest in testing its efficacy. Angel magic was the most powerful of all magics in the mortal realm. But if handled improperly? The witch may wish herself dead as opposed to experiencing the brutal backlash.

But the alicorn continued to draw her interest. Unfortunately, fascination was quickly overwhelmed by a sadness that tugged at her very core.

"There's so much positive energy leaking from the alicorn now that I've cleansed the room." Her heart shivered. "I could almost cry. Did a unicorn get slain?"

"I'm sure it was taken from a dead unicorn," Ed offered.

She gasped at his utter lack of concern, or perhaps he simply hadn't such knowledge. "Unicorns don't die, Ed. They are immortal. Oh, that's awful." She sipped the wine, not wanting to consider the alicorn anymore.

"Back to the questions about me," Ed said. She suspected it was an attempt to divert her from the alicorn. Good call. Maybe he was more attuned to her feelings than she suspected.

Very well. What else did she want to know, beyond that he could buy an item that had likely been stolen from a living being and had caused it much pain? *Don't think about it!* Her eyes strayed to his desk, which harbored only a closed laptop. She had no idea what he did. Buying and selling magical objects? He employed henchmen, as well.

"What do you do, exactly?"

"That's a faintly personal question."

"I mean here. In this office. What's your job? Is it to do with the collection on your wall? Is it related to you being a demon or is it a means to a living?"

He scruffed his fingers over the back of his head. "Let's say I head an organization dedicated to keeping the peace."

"That sounds entirely too heroic for—"

"For what? A demon?" He sighed and propped an ankle over his knee, rapping his fingers on the couch arm. "What *are* you wearing that keeps me at a distance from you? Is it a protection spell?"

"Huh? Oh. But I thought you…"

She thought he'd wanted to keep it all business. But instead he wanted to get closer? The man's duality was aggravating. Of course, he hadn't kissed her since she'd arrived. Unfortunately. And did his aggravation over not being able to get close to her have to do with his wanting to kiss her?

And why couldn't he— Hmm… She hadn't thought of that. "I always pull on a white light when I do a job. It protects me from any rogue elements or vengeful souls that I may not have control over."

"And demons?"

"From most breeds, actually," she said. "You can feel it?"

He tilted his head back on the couch, closed his eyes, then smiled. When he sat upright, he turned to her and touched her hand but retracted quickly as if bitten.

"Sorry," she offered.

"You must not have had the white light on earlier today when we kissed."

"I didn't. Your thugs surprised me and I wasn't calm enough to call it up."

"Could I ask you to take it off now?"

The look he gave her melted her insides and made her question if he'd asked her to take off her white light or, instead, her clothing. Yes, please?

She swallowed softly. "Depends."

"On my reason? I don't expect you to trust me, Tamatha. Or to feel safe. But I have kissed you, and… I'd like to do it again. But we can't do that unless I can sit closer to you and feel comfortable. It physically hurts me to be this close to you now. It's like tiny electric sparks are emanating from your body."

"Wow. I had no idea my white light was so powerful." Then again. "Oh, but, you know. Most powerful witch in Paris, here. Of course it's going to feel like that."

Whew! Fast save. She had to be careful. He had provided her a reason to keep him in her life; best not shatter that reason.

"If I take it off, will you tell me about those tattoos on your fingers? If that's not too personal a question."

"Yes, and it's a little personal, but some of the sigils on my skin are related to my genealogy."

Satisfied, she exhaled and then swept a hand over her from head to toe and pronounced, "*Exsolvo.*" The white light slipped away.

"I felt that. Like prickles skittering over my skin." He rubbed his forearms, then inhaled a deep breath. "Wow. Now I can smell your perfume. Lemons. I like that. It's different."

"I preserve my own lemons. My house always smells like a lemon orchard. It's a scent my grandmother wore, though I only know that because my mom told me. Grandma Lysia died long before I was born. So, those tats on your fingers?"

"Demonic runes. They are tribal. The history of them goes back centuries, maybe even millennia. They designate me corax and my location and alliances. As well, they provide protection within the demon community and rank me to others."

"That's a lot of information from a few crossed lines. Are you in a denizen?"

"Always been a lone demon. I prefer it that way. I, uh, don't play well with others."

"You're playing nicely enough with me." His smile was

a little shy and she liked that he was willing to relax now. "Tell me about those dark marks on your neck."

He slid closer and pulled aside his collar to expose the design. Tamatha leaned forward only a little. Didn't want to spook him. "These are demonic sigils that form on my body as I age," he said. "It's indicative of many demonic breeds but not all of them. Major life events imprint on my skin. And some are spells and wards."

"Really? That's so cool. I didn't know demons could do that. So a life event? Like what?"

"Anything. Dangerous encounters. Life-changing events. The move to Paris from Italy a decade ago. Defeating Himself's plans to send a dangerous demon into this realm. Growing into my horns. And I've already explained coming into my shifting abilities with the feather."

She eyed the hematite nubs at his temples and then tapped his gloved knuckles. Ed pulled away.

"Does that hurt when I touch them? I touched the ones on your temples earlier this afternoon when you had me pressed against the wall."

"I know you did. That touch was…" He blew out a breath laden with what she guessed was repressed lust. "Just take it easy, will you? Should you get cut, the thorns on my knuckles are capable of imbuing poison into your bloodstream, resulting in death. As for the horns on my temples…they are…sensitive."

"Oh." She'd take that sensitive as meaning *sensually* sensitive. Interesting. But she wanted to learn more about the thorns. They were a new bodily enhancement to her. "Poison? So you never take the gloves off?"

He clasped his hands together. "Only when I'm alone."

"Bummer. Must make for some weird—" She almost said "sex." Tamatha swallowed the last of her wine awkwardly. "So that mark on your lower neck looks like a scythe, actually."

"It imprinted after I got my horns. Puberty stuff, like the feather. This here." He traced his inner wrist, which featured a series of black wavy lines, almost as if a drunken bar code. "Was a fight with a werewolf. I won. And this one is a witch ward." He tugged up his sleeve to reveal a small, solid black circle on the side of his forearm.

Tamatha smoothed her fingers over the ward. He didn't flinch. Nor did she. "For or against witches?"

"It was supposed to be a sort of warning alarm should a witch come too close. Apparently, this one is bogus since I'm not feeling so much as a tingle from your touch. I'll have words with Sayne next time I see the guy."

"You had an ink witch tattoo you with a ward against witches? Doesn't that sound a trifle ironic? I mean, did you really expect it to work? It came from a witch."

He shrugged and a tiny smile softened his dark features. Compelled by his levity, Tamatha touched the corner of his mouth briefly. "I'm glad it doesn't repel me," she said.

"It has alerted me to other witches previously. I'm sure it's because you are so strong. Of course, that makes little sense. Unless you've a ward to repel my witch ward?"

"It may be my white light." Which she'd taken off. Hmm… That was weird, but not so startling she need worry about it. They were sitting here now. And he no longer seemed repelled by her presence.

And he leaned forward to kiss her, but stopped, their faces but a breath from one another. "I told myself I was going to keep it strictly business this evening."

"Me, too."

He considered it, frowned, but then nodded. "Right. So…" He tilted his head and nudged her nose with his. He smelled like leather and icy cedar. "I've always thought that nothing happens accidentally."

"Oh, it doesn't. There are no coincidences in this realm. I'm very sure our running into one another in the alley was destined. Though for what reason, we've yet to learn."

"Destiny is a big concept. Serendipity sounds cooler." He pressed his forehead to hers. A hint of wine on his breath compelled her closer and to close her eyes. "Demons and witches have a brutal history," he said.

Tamatha nodded. Witches had often been demon conduits through the centuries, along with their faithful familiars. But she didn't want to discuss their reasons for hating one another right now. Not when she could feel the pulse of his heart in the air and the cool hardness of his horn nub against her skin.

"This isn't history, Ed. It's right now. We're writing our own pages."

"I can get behind that. There is something I want to ask you," he said, breaking their connection by a few breathless inches, "but after I do, you'll not like me so much as you do at this moment. So I'm going to keep that one in my pocket for now."

"I can deal. Later will always be there waiting. I've asked enough questions for one night. I want to set work aside."

"No more business." He exhaled. "This you-and-I thing is really odd for me—"

Enough small talk. If he continued on that tangent he'd talk himself out of so much fun. "Kiss me, Ed."

She tilted up his chin with her forefinger and took the lead by kissing him. He responded nicely by not uttering another protesting word. Relaxing back against the couch, his hands spreading down her sides, he lured her on top of him. His hands glided down the purple velvet to her hips and she knelt between his legs because the skirt was too narrow for her to straddle him.

Lemon and cedar mingled as the two of them breathed in one another, tasting wine and anticipation, touching warmth, hair and the pulse beats of desire.

She spread her palm over his neck and felt a soft flutter. A demon sigil that marked him as corax. Cool. She hadn't read anything about sigils in her research so far, but knew she'd passed her hands over a book or two that detailed demonic sigils. When she returned to the Archives she'd head straight for those books.

"Do all demons have markings like this? Or wait, you said it was only certain breeds?"

He tilted a frown up at her, but it quickly softened to a light wonder. "Witch, do you want to research me or kiss me?"

"Honestly? Both." She teased a fingertip at the corner of her mouth. "But first I'd like you to stop calling me witch as if it were a bad thing."

"Sorry, Tamatha of the pretty green eyes." He clasped her hand and pulled it up to look at the side of her smallest finger. "Since we're asking about skin markings, what's this tattoo mean? Beatus?"

"Be-aye-tus." She pronounced the word properly. "It's Latin for 'blessed be.'"

"Special. A witch offering a blessing to a demon? Wonders never cease."

"I suppose I should be more cautious around you, but I can tell a lot about a person from his kiss."

"Is that so?"

"You're trustworthy."

She didn't miss his wince and then told herself she was being too trusting. She knew nothing about this man. But that was why she was there. To learn. And to learn one must set aside caution and dive in for the experience.

"So you must kiss a lot of people to have developed such a skill?" he proposed.

"I never kiss and tell." She traced a finger down the feather on his neck and delighted when it fluttered under her touch. "I'd like to see them all."

He waggled a finger at her. "That would involve removing clothing. And I suspect you're not that easy."

"Oh, I'm not." She tugged down her skirt and started to sit, but then immediately turned to lean into him. Because she couldn't not look into his eyes. "But kissing you is something I'd like to do more of."

"You perplex me." Grabbing the wine bottle and their empty goblets, he motioned she move aside so he could stand. "You say you want to ask me questions, do research," he said and set the bottle and glasses on the vanity, "but your body says something entirely different."

"What about you? The man who claims to be wary of witches and yet you were the one to ask me to take off my white light so you could get closer."

"Touché. You don't have a lot of fear, do you?"

"You keep assuming I should fear you. Is there something you're not telling me?"

There was. She could tell in his pause. Must be that thing he said he'd wanted to ask her, but that would make her not like him. Should she ask him about it? Asking might bring whatever they'd started to a screeching halt. Must be the history he had with witches. Well, she'd have to change his mind and teach him that some witches were trustworthy.

Tamatha stood and placed a hand on her hip as she paced before the couch. "Let's make a deal. We both want something from each other, yes? And whatever it is you want from me, I am going to assume it's not a simple office cleansing."

He nodded and swiped a palm over his mouth, and behind that swipe she saw his smoldering smirk. It was sexy, yet secretive, and the unspoken lust in his eyes made her heart thunder and parts of her simmer and grow wet. Oh, so wet.

"Whatever you want from me is a doozy," she decided.

"On the scale of trivial to doozy, I'd say you are correct."

"Must be dark and dangerous if you're so nervous about it."

"I'm not nervous. *Nervous* is not a word in my vocabulary. I am confident."

"If a trifle cautious."

"Caution is smart."

"Like I said, I can read a person, and you are nervous. You can't stand close to me. You keep touching your face, fidgeting. And you won't look me in the eye."

"And you are too perceptive. But I'll let it go because you're so pretty."

She twirled a finger within her hair. "You think?"

He clasped his hands together before his mouth and considered it a moment. Were it not for the black markings, he would appear a businessman standing in his high-tech office. An organization that sought peace? Dare she believe such a ruse?

"I need a witch," he finally said. "At least, I think I do. It's to do with my mission to keep the peace."

So it was a mission? That was…big. And magnanimous. Yet what reason could he have to be so secretive about it?

"I feel as though I need powerful magic to help rectify the situation." And at that moment his phone rang. He put up a finger that he needed to take the call. "Yes," he said to the caller. "Another? I'll be right there." He tucked the phone in his inner suit coat pocket. "I'm afraid I've an urgent appointment."

"Oh." She bent to gather her wand and athame from inside the salt circle. "Right. It's late anyway."

"After midnight."

"Yep, and I have work in the morning."

"Where do you work?"

"In the Council Archi—er...hmm." Should she actually reveal that to him? She hadn't been told to keep it a secret. It wasn't as though she worked with secret stuff. And most paranormal species were aware of the overseeing Council.

"The Council Archives?" he guessed. "Sounds like a bunch of stuffy old books."

"It is, but books are awesome. I could live in the stacks, reading everything about all things. I never want to leave. My boss usually has to remind me to go home."

"There is something about librarians that arouses most men's imaginations."

"Is that so?" She stood from collecting her things, then swiped the toe of her shoe through the salt circle, effectively rendering it but a broken circle of salt and no longer a protective barrier. "I've never considered myself a librarian. Bookish, I guess. But I know how to party it up. I'm down with all that."

Ed chuckled. He took her hand, and when she thought he would lead her to the door, instead he kissed the back of it. Clutching a candle and the knife to her chest, she sighed at the chivalrous move. But when he licked her skin, she flushed to her core. Goddess, what would that feel like on other places on her body? Like her breasts?

"Tasting me?" she tried lightly.

"We demons can tell a lot from taste," he said. "That's a freebie for your research."

"It's only a freebie if you explain yourself. What can you tell about me from tasting my skin?"

"Let's talk on the way out, shall we? That call was urgent." He led her down the hallway, and as they waited for the elevator, he again clasped her hand. "I can taste the wine in your blood and a salty remnant of the *pommes frites* you downed five or six hours earlier. Possibly on your way home from our less-than-stellar encounter here earlier."

"There's a Greek restaurant down the street from my apartment. I love their fries and chicken gyros. Tell me more."

"Your blood pressure is slightly elevated." He winked and smirked. "I'll attribute that to being here with me, your hand in mine."

She shrugged, acquiescing to that one.

"You are indeed very powerful because I could feel those electric vibrations tingle at my tongue, as if the white light, but I can differentiate and know it is your magic. You've been on this earth for about a century…" He tilted his head. "I can feel the ancient ways in you, but not so old that I sense you were around preautomobile."

The doors opened and they stepped into the elevator.

"You're very good," Tamatha said. "I was born in the 1920s."

"I assume you've taken a source?"

"A decade ago."

When a witch wished to maintain her immortality, she had to consume the live, beating heart of a vampire once a century. Witches called them sources; vamps called them ash. Nasty work, but immortality was well worth the mess and vulgar taste.

"And you emanate light," he finally said. "And joy and curiosity. But I didn't have to lick you to learn that. Such lightness is written all over—" he spread his hands before

her to take in her shape "—this gorgeous piece of work."
He exhaled. "I've that thing to get to."

And she sensed he was giving her an escape from what
could turn into an evening of debauchery. That neither of
them would protest. Yet she wasn't quite ready to dive in
so quickly with this intriguing yet deeply mysterious man.

"Tomorrow night?" she asked as the elevator doors slid
open. "Another research date?"

"I'm…hmm. Can I get back to you on that one?"

"Oh? Sure." She'd expected a quick response that he'd
love to see her again. Didn't he want to drop the big question on her? So her shoulders dropped as she headed for
the door. "I live in the 6th," she said.

"I know. By the Luxembourg."

She cast a look over her shoulder.

"I can smell the pear blossoms and roses from their
gardens in your hair. It's a unique blend indicative of the
garden on the Left Bank. If I want to find you, I will. We
demons retain scents far better than any werewolf can.
You're in me now, Tamatha."

And he turned to stroll toward a door set near the elevator bay. Without a goodbye or an *au revoir*. As last night
when he'd left her in the alleyway after that devastating kiss.

Tamatha stepped outside under the moonlight and
stroked the back of her hand where he'd licked her. With
a shiver, she decided to draw her white light back up.

Chapter 6

The last of a few black feathers dissipated as Ed's body re-formed into human shape. He tilted his head to the left and right to stretch the kink in his neck, then shook his shoulders to shake out his clothes and return to normality. Or as normal as it got shifting from a conspiracy of ravens to demonic flesh and blood.

There were other terms for a group of ravens, such as an *unkindness*. He'd stick with *conspiracy*. As it was, he got enough bad press.

The phone call had come from Inego, whom he'd directed to post guards at the Montparnasse. There were no dead witches in the cemetery this time that he could see. Nor a dismembered demon corpse. But between two mausoleum fronts with rusted iron doors he did find a telling pile of ash. Obsidian flakes clued him in that one of his own had died there. Recently, for the red embers and lingering sulfur that tainted the air.

Yet the sickly smell of rot clinging to the air was not demonic. And the ward on his forearm tingled.

"Witches," he muttered. "Again. How is it possible? Unless they are alive and just really ugly?"

No, he'd seen exposed bone on more than a few of them the night he'd witnessed Laurent's murder. Whatever the creatures were, they could not be alive. And they seemed to have a death wish for demons.

Perhaps the situation was more urgent than he'd initially thought.

Kneeling before the ash, he held his palm flat over the pile without touching it. Rising warmth teased at his skin, as if the essence yet remained. He couldn't get a read that would clue him in to what breed of demon it had been or if it had been male or female.

Scanning the surroundings, he wondered if the demon had been wandering about the cemetery—for what reason?—or if he or she had somehow been lured here. Because it was the same cemetery. It seemed too coincidental to be mere happenstance. Could dead witches do such a thing? Or was someone else luring hapless demons to a sure and terrible death?

The thought was disturbing. And he would find answers.

From a witch like Tamatha Bellerose? He wasn't sold on her being the most powerful in Paris, but he wasn't yet prepared to admit to that doubt. She seemed open-minded. She'd even suggested she was not into summoning and then commanding demons to her will. With hope, she would at least hear him out regarding this situation.

He should have been direct with her earlier. But after watching her smudge the office, the whole time he'd slid his eyes over her gorgeous figure and had thought thoughts he wouldn't want anyone to know about. Lust had altered his initial goal. He'd been thankful for the phone call only because he was pretty sure he might have pushed her down on the couch and made out with her right there in the office.

And what was wrong with that?

"Everything," he muttered. "She's a witch."

He stood, then strode quickly toward the south entrance and slipped through the unlocked gate. He spied Inego parked down the street in a black Audi and slid into the passenger side.

"I posted guards at the front gate like you asked, boss."

Ed rubbed his lower lip, in thought. Would any future victims really enter through the front gate? If the victim was demon, he or she could enter by a number of means, through shifted shape or by simply leaping over the fence at any point in the periphery. More guards may be necessary.

Beyond setting a demon out for bait, he had no idea why these killings were occurring. "Do you have any idea who the demon was?"

Inego shrugged. "He was in the process of being made dead when I decided to get the hell out of there. But he did have this." The lackey handed a bowie knife to him. "It was lying on a stone sarcophagus. I grabbed it 'cause you know how I like weapons."

The blade was crude iron, not polished steel. Demons worked well with iron, especially cold iron. The inlaid pearl handle was etched with a demonic sigil, but it was so worn it was difficult to determine the original design. In the hands of its owner the sigil may even glow and provide strength or serve some fierce magic.

"This sigil...the curve of it and that crossed line... It looks familiar, but I'm not sure. I'll have to clean it up and see if I can match it to a sigil on file. Looks like it's back to the office."

"Will do." Inego shifted into gear and turned the vehicle toward the Right Bank.

Ed had shifted the other night and again tonight. Too much, too fast. Already draining numbness toyed with his brain, thanks to the most recent shift. He probably wouldn't get farther than the couch in his office before falling into a dead sleep.

He closed his eyes and tried to banish the dreadful scent of death and rot from his senses. Dead demons generally did not smell when they dusted, but this one had reeked of sulfur. It could have been ripped limb from limb. There was no way to know by studying the remaining ash. As with vampires who ashed when staked, so did demons. But also similar to vampires, the younger demons could die and remain in bodily form or even only ash partially. So Ed knew the victim had to be at least a few decades old. Which helped him little in identifying the demon.

He absently tapped the blade on his thigh. The sigils could help in identification. He'd do that at the office. If he could get the memory of that awful smell from his nose. *Think of something sweeter.* Roses and pear trees that dotted the Luxembourg grounds. And lemons…

"Why do I keep kissing her?" he whispered.

"That pretty little witch?" Inego asked.

"Huh? Oh." He'd drifted into a reverie, lured by his exhaustion. He didn't want to have this conversation with the idiot who would put a plastic bag over someone's head thinking that was safe.

"We did get the right witch for you, yes? If you'll pardon me, boss, you two seemed familiar with one another."

"Yes, she's the right one." In ways even he couldn't comprehend. Yawning, Ed settled, flexing his spine into the comfortable leather seat. "I've kissed her both times I've seen her. And I don't know why. Witches disgust me. I had no intention—"

"You're bewitched," Inego offered. "The witch *made* you kiss her."

Bewitched? At the time, he'd jokingly suggested that she had made him kiss her. Because if he had been in his right mind, he would have never so boldly done such a thing. Maybe?

Bewitched. That made…a lot of sense. And what reason had she to tell him the truth? She'd wanted to soften him, keep him from harming her. Of course she had used witchcraft on him.

The car stopped behind his building and Ed stepped out, telling Inego to remain on call and keep his guards posted at the cemetery. Next time, he said, call him at the sign of anything suspicious. He needed to catch the demon before it was torn asunder.

"Bewitched," Ed muttered as Inego drove off. "She isn't playing fair."

Balancing a shoulder bag full of books on demons and curses and sigils, along with her purse, a plastic sack that held the high heels she'd traded for flats for the walk home, and the small plastic cup of pineapple gelato she had picked up when walking down the rue de La Huchette in the 5th, Tamatha licked the tiny plastic spoon clean and almost groaned out loud at the goodness of the tangy Italian ice.

On the days when she walked home after work, she always treated herself to gelato from Amorino. But as the first drops of rain hit the creamy treat, she cursed and rushed across the pebbled grounds of the Luxembourg. Her apartment backed up to the royal garden.

Pausing outside the lush hornbeam shrub that bordered

the park because the angle of the rain didn't reach her there, she finished the last of the gelato, then made a toss for the nearby garbage bag the city posted near trees and street poles—when a demon caught the empty cup and made the slam dunk for her.

"You."

"Me," Ed said as he approached. An irrepressible smile curled his mouth into something she could only wish he would press against her lips. "You didn't expect me? Didn't we have a date?"

"I thought you needed to think about it?"

"I thought. And here I am."

"Well, then here." She handed him her heavy bag, and when the rain began to pummel them both, they dashed down the alleyway that hugged her building. Once inside the cobblestone courtyard and sheltered by the roof over the landing, lightning crackled the sky.

"Inside. Quick," Ed said, and Tamatha followed orders without even thinking that he'd sounded demanding. "We've got to stop meeting in the rain," he offered as he followed her up the three twisting flights of timeworn stairs.

"I like the rain."

"It annoys me. And sometimes it hurts."

She pushed her key in the lock, turned it and shoved the door inward. "It hurts? I think I read something about that. No, that was faeries. Rain in the mortal realm can burn their skin."

"It works the same on some of us demons. Especially so when there's lightning. It crackles in my veins like electricity and messes with my ability to shift."

"Oh, I'm sorry. But I'm going to make a note of that."

"I'm learning to expect nothing less from you."

"You can drop my bag there by the door."

She strolled past the tiny kitchenette and into the living

room. Her bedroom was on the opposite side of the room
beyond the curvy pink velvet sofa. With a dash she de-
posited her shoes before her bed, then returned to the living room to find Ed looking around. The pale pink sheers
were pulled back to reveal lightning splintering the sky.

"It's not the Shangri-La, but it's my home. So, another
date?"

"Sure, but first I'd like to get straight to the point."

"The point?"

He walked right up to her and grabbed her by the shoulders. Not so gently. And he wasn't giving off "I'm going
to kiss you now" vibes. "You've bewitched me."

"I—" Tamatha's apprehensions dropped. Aww. What
a sweetie. Mr. Darcy redone in demonic flesh and blood.
Although…he hadn't said it in quite the manner Darcy
would. Not a hint of romance in his tone or mention of his
body and soul. Which meant… "Are you serious?"

"That's the only explanation for my compelling need
to kiss you every time I see you."

Was he for real? The guy couldn't accept that maybe
he *wanted* to kiss her? Way to make her feel special. Not.

Tamatha pulled from his grip and pushed her rain-jeweled
hair over a shoulder. "I don't work love spells or anything
romantically related. That's trouble waiting to happen. No
spells cast as a means to provoke you to kiss me, I promise.
Though, *bewitchment* is a term that encompasses a certain
romantic desire or feeling toward another. Seriously, you
think I'm *making* you kiss me? And you can't imagine any
other reason, on this entire planet, why you'd want to kiss
me? Maybe you just…want to?"

"Well, sure, but…" He sighed and swiped a hand through
his hair. The move made her yearn to know the feel of his
fingers gliding through her hair. "I thought… Uh…hmm…"
He tapped his lip. "Because when we do kiss, it's so easy.

And I've never been this way around a witch before. Because I have trouble with— And things never seem to last. Most especially if she—"

"She what? Ed?" She touched his cheek and then dared to stroke across his horn nub.

He gripped her hand quickly. "You shouldn't do that."

"What? Touch your horns?"

He tilted a serious stare at her.

"Does touching your horns make you…horny?" She tried not to laugh, or even giggle, but the idea of it was clearly ironic. "I'll keep my hands to myself. I didn't know."

"Yes, well, now you do. Lesson number one in Basic Demon Knowledge. Don't touch the horns unless you're invited to."

She nodded respectfully. "Kind of like faeries and their wings. You touch their wings and it's supposed to be sexual, like touching their breasts or their…" Her eyes dropped to his crotch, where a noticeable thickness caught her attention. "Wine! I'm sure you'd like some wine."

She hustled into the kitchen and was glad for the half bottle in the fridge. Needed to restock. And ugh, this was a white. Not the most romantic of wines. But then, apparently the demon was feeling put off by romance. Unless, of course, she considered what had appeared to be a hard-on.

So was he hot for her or not? She couldn't shake the awful feeling that he believed his kisses had been commanded by a force outside him instead of a reactionary pull to make contact with her.

To her, using magic to mess in the affairs of love and romance was almost as big a no-no as commanding demons against their will. Love spells could be quite effective. Until they were not. Be careful what you wish for and all that.

"Stick to business," she reminded herself. "But he did mention something about a date."

And she was keen on love. Often. But to be clear, the family motto encompassed all kinds of love. Familial, friendly, social, romantic, love for animals, love for food. Heck, love for bugs, grass or old cars. One must simply love life.

Out in the living room, Ed had opened one of the tall windows, and the noises from the restaurant below mingled with the clatter of rain on the windows and streets.

"Close it halfway," she said. She straightened the black velvet pillows on the pink sofa and cast about a glance to make sure no stray underthings were lying about. It was a chick's apartment; that stuff happened all the time. "Or the pigeons will come inside. I hate to bespell those poor things. They never seem to fly right afterward. Though I do use the occasional stray to practice ornithomancy."

"Divination by birds," he said and adjusted the window to make sure the opening wasn't quite so pigeon-wide. "That should make for interesting times, me being a corax."

She hadn't considered that, but cool. "Would you allow me to divine your conspiracy?"

"That sounds strangely sexual," he said with a wink.

And Tamatha actually blushed. So he did know how to flirt.

"White," he said as she handed him the goblet. "I do love a dry sip."

"Is that a demon thing?" she asked, slipping into research mode. From the table she grabbed a notebook that she always left lying around for moments of inspiration. And she put on her glasses, as well.

"No, I just love a good white. So we're right to business." Ed sat next to her. "I guess our dates always start that way, eh? That's cool— Wow."

"What?"

"Those glasses are incredibly sexy on you. All the

rhinestones and the way they draw focus to your bright green eyes."

"Hmm, must be the librarian thing you mentioned."

"You're not put off that one of my fantasies is exactly what you are?"

"Why should I be?" She leaned in close enough that his cedar scent overwhelmed the wine. It stirred her desires and softened her muscles so she felt like falling into his arms. "I like to play with danger."

"Right, the dangerous-demon thing. I'll give you that. I'm not safe, by any means."

"And how does not being safe play into your work, which is to bring peace? I don't understand that. What kind of peace and between whom? Other demons?"

"I said that was personal. You want basic demon facts, and that's what I'll give you. You know about our sigils." He pulled back his coat collar to show the black ink work, which wasn't ink work at all but an innate coloring in his skin. "You know about our sensitive taste."

"Right. And you can travel by shifting to a conspiracy of ravens. Can I see you do that?"

"Not now that I've learned you might like to use my ravens for divination. Besides, I'm all tapped out for a while. Just getting my strength back after doing it twice in a week."

"It drains you that much?"

"Shifting to dozens of birds and then re-forming back to a complex human body? That requires a lot of energy."

"Then why did you do it recently?"

"Next question."

She didn't like that he felt he couldn't be totally honest with her, but Tamatha would use caution. He was here and that was what mattered. "You know, I could help you with recharging your energy after a shift."

"How so?"

"I'm sure I've a spell of some sort that'll hasten your healing. Because that's what it is. Healing from the shift."

"Something to keep in mind. But pardon me if I maintain a healthy distance from your witchcraft."

"Right. You and your caution."

On with the research. And yet she wasn't as compelled to learn about the textbook stuff so much as delving deeper inside the man. A man who had just flirted with her, even if it may have been accidental on his part.

"Tell me something daring. Intimate. Do demons have sex the same way most other species do?"

He chuckled, shook his head. "Yes, we do. Though we come in all shapes and sizes, with different means, muses and fetishes. And some of us fellows are ribbed." He winked and sipped his wine.

"Ribbed?" She again averted her gaze to his crotch. "Like…you mean?"

He nodded, his grin irrepressible. "For your pleasure, my lady."

Mouth open in awe, she didn't know what to say to that one, so she let it sink in. Interesting. And…oh, baby. Now he expected her to continue with the interview without wanting to make out?

"That was too much too soon, wasn't it?" His gaze over the rim of the goblet reached in and caressed her thumping heart. Oh, how he had mastered the smolder.

"No, that was perfect. Great. I'm writing that one down."

He tugged the notebook from her grasp. "I don't want to be a footnote on your pages, Tamatha. Let's stick to conversation and leave the dictation for some guy with an ego. Is that okay?"

"Fine." She crossed her legs and settled back with the wine goblet in hand. A ribbed penis? *Oh, mercy, think about something else.* Like her pattering heartbeats. No. Her moistening hands. Double no! "So you know how old I am. What about you?"

"Thirty. Just turned."

"But you are immortal?"

"Unless someone stabs me with a salt blade or injects my veins with a salty brew. That stuff is killer. And it's everywhere. You can buy it at the local *supermarché*. It appalls me. I had to call in the building housekeeper to clean up the salt you left on the floor."

"I thought you said you had a secretary."

"Out on maternity leave."

"Aww, babies are so sweet." She caught his lift of brow and figured she'd better explain. "To look at. Not to have. Dear me, I don't know that I'm very maternal. I like to play with them a bit, then hand them back to the mother when they start to cry."

"So you won't be continuing the Bellerose family through your progeny?"

She shrugged. Babies were so far off her radar right now. Had always been that way. And she suspected the conversation would never get where she wanted it to go if she delved into talking diapers and snotty noses.

"Can you eat salt in food?"

"Minimal amounts won't kill me, but I have a chef who cooks meals for me once a month and leaves them in the freezer. Salt free."

She loved to cook, but sometimes cooking for one was a pain. Part of her desire to find a man who lasted longer than the family curse was so she could actually settle into the domestic-goddess mode and see if she liked it. Creating delicious meals for someone she loved? Sounded divine. Having children? She'd reexamine her priorities if and when she ever found a lover worthy of giving her children.

"Have you ever killed anyone?" she asked Ed.

"That's a personal question."

"Sort of. Sort of not. If it applies to a demon's necessary means to survive—"

"It does not. I am not a vampire who sucks the life from mortals, nor do I thrive on skin contact as would an afferous demon."

Tamatha reached for her notebook, then relented. "I'll remember that one. Maybe. Probably not. I'll survive. So, no killing."

"Killing is sometimes not necessarily murder."

"Oh. Yes, you're right. Murder is premeditated. A man might be faced with the kill to protect himself…"

Yet the fact he had to designate the difference— No, she wouldn't go there. Couldn't. Not with him sitting right there, but inches from her, overwhelming her senses with his ice and cedar scent and his—his very being. Yes, just being nearby, the man captivated her. And he made her desire. And want. Simple as that.

"Do demons possess a form of bewitchment?"

He quirked an odd look on her. "Not that I know of. You feeling bewitched, little witch?"

She nodded and then caught herself. "Course not." She took another sip of wine. "Oh, goddess, yes. I'm not much for avoiding the truth. There's something so compelling about you."

"It's your voracious need to learn what I am, to peel back my skin and study my innards."

"Oh, I don't do innards. Can't even manage most spells that require viscera or organs. Gross. It's your outsides and what's in here that interest me most." She tapped his temple below the horn nub. "Can I see your horns? They must extend out, yes?"

"They do, and I will not bring them out."

"A sex thing?"

"No, more like I'm not willing to display myself like that for you to preen over. Besides, they react more with my anger than anything."

"Oh, well, then I'm all for keeping you happy. But you did say something about having your horns touched making you horny."

"Tamatha, I can handle the questions. Even flirtation. But whether or not you realize it, your fascination is ribald."

"Really? What if it's genuine curiosity?"

He clasped her hand and squeezed it. "I'm trying not to push you down and kiss you right now. Is your intent to spoil my focus?"

Yes, yes and yes! "Wouldn't want to unsettle you."

"Now you're teasing."

"I won't deny that. What would you say to my research involving trying some spells on you?"

"No more binding. That hurt like hell. Much worse than lightning stinging in my veins."

"I promise I won't use such a dangerous spell again. Nor would I try to cast you out or eviscerate you."

"I appreciate your thoughtfulness. So I must subject myself to lab experiments now?"

"Would you?" she eagerly asked. "I might like to try a spell or two to connect with the sigils on your skin. See if I can divine—"

"You are entirely too excited about stuff you should not be."

Her lips formed a moue.

And he noticed her waning enthusiasm. "But I like that about you. You are uncommon. And I suppose being the most powerful witch in the city, I should expect as much from you. Always eager to learn and try new things?"

"Absolutely."

"I can't agree to be your lab rat. I admit, I'm protective of myself. Don't want anyone messing around…inside me, with magic or otherwise. But I will consider things not requiring evisceration if you give me some time to…"

"Trust me?"

He nodded. "Exactly. And now it's my turn to do a little research." He tugged her hand, bringing her closer to him, and nudged his nose against her neck. "Lemons. Delicious."

A pleasurable shiver traced her skin as his explorations moved him slowly along her neck and up toward her ear, where he kissed the lobe, then nibbled it softly. She clasped his hand tighter, wishing he were not wearing the half glove but knowing it was for her protection. His warm fingers twined within hers, and that was enough.

"Have you any witch marks?" he said after a kiss to the underside of her jaw.

"Why? Are you suddenly on a hunt?"

"No, just curious. You got to ask your questions, so I thought it fair to ask a few myself. Let me take a closer look at this tattoo on your arm." He slid down her dress sleeve, exposing her shoulder and bra strap, and traced the tattoo with a finger. "Looks like a rose, but bell-shaped."

"You got it on your first guess." His touch rubbed against her skin. All parts of her softened, luxuriating in the sensation. Tamatha wanted to fall forward, crushing her breasts against his chest, but she cautioned her eager need for the sensual connection. "That's the Bellerose family crest."

"Is it a magical tattoo?"

"No, just pretty."

"What do the words mean? Is it a spell?"

"*Amor Modum Saepe*. It's Latin for 'love often.' It's the

family motto." But she wouldn't tell him the unspoken part. No man deserved such cruel knowledge of his future.

"So have you loved often?"

"I've loved my fair share for a woman who has been on this earth for nearly a century. What about you?"

He shrugged and leaned back against the sofa. She sensed she was losing him to his intense need to keep his personal stuff private.

So she quickly said, "And so you know, I've not any witch marks. At least, not that I've seen. Though when I was little I wanted to have a beauty mark at the corner of my mouth like a glamorous movie star. I used to put a dab of chocolate there after lunch."

He leaned closer again, his eyes dancing over her mouth. "Too bad you don't still do that. I'd love to lick it off."

He kissed her and Tamatha sighed into him. The man had switched from business to pleasure and she wasn't going to point that out to him.

The kiss wasn't like most. It wasn't greedy. It didn't try to command. Instead, it was more tentative and perhaps a little cautious. Even when he traced her teeth with his tongue and pressed a hand across her back to draw her closer, she felt he wasn't quite relaxing into her. The man had a healthy fear of witches. So perhaps kissing her was more daring than satisfying.

Still, his mouth on hers felt marvelous. And she could allow him the slow exploration because that would only grow the trust between them. Her fingers glided along his neck and she felt the feather sigil flutter. As if a bird beneath her touch, ready to take flight. The energy was incredible, the power. And yet it never took off. And she remembered his mention of being drained from the shifting.

Suddenly his mouth left hers, and Ed stood.

"Put your shoes on." He tugged her up from the couch

and waited for her to slip into her shoes, then pulled her down the hallway. "It's stopped raining. Let's go to the park."

"Why? We were doing fine…"

"Because if we're out in public then I won't be able to ravage you."

She tugged him to a stop at the front door.

Ed bowed to study her face. "You're thinking about getting ravaged, aren't you?"

She nodded and her smile burst.

He slid his hands up her arms and pinned her wrists above her head. He kissed her there against the wall and she felt his erection nudge her hip. And then he pulled her down the stairs and into the safety of the public courtyard.

He wanted her. And she wanted him. But he was ever cautious.

She couldn't think of a single reason why someone would fear her so much. "I thought we were going out?"

"We were—are. I need to ask you something but I'm not sure how."

"It must be really bad if you can't bring yourself to ask me. Don't you think I'm a big enough girl to handle it?"

"I think you're a powerful witch who might have the answers I require. And I also think you need to trust me more before that happens. And I need to trust you."

Tamatha sighed. "Fine. But I'm not a very patient woman. I'll keep bugging you about this. And you've no one to blame but yourself. You did bring it up."

"That I did. I'll just have to distract you." The phone in his pocket rang and he kissed her instead of answering it. Points for ignoring the technology.

But after five rings, a pause and a renewed set of rings, she pulled from the kiss. "Answer it."

"It's one of my…" He checked the phone and smirked.

"Minions?" she provided. "You know how weird that is, to lay claim to having minions?"

"I prefer to call them field assistants."

"I distinctly heard you call them minions when I was at your office."

"Fine. I am Edamite Thrash, the evil overlord of the demon sect in Paris. Are you happy?" He turned from her to talk to the caller.

"Edamite Thrash?" she whispered. That was the first time she'd learned his whole name. Well, it didn't include his middle name, so she still couldn't control him with a spell. Not that she wanted to. Or needed to.

The name was indeed of the evil-overlord persuasion. Yikes.

"I've some details regarding an urgent matter I need to attend to," he said, tucking his phone away.

"Once again rescued by the phone call," she said.

"That's not fair."

"I count three times you've been whisked away from kissing me by that blasted thing."

"I'm sorry. Evil-overlord stuff."

She blew out a breath. That title was not as funny as he apparently had hoped it would sound.

"To make it up to you I promise if you'll meet me tomorrow night I'll turn off my phone."

"Can we talk then? Will you reveal the evil overlord's ultimate plan to take over the world?"

He smirked. "I should have never said that."

"I know you're kidding."

"Do you?" He kissed her on the cheek and then opened the front door of the building. "Tomorrow, then. Thanks for the wine and kisses."

"Don't ever thank me for a kiss," she said. "Just spending the night missing me will suffice."

"I can do that." He winked and closed the door be-hind him.

And Tamatha blew out a breath. "I don't know what is up with him. He's cold and then hot for me, and then right back to business. Maybe I *should* look into a love spell? At least then I could have him all to myself for more than an hour here and there."

Edamite Thrash?

She sucked in her lower lip. She'd have to look up that name at work tomorrow. Just for research's sake. Not be-cause she suspected he was the evil overlord he jokingly claimed to be.

On the other hand, she didn't know him at all.

Chapter 7

After cleaning the knife Inego had found at the cemetery and applying a bit of demonic magic to the blade to lift the engraving, the sigil was then easily matched in a database Ed kept on the local demon denizens. It was Laurent's Libre denizen, and the second victim had been a friend of Laurent's whom Ed knew, but not well. That was why the sigil had seemed familiar to him.

Pacing beside his desk as he racked his brain on what to do next, he suddenly noticed…something. Like a darkness humming above his head, yet it wasn't something he could see, only feel. It was odd, and it lingered.

He stretched his arm up and tapped at the air. He didn't feel anything tangible, but instinctively it felt intrusive.

"Dark magic? I thought she'd cleansed this office?"

He cast a glance toward the genie bottle displayed on his wall. That thing was always lit from within, and at times it would roil with an angry redness that wanted out. He'd never let the genie out, no matter the three wishes he should earn. Because after a man had been granted those wishes? The genie was granted freedom.

The city of Paris would never be prepared for the wrath of a genie who had been contained within a tiny bottle for millennia.

Blowing out a breath and shaking his head, he dismissed the odd feeling as angry genie vibes. Or it could be nerves after everything that had happened lately. A demon had a right to be on edge after the things he'd seen in the cemetery.

"Zombie freakin' witches. Whoda thought?"

He couldn't erase the memory of watching Laurent being torn asunder. Had the same happened to the demon who had owned the bowie knife?

The Libre denizen traced back centuries, which was how Ed knew Laurent. Their respective grandfathers had founded the denizen together, choosing the name Libre, which meant *free*, to signify their escape from the domination of their witchy owners who had originally summoned them to this realm. So the sigil on the knife had also been Ed's grandfather's sigil. And while Laurent currently oversaw the Libre denizen—or had when he'd been alive—Ed had never any desire to join them. He stood on his own. No one told him what to do.

Were the witches in the cemetery going after the demons in one particular denizen? He had no idea if these were the first two deaths or if others had occurred. He'd send Inego out to locate the acting leader of Libre, to ensure all other members were accounted for. It was the only lead he had.

It was time to get over his mistrust for witches and tell Tamatha what he knew. With the access she had to the Archives, perhaps she could fill in some of the missing spaces for him. Such as more information about *Les Douze*. What were they about? And were they actually dead or just really old and decrepit?

"No, have to be dead."

He typed Les Douze into the browser search and it brought up a paragraph he'd read earlier detailing the mass burning of a dozen witches in the Place de Grève in the eighteenth century. The article didn't detail their crimes, save only that a group of men and women had accused the witches of heinous occult activity.

Of course, hundreds of years ago, a woman merely had to look at a man wrong or even refuse his vulgar advances and he'd accuse her of witchcraft. True witches had managed to avoid capture and ultimately a hideous death. Though, not all. Ed knew well a good fear of a specific breed could cling to a man's psyche even after he met one who he felt should not be threatening.

Tamatha could be threatening. She was very powerful, and he had the memory of the binding to prove it. But he didn't fear her. Not physically. Emotionally? Hell, he didn't want to answer that one right now. But he did know she could sense his reluctance to simply relax and trust her.

He was stronger than that. He'd once faced Himself and defeated a nasty crew of wraith demons. He wasn't going to let one little witch make him shiver.

He tapped the computer screen. One of the accuser's names was listed. LaVolliere. He had the same surname as Laurent. A relative? But Laurent was demon. Demons weren't big on surnames or carrying them through the generations. Ed had always assumed it was a name Laurent had taken to make him fit in with humans.

And besides the surname, mortal men had accused *Les Douze*. Maybe. That was according to reports, which had been detailed by a human. Of course, a human would only assume the accusers had also been human. Demons were once expected to appear as creatures, hideous and deformed with tails and hooves.

Had demons in corporeal form accused the witches? It would serve adequate reason for those *things* in the cemetery to want revenge against their accusers. But why now after so many centuries? And how had they managed to rise from the grave to achieve such revenge?

He was missing something. He needed to clear his mind and think about other things. Only then would his distraction allow focus to the fore.

He picked up the phone and dialed Tamatha. With luck, she would forgive his hasty retreat last night and meet him for dinner. And he'd show her how relaxed and trusting he could be in her company. He could get lost in her eyes. The best distraction he could imagine.

"That place salts even the desserts," Ed offered as he strolled arm in arm with Tamatha down a narrow street in the 1st arrondissement. He'd asked for her recommendation for a restaurant but she hadn't any in mind. He wasn't hungry and neither did she seem to be in a rush to eat. And walking closely as twilight settled the sky in violets and pinks was some kind of all right.

"The new park layout is pretty," she commented and veered down the narrow, cobblestoned aisle leading toward the Bourse de Commerce, the old Commerce Exchange, which now housed the Paris Chamber of Commerce. "Let's check it out."

They filed around the domed structure, past the Medici column and into the recently remodeled gardens of Les Halles, beneath which stretched a massive shopping complex that offered everything, including lattes, music, movies and high-end diamond watches.

They strolled across a lawn and Tamatha inhaled the scent of flowers and commented on the green texture of the air. Ed had never considered air to have a texture but he had to admit it did. Clear and crisp and, indeed, green. The water feature dribbled over smooth cement forms and he felt the whole experience surreal. He was holding hands with a pretty woman and talking about the scent of flowers. As if normal humans on a date. As if there was nothing whatsoever odd about him—or her, for that matter—and everything was peachy.

Maybe it was all romance and roses? This feeling of comfort with a witch was new to him. The difficult part was to not rush away from it. To just enjoy. He liked holding hands with the girl. A pretty woman who had chosen to spend time with him. And he felt a sense of pride that she deemed to walk alongside him and no one else. She could be his girl.

No, she can't.

And that, he realized, wasn't even a witch thing. It was just that he didn't know how to do the romance thing, and even if he tried, it could never end happily.

Enough sappy stuff. He veered toward the cobblestoned street that paralleled the Saint Eustache Church and noticed the farmers market. Some stands appeared to be packing up for the night, but a few were still accepting patrons and serving food. The spicy rich saffron, rosemary and sausage carried on the air and wove it into a fiery, yet enticing texture.

"Paella," Ed said and tugged Tamatha along.

He paid for a huge plate, grabbed two plastic forks, and then they found a spot on a concrete step before the park and shared the meal. A trio of dancers had set up a boom box and were busking for tips with some stunning moves.

"This is delicious," Tamatha said, her knee touching his as she sat close. "I've never tried it before."

"Really? I love this mishmash of rice and sausage and veggies. If I had any cooking skills at all, I'd make it once a week. And this is not salted. I know the guy. He's got a heart condition, so he watches salt as if he were a demon."

"Awesome. I happen to have some mad skills with the pots and pans."

"Is that so?" He waggled a brow as he forked in another steamy bite.

"I like to try new things. I'll have to look up a recipe for this online."

"I volunteer to be your taste tester."

"Deal." She tilted her head onto his shoulder. "You know, I'd love to have a guy to cook for all the time."

Ed mocked a choke on his next bite. "Did you just say, in a roundabout way, you are looking to get married?"

"Did I? Oh, no. I mean, someday. But no. I didn't mean that about us." She spooned in a bite of rice.

Ed would love to have a woman cook for him. But marriage? Absolutely not. Well. Yes, someday. Maybe? Ah, who was he trying to fool?

"I don't think I'll ever marry," he said, casting his gaze beyond the dancers and across the park where a half-dozen young men tossed a Frisbee back and forth. "Never had much luck with women."

"Really? There's always men."

"I prefer women," he said, tilting his head to bump it softly against hers. "But thanks for offering me hope." Then he laughed and folded the empty plate in half. "I have never discussed anything remotely domestic with a woman before. It's usually…"

"Wham, bam, thank you, *mademoiselle*?"

"Uh…" Close, but he wasn't going to reveal that to any

woman he was interested in. Especially not a woman capable of retaliating with magic.

"It's okay. Like I said, I'm not in the market for marriage."

"Just following that family motto, eh?"

"It does include more than romantic love. It could mean loving paella. Which I do. And going for walks with a handsome demon. Which I also love."

"All right, then, let's continue the walk and talk. Where to?"

"How about we check out the church behind us? I've heard it's beautiful inside. Can you go inside?"

"Of course I can. What? You think I'll sizzle to ash if I encounter the holy? You don't need to research demons to know that holy symbols are just that, Tamatha. A symbol. Belief is what holds all the power."

"True. But baptized vamps can't touch the holy."

"So there are some exceptions." He stood and offered his hand. "Come on. Let's go see if this demon starts to sizzle."

Ed stood before the stone statue of some pope flanked by two angels in the narthex of the Renaissance-style Saint Eustache Church, the largest church in the city. He did not feel as though his skin would begin to sizzle and flake off until he had been reduced to a heap of black ash at Tamatha's feet.

On the other hand, he did feel...odd.

Never before had he been in a church or cathedral. He did not subscribe to religion. It seemed to be the root of war, greed, patriarchy and hatred among the human population. He preferred a spiritual approach to life, blessing the nature and earth he lived upon and giving thanks for his existence. All were equal and came from the same star stuff, after all. Yes, he was a fan of Carl Sagan.

So while he hadn't known what to expect when crossing the threshold into this holy structure, he had prepared to not be surprised at whatever may come. And right now he felt a weird compression against his skin. As if something were trying to intrude, move inside him.

He shook his hands, hoping to fend off the feeling.

"It's gorgeous, isn't it?" Tamatha spun and cast him a beaming smile. Tonight she wore a peach dress with a lacy neckline that danced about her full breasts. Her hair was coiled in victory rolls on each side of her head and trailed down the middle of her back. She studied the massive stained glass window, which was surprisingly heart-shaped. "I do love stained glass."

Well, there. An opportunity to escape this infernal establishment and hopefully save face by not turning into a raging madman as he tried to shake off whatever it was pushing into him. If he thought about it, it was similar to the intrusion he'd felt in his office last night.

"You've seen one church window, you've seen them all." He clasped her hand and tugged her toward the entrance doors.

"But we've hardly looked around. You're starting to sizzle, aren't you?" she asked as he pulled her outside into the night.

"No, sweetness, I am not sizzling." He tugged at his tie and assessed his composure. The intrusive feeling was gone. Whew! Maybe he would have started to sizzle? "I have stained glass windows at my place."

"You do?"

"You'll have to come over sometime if you admire stained glass. They are quite remarkable."

"That sounds like you're suggesting another date."

When he nodded, she bounced on her toes. He liked her enthusiasm, yet he could never be sure if her excitement was that she got to spend more time with him or that she was gaining opportunity to research and study. Should it matter? It meant he got to spend time with her, and that was all right.

"Tomorrow night," he offered. "I'll order in."

She kissed him, there in the shadow of the church's sacred walls. Passersby strolled on the cobbled path between the church and park, not paying them any attention, or perhaps they were and Ed didn't notice their reactions. Because he couldn't focus on anything but Tamatha when they kissed. She may not have used witchcraft to get him to like her, but he truly did feel bewitched.

And there was nothing whatsoever wrong with that.

Chapter 8

After pulling on a white light, Tamatha strolled the stacks in the demon room. Set into the far wall was a small iron door that led to the live and pickled specimens. A person had to bend over to pass through. And about the door flurried a constant blizzard of snow. She could feel the chill from here. She'd been in there a few times, but today she merely wanted to look up the corax demon.

An entire wall of books focused solely on defining the various demon breeds loomed before her. A few crooked volumes straightened as she approached, and dust flew off the pages to sift through the air. Suppressing a sneeze, she reached for a volume labeled *C* that sat with its alphabetical compatriots. It was thicker than most, but not as thick as the *S* and, surprisingly, *Z* volumes.

Back at the study table, where she'd left a steaming cup of peppermint tea and a plate of chocolate biscuits, she settled in and paged through until she found the corax entry. Rather short, but it did provide a few details.

Tens of thousands of years old, the breed was originally entirely raven in form until they began mating
with other species that had mastered human shape.
Their evolution was swift and they quickly became
a trusted entity among their kind for their ancient
heritage yet progressive manner. The demon's sigil
is the line of raven feathers down their spinal column and their sense of taste is especially valuable
for reading others.

"They gain knowledge by consuming the hearts of those
who hold such knowledge? Ugh." She set the book on the
table and pulled her legs up to clasp her arms about her
ankles. "Ed eats hearts? That's…"

She couldn't pronounce the vocation awful, because she
had done it. Once. But if he murdered innocents merely to
gain knowledge? Or did he consider it killing? Either way,
it was awful. And it didn't seem as if it were a part of his
nature, that he needed to commit such an act to survive.
Knowledge was an enhancement to one's wisdom.

"Maybe I shouldn't have looked you up," she muttered.
"Ed, the demon who looks like a gangster and has minions like an evil overlord, and yet…he can't be. He's very
mannered and…his kisses."

She sighed and clasped the clear quartz crystal sus-
pended around her neck. For clarity and truth.

"Who are you, Edamite Thrash?"

He trusted Tamatha. He did. Maybe. Hell, with another
demon death he didn't have time to waffle. But could he
spring it on her? Tell her why he'd sought her in the first
place? She had expressed exasperation over his avoidance
of the subject. Certainly she wanted to know what he had
to ask of her.

But accepting that information could be difficult. Could a witch work against her own? *Were* they her own? Those decrepit monsters in the cemetery couldn't be from the Light. Of course, he didn't know for sure.

One thing he did know: witches ran in tight circles, or rather, covens. All for one and one for all the cackling hags. Dread to those who went against one of them. Witch Number Two from his past had garnered much of her power from her two sisters and they in turn had met with their coven weekly. It made him shudder now to remember how easily she had seduced him into trusting her. Her dominatrix tease had fired his desires. He'd been crushed by his own lascivious curiosities.

His phone rang and Tamatha's profile displayed a female silhouette against a pastel square. He'd have to snap a pic next time he saw her. Trust her? Probably never. But he did need her and he did know how to play nice.

"Sweetness," he answered.

"Aww, I like when you call me that. Cheers me up."

"You need cheering up?"

"A little. I've a terrible backache from crouching over the floor all day on all fours. I hit a smelly spot in the demon room here at the Archives and discovered a stack of molding books. Had to scrub the floor but I think I salvaged most of the books."

"Would a back massage do the trick?"

She cooed and Ed could feel her anticipation shiver up his neck in a pleasurable way. Yes, he wanted her here. Now. In his arms. At his mouth. Wrapped about his body and filling his senses with lemons.

"Come over," he said. "I'll make dinner."

"I thought you didn't cook?"

"If you promise not to notice the containers in the garbage, I'll pretend to plate the meals with such a flair you would never bother asking if a chef made it."

"Deal. I don't know where you live."

He gave her the address to his place, not far from where his office was in the 10th, and the warning that she mustn't be surprised at the building. It had been in the family for ages, and it had once belonged to a religious organization.

Smirking, he hung up and glanced out his office window to the stained glass windows a few blocks away that curved along the wall in his penthouse apartment. From one of the windows, the archangel Michael pointed his sword directly at Ed. He always got a kick out of that one.

He tried to keep his nose clean and avoid angels. Wisdom any demon would do well to follow.

The man's place was fancy, yet the gorgeous gray-and-turquoise palette added a subtle tone. The main floor was open, and the kitchen was set off the living area and two steps up. Everything was tiled in gray marble. And the place was not square or rectangular—but circular. Not a straight wall in the place—at least, not on the main floor. He told her the bedroom and bathroom were up the open stairway that was railed with ultramodern steel cables.

One half of the circle was walled along the kitchen; the other half, in the living area, emitted the setting sunlight in shards of myriad color from the stained glass windows that curved about that side. Once a former headquarters for a Catholic diocese in the nineteenth century, Ed had explained. Tamatha got a kick out of learning it had been in a demon family for half a century. The saints depicted in some of the windows must surely cringe whenever the current resident passed by.

She wondered if he'd had to have the place unblessed. She had read how to do it once, but hadn't ever thought it an important skill. So many strange yet wondrous facets to the man's life.

She could fall in love with a guy like Edamite Thrash if she didn't think he was hiding something huge. Or that he killed. But if love weren't in the cards, she wanted to have fun with him. And sex. Ribbed for her pleasure? Oh, mercy, she needed to further her studies on that.

Two warm hands suddenly massaged her shoulders from behind, and he leaned in to kiss her on the cheek. "You like coq au vin?"

"Love it. Smells delicious. You were right about this place being startling."

"It takes some getting used to, but I enjoy the colors streaming in more than focusing on the pictures depicted in the glass. Religion can be so theatrical, yes?"

"I bet some long-dead church elders would roll over in their graves to learn who lived here now."

"I think I felt that group roll when I moved in. Had the place cleansed."

"Whoever did it performed a much better job than in your office."

Though she did sense a tendril of…something. It was almost like a sheen over her head, something shaded with darkness. Perhaps it was just Ed's presence. The demonic inhabiting this former religious haven? That had to mess with the room's aura.

His hands worked down her spine to just below her bra strap and she cooed in pleasure. "Oh, yes, right there."

"Why does the Council have you doing the dirty work of crawling about on your hands and knees as a maid?"

"I didn't mind the cleanup work. And if I hadn't done it, the mess would have sat for decades longer, surely. The Archives are ancient and I'm sure some books haven't been touched for centuries. Goddess, that smells so good. I'm a lot hungrier than I realized."

He ended the all-too-short massage with another kiss to her cheek, then wandered into the kitchen. "Wine?"

"Yes, please."

She sat on a stainless steel stool before the glass-topped kitchen counter, where he had placed two settings and poured her a goblet of red. He placed a plate of food before her, along with silverware, which reacted to her by straightening alongside the plate.

"Really?" he said.

"What can I say?" She lifted a fork and dived in without further explanation. If he were around her for any length of time, he'd get used to her OCD magic.

The kitchen was a stainless steel and glass marvel. Tamatha felt as if she were sitting in a nouveau chef's laboratory, tasting his wares. The meal had been premade and featured small servings à la high-tech cuisine, but man, how good was the side of caviar soaked in kir?

It was weird to watch Ed eat with his half gloves on. She bet he took them off when he dined alone. Had he ever harmed anyone with his thorns? She stopped herself from asking, thinking to keep dinner light instead of veering toward research. Besides, the side glances he cast her and those tiny smiles during their conversation about the history of the building were enough to satisfy her. The shiny nubs at his temples didn't bother her at all, though she did want to rub them again.

To test his lust.

And when she moaned over the grapefruit mousse, Ed gave her a raised eyebrow. Realizing she'd been imagining a lusty embrace instead of the food, Tamatha blushed and used the napkin to hide her foray. "So good," she murmured. "My compliments to the chef, whoever that may be."

She finished the fruity mousse and set her plate in the dishwasher. She cleared Ed's dishes as well, finding she liked stepping into the domestic role. Taking care of a man. At least, as much as he would allow it. She did know he was protective of himself and his surroundings. A closed man.

When he was not making out with her.

Her demon boyfriend? Yes, she could consider having him as a boyfriend. But if she went that far into the relationship, then there was always the family curse to consider. So she wouldn't label him yet. For his own safety.

She paced in the living room before the stained glass windows. He'd eaten without even tasting his food, she guessed. He was preoccupied. And she could guess with what. The same thing he'd had on his mind since that day he'd ordered his henchmen to bring her into the office.

But what she was more curious about was his morals.

It was time to get some answers from him. And maybe he'd pop the question he so wanted to ask her. For good or for ill, she wanted to hear it.

Pushing her hair over a shoulder, she smoothed down the blue velvet skirt that flared out at her knees. Her heels—black with blue lace around the edges—clicked on the stone floor over to where Ed paced, and she stopped before him and took his hand.

They both spoke at the same time.

"Do you kill?" she asked.

While he asked, "I need you to cast a spell. Kill? Tamatha? I thought we'd discussed this already."

"I know but—it wasn't really a discussion." She shrugged. "I looked up the corax demon. There was something about eating hearts…"

"Ah, that little detail."

"Little? I think it's a rather big detail myself."

"I suppose, but no. I do not kill. It is not necessary for my survival. My breed can gain knowledge by consuming the hearts of others, but people die every day in a big city like Paris. I just have to be there when it occurs. It's not a difficult task. I don't touch them. I tap into their heart. If I need it. Which isn't often. Rare, even. I'm not making this sound very good, am I?"

She didn't know what to say to that. It sounded weird. Then again, who was she to waggle her finger in blame over eating a heart? She'd done it to maintain her immortality. Of course, she had done it only once.

"What kind of knowledge is so important you would commit such a grave act?"

"Information on local denizens. Or other species that may have invaded the city. It's all a part of the keeping-the-peace thing."

"That you don't want to elaborate on."

"It's what I am, Tamatha. We eat knowledge. I was born that way. Can't change it. Though trust me, I wanted to when I was a teenager. Teenage angst, you know. Even we demons have it."

"I can relate to having problems when I was younger. Though I can't remember a time I've ever had angst about being a witch. Maybe knowing about how cruelly some treat my kind. I mean, witch burnings? What kind of history is that to grow up with?"

"I can't imagine. Your breed has endured much through history."

"Thank you. I just needed to know…"

"I'm not a murderer?"

She shrugged. "It would have been a deal breaker."

"I see. So we're at the deal stage?" He crossed his arms

and strode to a window. Red and azure light beams spilled across his face and the sigils on his hands. He was beautiful. And dark. And an enigma she never wanted to completely learn, because to do so would spoil his mystery.

"No," she said, "I just— Well, you know. I couldn't have continued to see you if that had been the case."

He nodded, not turning to regard her. "Are we doing something here? The two of us? Beyond the obvious need for knowledge we seem to want to get and give to one another?"

"Uh, don't you think we are? It's not necessary to kiss a woman to answer her questions. I just thought…"

This time the look he cast her felt genuine and real. His smile wasn't cold. And a bit of the smolder filled his eyes now. "I do like kissing you. You'll have to forgive me my skittishness. I thought I was over that with you."

"Your thing about bad luck with witches."

"Yes." He held up his hand, the half gloves revealing only the heavily tattooed and sigiled fingers. "Unlike many species who can walk among the humans undetected, my differences are visible. Women get a look at my thorns, or wonder about the weird black growths at my temples, and let's just say it spoils the romantic mood."

"But witches should understand."

"Yes, well, your kind tend to be either oddly fascinated…" He grinned at her and Tamatha felt a thread of guilt heat her face. "Or… I'd rather not explain right now. I had a bad experience with a witch. But that's my past." Again he assessed her with that knowing accusation. "I think I should probably not question this thing we have too much. Maybe just enjoy it while I can."

"Good plan. Love often," she provided.

"Yes, that family motto of yours."

"Good words to live by. Love is good for everyone."

"You are quite the optimist."

"And you tend toward pessimism."

His shoulders dropped with a heavy sigh. "I suppose I am. But I won't offer excuses. Take me or leave me."

"I'll take you." She winked and danced her fingers along his arm and up to thread them through his hair. "Tell me, Ed. What was the reason you needed a witch to cast a spell for you? Are you calling up a fellow demon? If it's bad, I still want to know. I need to know. You can trust me."

"I do know that. I want to tell you exactly what I've been involved in lately. I need your help. But…" He glanced around, limning his gaze along the walls and even the ceiling. "I've felt the intrusion lately. Like a sort of supernatural spy cam. I think someone is tracking me or somehow… listening."

"Really?" She joined him in his search of the invisible snoop. If she focused she could match her earthbound vibrations to that of the marble inside his home and sense any anomalies. She had noticed something earlier that seemed a bit off but had thought it from him.

"Might be a witch," he added. "I can't tell."

"I can put up a shield for us to talk under so no one can hear."

"You can?"

"No problem. Uh…" She tapped her lips as she sorted through the possibilities. This was fun stuff. She rarely got to utilize the shield of silence. "The bathroom is upstairs? You secure the front door and meet me up there."

Grabbing her shoulder bag, she skipped up the black metal stairs and into the bathroom, where she pulled the shower curtain aside to reveal the freestanding black clawfoot bathtub. A narrow stained glass window featured a white lily, but the sun was on the other side of the building, so it was muted. The lily was the heraldic fleur-delis and symbolized chastity and virtue. "Yes, perfect for keeping secrets."

Inside her bag she kept an emergency kit of supplies. Enough salt to pour a thin circle around the tub. A small red-and-black candle she set on the vanity. Some crushed valerian sprinkled over the salt for silence. And a spritz of lemon oil around the door frame to block intrusive entities finished the job.

By the time Ed stood in the bathroom doorway, she had completed preparations.

Kicking off her heels, Tamatha climbed into the tub and, peering through the parted gray fabric shower curtains, gestured to her reluctant demon lover to join her.

"Seriously?" He approached, arms crossed over his chest, and sniffed the lemony air. "This is going to work?"

"It'll give us the privacy we need. I promise. Careful. Step over the salt. And kick off your boots. You shouldn't be wearing boots in the house anyway."

"Yes, ma'am." He studied the salt circle for a few long seconds, then drew in a deep breath and did as requested, climbing into the tub and crouching on the opposite edge, facing her. The curtain darkened their little tent, but a candle placed between their feet glowed up beneath their faces.

Tamatha reached out and adjusted the broken salt line to close it up, containing them within the circle. Ed reacted instantly. His head jerking backward, he grasped for the tub edges and grimaced, jaws tight.

She placed a palm over his heart to adjust the volatility of the circle. Whispered a few Latin words, "*refragatio subsisto*." His heartbeats thundered and then slowed.

Ed relaxed and exhaled. "Whew! This is a powerful circle."

"I never do anything half-assed," she said and leaned

forward to kiss him. "Most powerful witch in Paris, remember?"

"That is probably the first time I've ever voluntarily stepped into a salt circle. You do bewitch me, Tamatha."

"Never purposely. Now." She clasped his hands between them. "Tell me—what has been troubling you so much you resorted to kidnapping a witch?"

"Will you ever let me forget that one?"

"Probably not. But you've been wanting to ask me since then, right?"

"Yes, but I had to know I could trust you first."

"Hence the romance and wine?"

"Honestly? Whatever happens romantically between us is separate from this, which I consider business."

"Good to know. So you do consider this a romance?"

"It's certainly not a tragedy." He kissed her.

She was miffed he couldn't claim the word but decided to mark it off as caution instead of lack of interest. "So tell."

He clasped his hands before him and pressed his fists against his mouth. She sensed his anxiety, but wasn't about to give him a pass on this one. She needed to know what it was he was so passionate about that destiny had brought the two of them together in a means neither could have resisted.

"I need you to perform a spell for me. Maybe a spell. I'm not sure. But a searching spell might be a good start."

"I already said I could do that."

"Right, but it might be vast or maybe small. I feel as though I'm asking a lot. It's to do with…other witches."

She gaped at him. She'd expected demons. What could he want that required a spell against her own? She didn't perform magic against the Light. It was unthinkable.

She leaned forward, feeling the heat from the candle

flame warm her hands. "I know witches aren't in trouble with vamps again. Has it to do with demons?"

"Demons and witches. A particular denizen of demons and perhaps one particular coven. Maybe. I don't know. I'm trying to piece things together and I need your help to do that."

He took her hands and held them above the candle flame. The amber light warmed their grasp. "Demonic magic won't work because we've very little sway against witches."

"As do witches against demons. We generally can't command a demon to do our bidding unless we've conjured that demon to this realm in the first place."

"Right, but you can take us out and...bind us."

"True." She hadn't considered that at the time. Why had she been able to bespell him in the binding? Were there exceptions? Another note for her research list.

"I need a witch to perform a spell that will— Let me explain first."

Within the glowing confines of the bespelled bathtub, Ed told her everything.

"I witnessed a coven of witches murder a demon a few days ago, not ten minutes after I ran into you in the alley. And the other night after you cleansed my office, that phone call I got sent me to arrive after another demon had been slaughtered. I had initially thought it was a random killing, but now with two in the same cemetery and possibly by the same witches, I'm thinking this could escalate, and I don't want that to happen."

"Keeping the peace?" she asked.

"Exactly. I've been able to piece together some basic facts. But I still don't know exactly what is going on. The demon killed was a friend of mine. Laurent LaVolliere. And the second demon was from Laurent's denizen."

"And you think a coven is killing off a denizen of demons?"

"I don't know. Are the witches going after any demon they can find? Or maybe they are focusing on a specific bloodline that originated in the eighteenth century. Or it could be that specific denizen."

"What makes you think it's related to a bloodline from the eighteenth century?"

"Tamatha." He clasped her hand to the side of the candle. "You know how witches use familiars to call up demons and then can control that demon to do their bidding?"

She nodded. "I've never done it myself. Seems cruel."

"Exactly. The demon never asked for such slavery. But generally after the intended task is completed, the demon is released or escapes. But a coven in the eighteenth century used to enslave their demons and use them until they literally burst into dust or collapsed from exhaustion."

He splayed his hands out and continued. "What I have learned from some online research is that, in the eighteenth century, a coven was brought to the pyres and burned right here in Paris where the Place de Grève used to be."

"In the courtyard before city hall."

"Yes. In the article I read, two accusers were listed by name. And of course, no one assumed anything at the time but that they were human. I suspect they may have been the very demons the witches had enslaved. Yet they had been able to occupy human bodies to make the accusations.

"It was clever on the demons' part. Revenge against their oppressors. And it did serve to set them free, for their persecutors were burned."

"Clever indeed. And I can hardly feel sympathy for a coven who would do such a thing." She stroked his hand reassuringly. "How do you feel this is related to the demon deaths you've witnessed?"

"I believe the coven that was burned is the very same who are now murdering descendants of that denizen who accused them," he said.

"But if they were burned at the stake...how is that possible? They'd have to be...revenants."

"You said it, not me. But that term perfectly fits what I've witnessed. They've risen from ash, Tamatha. I don't know if they were conjured by another witch or were able to manage the transformation back to life themselves, but I know the coven's name because it was the last thing Laurent said before he died. They are *Les Douze*."

"The Twelve?" Suddenly Tamatha's heart thudded against her rib cage. She clutched her chest. "I've heard of them before. But from whom and why? I can't recall what I know about them."

"Whatever they are, I think they're back. As zombies."

Chapter 9

He'd confessed his idiotic thinking. And she hadn't laughed at him. Did she trust him after all?

"And you learned this by witnessing one of your friends being killed by these zombie witches?"

Ed nodded and rubbed Tamatha's clasped hands softly. "Laurent and I were close because our mothers were when we were younger. Our distant relatives were in the same denizen that Laurent led, or used to lead. That denizen was formed in the eighteenth century after they escaped enslavement by The Twelve."

"But you're not in the denizen?"

"I'm not affiliated with a denizen. Evil overlord, remember? I'm a stand-alone kind of guy."

And after discussing his ability to gain knowledge by eating hearts, he kicked himself for not considering such in the graveyard. If he had tapped into Laurent's heart, he might have some answers. Of course, it wasn't a practice he utilized often, so it hadn't been fore in mind. Hell, just getting out of there had been. But he wouldn't reveal that moment of lacking bravery to Tamatha.

"Come on. I've laid something incredible on you, and I'm feeling drained by this salt circle." He leaned forward, pressing his nose to hers and kissing her lips. "Can we get out of the cone of silence now?"

"Yes, I'm sorry. I forgot about that. Let me clear the salt for you." She did so with a shuffle of her hand over the salt line, and once he was out, he turned to help her from the tub. She snuffed the candles and set them back on the vanity. As she cleaned up her supplies, Ed noticed she wasn't even touching the things as they straightened and aligned on the vanity. That OCD magic could come in handy on cleaning day.

When finished, she leaned against the vanity and crossed her arms. Candlelight kissed her glossy lips with an enticing glint. "I need to think about this, Ed."

"Of course you do. What I ask of you is immense. I'm not even sure what it is I'm asking you for. *Is* a spell required? What *are* those witches? They look dead to me. They must have been summoned by someone."

"Who else could be involved?"

"I have no clue. I need to do more research, but I don't have a very extensive database or the means—"

"The Archives. Now that I know what is going on, I'm sure I can find information in there." She hastened down the stairs, and when he thought she would rush away, she sat on the stool before the kitchen counter. "I think we should finish the wine."

He poured her a goblet of wine and none for himself.

"You don't seem very worried that a gang of dead witches might come for you."

"I don't worry so much about myself as I do other demons getting killed and the possibility of chaos should this coven become sloppy and reveal themselves to humans."

She tapped a beringed finger against the goblet rim. "You and that 'keeping the peace' thing?"

"Exactly. Let's say I make it a point to ensure Paris stays relatively demon quiet. In the long run it's good for us all."

"You really are a good guy," she said on an incredulous whisper. "I think an evil overlord can be beneficent if the henchmen he leads are doing good. But what bothers me is I don't know how those witches could have risen from ash."

"Witchcraft? Do you think someone else—another witch—could have summoned them?"

"Makes more sense than dead witches rising on their own. Oh." She pressed a hand to his chest. "We shouldn't talk about this out here. I haven't warded this area."

He swept her into his arms. "What was shared in the cone of silence stays in the cone of silence. Promise?"

She nodded. "But—" Another shiver and this time she pushed out of his arms. "Agreed."

"You want to leave?"

She looked at him and shook her head. "I'd much rather finish our date. And this wine."

"We could watch some television, chatter about random things. Kiss?"

That got a smile from her. But he was pushing it. He'd dumped a huge revelation on her. He could hardly expect her to want to make out. It was really hard for him, though, not to think about kissing her. All the time.

"I want to ward this place," she said with determination.

"I have wards."

"Against witches?"

"Surprisingly? Not. Else you would be in pain right now."

"I felt the intrusion you spoke of when I first entered. There's something not right about this place."

"It's probably the same thing I felt. Heavy, like it's trying to invade my skin."

"Yes." She shuffled through her shoulder bag. "I'll need more supplies. I'll have to do it next time I visit. If it's a witch who has been getting into your place and spying on you and we want to have a conversation without worry of it being broadcast, a ward is necessary. Would you let me try?"

He clasped her hand and leaned across the counter. "But if you ward against witches, then I won't be able to bring you home and ravish you."

A flutter of her lashes teased. "Ravishing sounds wonderful. I'll put a niche in for me. The warder usually does that anyway. Did you know that? Whomever you have ward your home generally leaves an entry for themselves. I hope you trust the person who warded it previously."

"I did not know that, but I do trust the fellow. And I trust you." He walked around the counter and took her hand as she got off the stool. "I'm suddenly compelled to do this."

He kissed her below the jaw, there at the base of her earlobe where he loved it most. Always her hair spilled over his face, tickling, and the scent of lemons was sweetly fresh.

"Mmm," she cooed and slipped her hands up his chest. "Let the ravishing begin."

Ed spun her and her shoulders met the wall. He kissed her mouth, tasting wine and her sigh. Her dress buttoned from breasts to hem, and he unbuttoned the first and then the next. "Do you mind?" he asked.

"No, this is just the thing we need to take our minds from more dire things. It's not wrong, is it?"

"What?" He kissed the top of her breast as he unbuttoned

yet another button. Mmm, soft, luscious, flesh-smelling, tangy sweet.

"Us ignoring that other thing."

"The world will be fine for a few minutes. We need to do research, yes?"

"Right. Oh…yes. That's nice. You going to go…all the way down?"

"I am." His fingers danced over her stomach and continued to unbutton. Tamatha tilted her head against the wall and closed her eyes. "Pink lace," he commented on her matching bra and panties. Two more buttons, and he spread her dress open to look over her long, lithe figure. A tattoo at her hip featured an owl, wings spread, soaring toward him. "What does an owl symbolize?"

"Athena," she offered, "the Greek goddess of learning."

"Most definitely you." He glided his hands over her stomach, feeling the muscles beneath tighten and release in his wake. "You are gorgeous, witch."

She smirked. "You didn't say that with quite as much accusation as you once did."

"You are undeserving of my scorn." He licked from one breast to the other and cupped them in his hands, cursing the fact he must wear the half gloves. But it was for her protection. "You smell so good. I want to taste you."

"No objections to that. But when you taste things, are you always getting a read like you showed me in the elevator?"

"Not unless I want to." He dashed his tongue from between her breasts and up her neck. "Anything you don't want me to know about you?"

"No. And I much prefer this method of your gaining knowledge to the 'eating the heart' method."

"Agreed."

"Let's get you a little more comfortable." She unbuttoned his shirt and he helped her to pull it off. When she tapped his gloves he shook his head.

"My thorns contain poison. One little slice…"

"Yes, I won't forget that. I can deal." Her hand spread across his chest and her eyes danced with marvel. "So much dark hair. And so soft."

He chuckled. "If I got anything from my werewolf father, it was thick hair. Good thing, too. I don't worry about going bald."

"Mmm, and it goes down further." Her fingers walked down his muscled abdomen and teased at the dark hairs below his navel. "Your father is a werewolf? I didn't know that."

"Was that something I was supposed to provide during your questioning?"

"Maybe, but I've realized you protect yourself, first and foremost. So, half wolf, half raven?"

"I've never thought of it that way. Raven-shifting is simply an innate skill of mine. If I have to label myself, it's simply 'demon' because I have no werewolf qualities beyond the abundant hair."

She tickled her fingers up through his chest hair and tapped his mouth. "Let's go up to the bedroom, demon. I want to get you naked."

"More research?"

"I'll never tell."

"That means yes."

"Maybe."

Oh, it was a yes. And he didn't mind at all.

Ed grabbed her hand and led her up the stairs. He flicked on the lights, which were set around the ceiling cornice and beamed subtle halogens every ten feet around the room's circumference. Not too bright, but enough light so he could admire every sensual curve that designed her body.

Tamatha strode across the room, dropping the blue dress in her wake. Pink lace panties barely covered her sweet, peach bottom. She turned a teasing wink over her shoulder and crooked her finger for him to come to her.

Ed unzipped his trousers and Tamatha slid them down his legs. As he stepped out of them to stand in nothing but dark blue, form-fitted boxer briefs, she walked around behind him, her fingertips drawing over the sigils on his shoulder and gliding down his back where the black lines formed an art gallery of life events.

"You have so many marks back here. These feathers trace your entire spine. The same as the one on your neck. Oh! They connect."

"Yes, it's one long trail. The feathers are indicative of the corax breed," he said of the long black sigil that started at the side of his neck and trailed down his spine to the top of his buttocks.

The feathers were thorned along the shafts and seemed to have a depth, as if she could push her fingers into the blackness. Tamatha stroked the feathers and marveled over their subtle movement upon the steely muscle that wrapped his body. It was a two-dimensional drawing that took on three-dimensional life under her touch. Amazing. This was going in her notebook.

"Born with it," he added.

"Really? A baby with tattoos?"

He shrugged. "A sigil. Unlike tattoos, sigils alter and grow as I age. I imagine it was but a fine line down my spine when I was a baby."

He let out a pleasurable moan as she danced her fingers along the pale gray marking at the back of his hip. It was circular but again thorned and tribal in style. Most of his sigils were, and she associated it with the deadly thorns on his knuckles he wouldn't allow her to study.

"First official fuck," he said with a gasp. "That one."

"Really? You've a sigil to mark the first time you had sex? Do you have one that tallies every time you get it on?"

"Cheeky of you, but no. You think I would have a back full of hash marks?"

"Would you?" She rested her chin on his shoulder and hugged him from behind. "Don't tell me. It's not important. Besides, I've lived four times as long as you."

"Should I be asking about your tally marks?"

"I take my lovers with a discretionary eye. I have had my share over the decades. Let's leave it at that."

"Love Often, eh?"

"Exactly."

Returning to stand before him, she glided her fingers through his chest hair, marveling over the soft thickness. His abs were hard and ridged, a count of three rises and falls as she moved lower. She stopped at his boxers but then couldn't stop herself from pressing a hand over his very obvious erection.

"Oh!" She met his curiously wondering gaze. "You really are…"

He nodded. "For your pleasure, my lady."

"I need to take a look at this."

He gripped her wrist, halting her from tugging down the boxers. "Tell me first—are you curious or is this for your research?"

She shoved him backward to land on the bed. "Both."

Tamatha's demon lover winked and clasped his hands behind his head as she shimmied down his boxers and tossed them aside. His erection was impressive, regally straight, and—

"This is so cool. It really is ribbed." She ran her thumb

over the definite ridges that circled from below the bold, thick head of it. She counted four and they were spaced about a finger's width apart. "This is going to be fun."

"I have never had a woman take such delight in my penis before."

"Really? I'm sorry for you."

"I mean—well, you know, it has never scared anyone off."

"I should say not. I want to play. You okay with that?"

"You play all you like, sweetness. Did you want me to join in while you're playing?"

"No. Lie back and—" she gripped his hard rod "—take it all in. I know I'm going to enjoy this."

"I'm going to have to change my thinking regarding your research," he said as she tickled her tongue around his penis corona. "Oooo, yes. Research. Goood."

Trying a few strokes up and down his length, she noticed he didn't have the usual salty tang that most did. He was clean and perhaps even a little cool, as if he'd come in from a brisk outdoor walk and the chill air lingered on his skin. Yet with every stroke she could feel heat replacing the coolness. Ed groaned and muttered something about her having her way with him being perfectly fine. She lashed her tongue over each of the ribs on his length. They were so firm and like a sex toy waiting for her to experiment.

Shimmying off her panties, she straddled his hips and directed the head of him against her folds. Wet and hot, she needed connection. His molten heat steamed her skin. Mmm, she pressed hard, using his erection to satisfy her achy need for contact. Rocking her hips, she rubbed the ribs against her clit, dragging his penis up and down, increasing the friction and luring her pleasure to the edge.

"You know exactly what you like," he said. "Ah, that's so good."

"Good? This is sofuckingsweet."

Now was not the time for chatter. Because the focused sensation of his hot cock gliding over her swollen clitoris was rapidly conjuring a heady storm in her core. With her free hand she clasped her breast and squeezed the nipple, rocking her hips faster and faster. Ed's encouraging moans spurred her to press his length harder to her.

And with a thrilling shout, an orgasm swept through her system, shivering and quaking and spilling through her pores. Tamatha gasped and stopped humping him as she quivered into the delicious surrender.

Ed sat up and swept aside her hair, then kissed her breasts. "You are incredible, witch."

The sweetest accusation ever.

"So good," she said on a gasp and kissed him quickly. Hungrily she devoured his taste.

"I can taste your fire," he said. "The hot, fiery magic within you. It's powerful."

He lifted her by the hips and she wrapped her legs about his back as he lowered her onto his stiff, wanting erection. The man groaned deeply as she enveloped him. He pulsed and swelled within her. Swearing, he hissed, then lifted her by the thighs to rock her up and down upon his shaft.

Still fluttering in the orgasm, she squeezed her insides about him, coaxing him to join her in the bliss. And with a few more glides up and down, her lover bucked beneath her and shouted. He clasped an arm across her back and clutched her to him as he came along with her.

Bodies trembling, breaths gasping, together they fell back onto the soft gray bedsheets, panting as they rode the exquisite wave.

Tamatha kissed him. He bracketed her head, dashing his tongue in deeply and mimicking the actions his penis had made inside her. He was still inside her, both at loins and mouth. Sweet possession.

She glided her hands through his hair and traced the glossy horn nubs. Breaking the kiss, she slid upward and licked one of the hard nubs, which felt like warm hematite against her tongue.

"Holy—whoa." Ed gripped her about the waist. "That's…"

"You like that?"

He nodded as she licked him again. "Never had a woman do that to me before. Actually, I never allowed it. Why, I have no idea. I'm going to come again if you keep it up."

That was an invitation she wouldn't pass up. She tested the other horn, and it was warm and solid, smooth, and didn't taste like anything. Ed's gasps and increased breathing enticed her to lick harder and to swirl her tongue about the circle of it. And *like that* his chest bucked, his hands slapped the bed, and within her, she felt his cock harden again as he came.

Her lover groaned from his very being and pulled her down to collapse on top of him. Tamatha nuzzled her cheek against his shoulder and clasped a hand within his fingers half-covered by the leather glove.

"That was incredible," he muttered. "How'd you know to do that?"

"Just being curious." She hugged her breasts up to his panting heat and nuzzled her cheek against his chest. "You're a nice big cozy snuggle."

"No one has every used *nice*, *cozy* or *snuggle* to describe me."

"It's the truth. Can you handle that, Evil Overlord?"

"My evil cred may take a hit, but yes. Bring it."

Chapter 10

Tamatha woke to a beam of red light dashing across her face and smiled to realize she lay in Ed's bed after spending the night snuggled next to his gorgeously muscled, sex-warmed body. But he wasn't in the bed now. Turning her head, she found he stood near the wall, looking up, as if following a spider along the ceiling. But she couldn't see anything.

"What is it?" she asked sleepily.

"You can't feel it? Something is trying to intrude." He shook his hands over his head as if to chase away the invisible entity. "What is it?"

She sat up and closed her eyes, tapping her littlest fingers together to invoke her connection to air magic. Instantly, a malevolent feeling fell upon her bare shoulders and teased at the back of her neck.

"Oh, shit, that's malefic magic." She threw aside the sheets and hopped out of bed. Grabbing her bra and panties and hastily putting them on, she then rushed down to the living room.

"What is it?" Ed followed her. He wore only boxers and his hair was tousled. He looked so eatable. And she would get to that. But first.

Emptying her bag on the couch, she sorted through the magical accoutrements and grabbed the amethyst-hilted athame. "I forgot all about warding this place last night. You distracted me." She winked at him.

He nodded acknowledgment. "I aim to please."

"You did please. More than a few times. But we forgot the important stuff."

"You said you had to go home for supplies."

"I do, but shoot. Maybe I can work with what I have. I have to do this now because something malefic is trying to get in."

"Maybe I've something you can use?"

"Unless you have a store of salt somewhere, I don't think you can."

"Fresh out of that condiment. What do you need me to do?"

"Stand back and let it happen." She dipped the athame into a vial of blessed rainwater, then walked to the center of the living room and stood before the stained glass windows that beamed in colorful morning sunlight.

"I have never seen a more beautiful witch," Ed commented.

Smiling to herself, Tamatha redirected her focus. Reveling in a compliment from her lover could threaten to lower the efficacy of any spell she attempted. Drawing in the air before her, she marked out the sigil against malefic magic and recited the incantation. Tapping her little fingers together, she activated her air magic and focused her inner eye to encompass the entire building Ed lived in, including the surrounding streets.

A pulse of power echoed out from her being and pushed through the air. Behind her, Ed swore in quiet fascination. And when the energy returned and entered through her soles, she closed off the ward and sealed it with a final dash of the athame across the invisible sigil she had drawn before her.

Turning to the fascinated demon, she nodded. "It's done."

"I felt that. But I don't see anything."

"Exactly. The best wards are invisible yet strong. That should hold. But not for long. I didn't have any sage to make it stick. And blood might even be required to really put up a good block against the intrusion. Malefic magic is way out of my realm. It's beyond diabology, which I'm only beginning to study. But I put it off for a while. You think whatever has been trying to get into your place might be involved with the cemetery killings?"

"Possible. In my line of work, I'm always dealing with nefarious people."

"Evil-overlord stuff?"

"Yes, but this feels like it is to do with the current situation."

"I need to do some research on *Les Douze* today. Do you mind if I shower here? I want to head straight to the Archives from your place."

"Not at all. You want me to join you in the shower?"

"Oh, yeah. Do you have a vacuum?"

"A, er…vacuum?"

She smirked at his apparent lacking knowledge. "You know that electronic thing that you push through the house to suck up dirt?"

"Ah. I have a maid who does that once a week."

Tamatha shook her head. "Bachelors. How about a broom?"

He winced. "Perhaps? Why the compulsion to clean?"

"I want to sweep up the salt around your tub so you can get into it with me."

"I think I remember where the broom is kept."

The depths of the Archives' room that harbored grimoires and all documents and tomes related to the species of witch was Tamatha's favorite room. It was the largest room with high, arched ceilings painted in the fresco style of da Vinci, though there were no religious scenes, but rather depictions of Samhain, Beltane and the great Hecate. This room contained twice as much information as any other. Witches were the most abundant of the paranormal species.

It was a workday, but Tamatha had nothing more pressing to tend to. Dusting and tidying she achieved by slowly pacing down an aisle of books. Her OCD magic took care of straightening, dust dispersed in her wake.

She paused at the end of the aisle where the fluorescent lights didn't reach. This far quadrant of the room repelled modern electricity. It was where the books on malefic magic were kept. Old-fashioned candle sconces provided lighting, and two beeswax candles took to light with a snap of her fingers.

A familiar shiver crossed her shoulders. Malefic magic had been trying to infiltrate Ed's home. That made her suspect whoever was behind whatever was going on was a witch who practiced malefic magic. But witches didn't practice such magic. If so, they were branded a warlock and shunned from both the Light and Dark.

The only warlock Tamatha was familiar with was Ian Grim. She didn't know him personally. Never had a reason to work with a practitioner of such foul magic. There were dozens of other warlocks, surely, but she'd need to do more research if all paths led that direction.

Stepping forward, she felt the shadows creep over her like black ink spilling over her skin. The hairs on her arms tingled. Hisses lured her to the left of the bookshelf. Scents of decayed thyme and earth infused the air. A low growl sounded more from within her head than before her. It was the magic toying with her.

She followed intuition, hoping it would guide her.

Something skittered off on a multitude of feet, not across the floor, but within the pages of the dark, bound volumes lining the shelves. Even though she fluttered her fingers along the spines, these books did not align as did all other things when reacting to her OCD magic.

"Most definitely malefic," she whispered. Quickly she pulled up her white light. "Should have done that earlier. You're slipping, Tam. Too much demon on the brain lately."

But, oh, what a demon. And she'd had him on more than her brain. Her lips, her breasts, her stomach. Mmm…between her legs. Her thoughts drifted to the king-size bed and Ed leaning over her, tending her every sensual hot spot…

One slim book slid out a quarter of an inch, dusting the air with a mist of emerald smoke.

"Really? And I was just getting to the good part of the daydream."

With a sigh, she snatched the volume, which moaned until she'd returned to the fore of the room and set it on the table right on top of the sigil carved into the wood that would render all magics useless. It was a contained spell and focused only on text, so it could not vanquish a spell tossed at her from a visitor or fellow archivist. Not that Tamatha worried. The Archives were secure.

She planted herself in a wicker chair that creaked, kicking off her high heels. Study of the heavy volume found the gold leaf had worn away from the title, but the words were impressed deeply into the scuffed brown leather. And the fore-edges of the pages were not deckled, but rather, when she pressed them tightly together and then fanned them slightly, revealed a scene that depicted horned and tailed beings. She loved surprises like that. Yet the book wasn't a malefic grimoire, but rather a genealogy.

"Weird. Why was it shelved with those dark books?" It felt safe now that she preened over it in the light. "Why am I surprised? Isn't as if there aren't hundreds of mis-shelved volumes."

She had been meant to pull out this volume, and that was the important thing.

It wasn't difficult to track down a page detailing the witches of *Les Douze*. They had been burned in 1753 in the Place de Grève. The area was now the square before the city hall, and a merry-go-round held court where once violent hangings, burnings and all sorts of criminal executions had taken place through the centuries. A couple decades later, use of the guillotine had literally stained the streets red during the Revolution.

The page in the grimoire shivered under Tamatha's touch and a minute twinge of sorrow entered her veins.

She quickly withdrew her finger from the book. "Whew! Powerful stuff."

Many a grimoire or book in the Archives were filled to the endpapers with whatever magics it detailed and often harbored memories and emotions that could bleed into a reader's very being. It was the reason most chose not to work in the Archives. Anything could happen. Including escape from the pages. CJ had captured an elemental the first week Tamatha had worked there. It had been left next to a book of cherubs, and the magics had combined. A drunken bacchanal had ensued. Of course, with no alcohol on the premises, the cherubs had stolen tea, and well, as CJ told it, tea could get a cherub drunk faster than vodka to a teetotaler.

Lifting the book to check the magic sigil was indeed directly beneath the volume, she set it down with a bit more confidence. She trailed her finger down the list of twelve, whispering each name as if a prayer as she did so.

"Macarius Fleche, Alyce Doran, Lucian Maldove." The list included all twelve coven members and ended with "Martine Chevalier and…"

She paused before speaking the final name written in tiny cursive. A name all too familiar to her. Tamatha's heartbeats sped. It couldn't be. Her mother had never mentioned…

"Lysia Bellerose?"

Her heart dropped in her chest. She gasped to catch her shallow breaths. That was impossible. Of course, nothing was impossible. And there were no coincidences. It was right there in black ink on the stained page.

Her grandmother had been one of the witches of *Les Douze*.

Chapter 11

After Tamatha had left for the Archives, Ed dressed, slipped on his gloves and selected a deep purple tie to go with the steel-gray business shirt. He pulled on the black Zegna suit coat and stepped into his leather shoes. He would go in to the office because he wanted to put contacts on the alert should he need them.

And figure how dangerous it could be to piss off a warlock. Though it seemed as though, if it really was a warlock, he was already in fine fettle. Ed didn't mind facing a new and powerful opponent, but he did like to know what he was dealing with. With hope, Tamatha's research could fill him in.

He took the elevator down and checked the part in his hair in the mirrored wall. His finger dashed over a horn nub but it didn't feel like it did when Tamatha did that. When she touched him there it was like sex coursing through his veins and congregating at the base of his cock to an instant hard-on.

For all appearances, he and Tamatha were hitting it off. Doing the boyfriend-and-girlfriend thing. But he didn't want to get his hopes up. Because…he wasn't boyfriend material. Women never stayed in his life for long. And when he finished with what he needed Tamatha for, she'd leave him. He felt sure of that.

He wasn't meant to have love.

Besides, he was merely research to the witch. She wanted to study him and, yes, even have sex with him to see what it was like to have sex with a demon. She might like to believe differently, but he knew better.

He sighed as the elevator doors glided open. Striding out the lobby and through the main doors, he headed down the street toward his office building. Once across the street he felt something pull over his skin and he stepped through it, as if emerging from a thickness.

He stopped and looked back over the street. "Her ward," he decided. "A powerful witch indeed. I'm lucky to have found her. She'll help defeat *Les Douze*."

And that should be all that mattered.

Of course, he knew better. Somewhere deep inside, the idea of love rattled his better senses and scared the crap out of him.

Hands shaking, Tamatha carefully sipped the mint tea. The one name on the list of twelve witches kept flashing at her like a warning light. Truly, was her grandmother involved in the terrible murders Ed had detailed?

It didn't make sense. Her mother had never spoken a disparaging word about Lysia Bellerose. Petrina had not talked about her often, but when she had, it had been to tell Tamatha of her grandmother's wisdom and spell-crafting expertise. Lysia had been kind, lovely and wise. Her magical knowledge had been vast. She'd had diabology under her belt and had sought to study angelology before her abrupt and cruel demise. She'd never caused a death, nor would she participate in magic that could result in such evil. Born in the early sixteenth century, she had lived two and a half centuries and had given birth to five daughters, three of whom had survived the birth. Yes, Lysia had been burned at the stake—the sad fate of many a witch who had tried to help humans by teaching them simple remedies that embraced herbology and healing skills.

"Burned at the stake alongside eleven others," Tamatha whispered.

To imagine such a horror chilled her veins. Had all twelve pyres been lit at once? Or had one been lit and then the next, so that the witches at the end had to endure the screams and agony of their coven mates before the flames got to them? The thought of it made Tamatha moan.

Tea spattered her lap, and she set the teacup on the saucer with a click. Blowing and whispering a spell instantly dried the dark skirt fabric, which didn't show a stain.

She turned the page in the book to read more. Within the fragile pages of a history ledger that detailed the bloodlines of witches of the Light, she located her grandmother, Lysia Bellerose. None of the females in the Bellerose family— should they marry—had taken their husband's name. It just wasn't done. If they fell in love and felt the need to make a home with the man, they did so. Without the official document. All their offspring carried the Bellerose name.

It was how witches often did things. The matriarchs were the strongest and wisest in most families. Male witches were often considered lesser, which wasn't necessarily true when comparing skills, but it was an old and revered train of thought.

Tamatha's father had been a witch, but he and Petrina had drifted apart after fifty years with one another. *People are not meant to have such long monogamous relation-ships*, her mother had once said. *But if it comes to you, try it, embrace it and welcome it for as long as you feel comfortable. But never stay beyond the expiration date*, her mother had also warned.

Love often.

"And deeply," Tamatha whispered. "For it never lasts."

The idea of marrying a man for the romantic ideal of happily-ever-after didn't fit when the twosome were immortal. Ever after took on an entirely new meaning when compared to the fifty or more years some humans enjoyed in marriage.

Yet Tamatha teased the idea of monogamy. Dating was tedious. Lovers were essential, though. And she'd never been bothered that they left her life more frequently than they stayed. Only three of her former serious lovers had died when they'd been dating. Henry had been a mortal who'd fallen off his bicycle, hit his head on a sharp rock and bled out. Joseph had been a fellow witch who had insisted that using arsenic in a spell was correct—he'd choked on his foaming saliva. The familiar had died after they'd broken it off. All the others she'd dated had come and gone with the same desire for freedom as she had. Save Byron, who had gone mad and had literally been carted away from her in a straitjacket.

And Ed, well…

Well.

She wanted him to last. To not go mad. To not die. And to be in her life longer than most. Because he fascinated her and appealed to her desire for the new and unknown.

But most of all, she wanted to help him. She'd agreed to help him with whatever he needed to figure out the situation of demons being murdered by witches. But could she? If worse came to worst, that may mean she'd have to kill her grandmother. That was, if Lysia Bellerose was really dead. And if the witches Ed claimed to have seen in the cemetery truly were the infamous *Les Douze*.

According to the notes on Lysia Bellerose and the others in *Les Douze*, each of the twelve had named their accusers as demons. The human witch finder had mocked them and further accused them of spewing lies and diabolitry. Could they not see the humans who had accused them were simply men and women? Demons had tails and fiery red eyes. Yet the witch finder had noted that he did not doubt *Les Douze* were in alliance with demons and the very Devil himself.

"*Himself,*" Tamatha corrected herself when she read the lowercased word. One always capitalized the name of the Dark Lord. And a wise witch would never say the name three times, for that would serve as an invite to Himself, who had a tendency to appear to a person in the guise of their greatest temptation.

She mused that should he appear on her doorstep, she might lunge into his arms and kiss him, for surely the Devil would appear to her as Edamite Thrash.

She shook her head of the terrible notion. Best not to spend time considering *you know who*. Back to the text.

"Grandma must have known something," she said. "Of course, if they were really demons, she would know. She was a diabolotrist. If anyone could recognize a demon on the spot, it had to be Grandmother. But why had demons accused *Les Douze*?"

Had Ed figured it out? They had to compare notes.

She pulled up the ledger against her chest and settled into the chair, clasping the book as if it would fly away. "How terrible to have been burned at the stake. Alive."

Prickles shivered her skin. Most witches shied from studying fire magic. Fire proved the witch's bane. If something went wrong, it could kill with ease. Tamatha had

taken decades to master it, and still, she never utilized it
too often. A sudden gust of wind could turn a fire spell
back on her. And to mix magics by applying water magic
to back up the fire would result in disaster. She was no
master at mixed magic, and it had resulted in more than
a few mishaps. Earth magic combined with air and water
magic could put a never-ending tangle of poisonous snakes
on a man's feet and render him insane.

But that was the past.

And now...

Had Lysia managed to come back on her own, along
with her eleven coven mates? Didn't seem possible. Which
only left someone else summoning the dead witches.

"What malefic magic has brought back twelve witches
from the dead?"

Tamatha set the book on the table and closed her eyes,
placing her fingers lightly over the pages. She inhaled and
exhaled deeply but could divine no hidden clues beyond
the printed text.

Dare she involve herself in this? It couldn't end well if
it resulted in her grandmother's destruction. And a witch
never worked magic against her own. It was unheard of.
The Light and Dark would ostracize any witch who worked
against them, which was how some became warlock.

But if Lysia truly were back and killing demons, Tamatha
couldn't stand by and allow that to happen. Why hadn't her
mother told her the details of her grandmother's death?

She had to give her a call, get to the truth.

Tugging out her cell phone from her purse, she texted
her mother. Petrina never answered calls. She preferred
her daughter text her and she would return a call when
she had a moment. She typed: Questions about Grandmother's death. Urgent.

If that didn't result in a return call within a few hours, she'd worry that her mother was hiding something.

Until then, she had work to do. But she couldn't concentrate on her demonic studies. Maybe there was something in one of these books about witches raised from the dead? Should she look up zombies?

Setting the teacup on the side table next to the teapot, she then pushed a tall wooden ladder along the dusty metal pipe to move it down toward the spell books. The books closest to her on the head-level shelves shifted to attention. This room was partially organized by topic, such as spell books, grimoires, herbals, incantations and hexes, et cetera. But within those categories there was no organization.

Looking over the vast shelves overstuffed with books, she shook her head. It was going to be a long yet interesting day.

Ed crossed a street lit with neon gleams from nearby restaurants and bars. It was midnight and he didn't want to sit in the office or at home. Tamatha had called to say she was spending a late night at the Archives and not to look forward to seeing her. He never thought he'd miss seeing a woman daily, but he did. He tried to remember her scent. It was lemons, but he couldn't summon the memory in his nose.

Really? He couldn't remember the scent of a common fruit? He was acting stupid. Pussy whipped? Yes, he was.

Best he focus on business. He'd send Inego and Glitch to check on the cemetery guard. He hadn't heard word from either, so he assumed no new zombie-witch action there.

A horn honked and he flipped off the driver as he crossed the street.

"Nice," a familiar voice called from behind the wheel.

Ed turned a look over his shoulder and chuckled. "Kir!

You see?" He splayed out his hands as he approached the car. "I knew it was someone worthy of my scorn."

He joked. But he always sensed if either of the two of them held scorn toward the other, it was his brother for him. His werewolf half brother. They shared the same father, Colin Sauveterre. Kir had a thing about demons. He hated them. Although, he was getting better. He seemed to tolerate Ed.

And as hungry as he was for family, Ed tolerated the wolf's tolerance.

Kir found a parking spot and the lanky wolf climbed out and gestured toward a tapas bar. Good call.

The place was touristy, but Ed and Kir found stools at the end of the bar where one of the neon wall signs had blinked out, and it was as far from the '80s-themed karaoke stage as they could possibly get.

Kir drank whiskey while Ed preferred absinthe. It had an acrid bite that appealed to his ultrasensitive palate. He could read old things and stale mossy forests in some of the better absinthes. This one was too processed, nothing but a chemical note.

"Thought that stuff was illegal," Kir said of Ed's foggy green drink.

"Only in the States. But it's no longer like they used to make it in the nineteenth century, I'm sure. Rarely do I get a buzz off this stuff."

"Maybe because you're not human?"

"Possibly." He clinked his glass against Kir's and the two tilted back healthy swallows. "So what brings my werewolf brother to the red-light district? I thought you were married now? Would your faery wife appreciate you venturing into dark, seedy bars so late at night?"

"Bea is in a mood and the baby is teething. She sent me out for some groceries."

"At midnight?"

"That's her form of saying, 'Don't bug me—I'm cranky. Go have a beer. Chum around with your friends.'" Kir leaned his elbows on the bar counter. "Thing is, I don't have friends after being banished from pack Valoir."

"Aww…" Ed finished his drink and slammed the glass on the counter, signaling for another from the bartender. He clamped a hand across Kir's shoulder. "You got me, bro."

"You're not looking much better than I am, my man. What's up? You nearly walked right into my car out there. Deep thoughts?"

"It's nothing."

"Right. And my wife is a bundle of peaches and cream all the time. What is it? A woman?"

Ed snickered and placed another ten-euro bill on the bar when the drink was slid before him. He tapped the silver spoon, on which perched a melting sugar cube. A small pitcher of cool water had been provided, but he didn't like to bring up too much of a louche, preferring the hard bite of alcohol.

"Does it have to be a woman?" he asked.

"It should be. 'Bout time you found one for yourself."

"So you and I can commiserate on the married life? Love isn't for me, my brother. It's just…" He wouldn't sigh, so instead he dipped a forefinger into the green drink and stirred the clouding mix. "She's a witch."

"So it *is* a woman." Kir signaled the bartender for another drink. "I thought you didn't like witches."

"Like you not liking demons?"

"I'm coming around. Give me some credit."

"I do. But you'll understand, then, that a healthy fear

of witches is a demon thing. History has proved we don't fare well when summoned by them. I remain cautious."

"So why did you decide it would be a good idea to do whatever it is you're doing with this witch?"

"I was out one night, minding my own business, and I bumped into her. Acting defensively, she cast a binding spell on me. Hurt like a mother. Then…" Now he did sigh before tilting back the entire drink. As it burned down his throat, he muttered, "I kissed her."

Kir broke out in laughter and smacked the bar with a palm.

"It's not *that* funny."

"Yes, it is. It's always the ones you least expect to be interested in that seem to wrangle you like a cow and hobble you to kneel before their pretty high-heeled shoes."

"She does wear pretty shoes. I think about dragging my tongue up the heel and along her ankle. A lot." The lingering burn from the absinthe helped to quench the stupid rise of desire he'd almost fallen into right before his brother's eyes.

"What about the clothes they wear?" Kir asked. "Bea likes to wear sexy, clingy stuff that hugs her breasts and her nipples point up under the fabric. So awesome."

"And those tight skirts that squeeze her pretty little derriere." Ed echoed the appreciation.

"Hair that smells like flowers."

"Lemons," Ed said. "She smells like lemons."

The wolf slapped a hand across Ed's back. "You're whipped, buddy."

"But I can't be. I don't do the love thing. It's not right. It feels wrong. Alien. And I don't need the distraction, what with the zombie witches and dead demons."

Kir swung a look at him.

"It's a weird story. I'm dealing with it. You know I like

to keep a finger on all demonic activity in Paris. Unfortunately, I need Tamatha's witchcraft skills to help me figure things out."

"Tamatha Bellerose?"

"You know her?"

"I know of her. Weird silver hair and kind of a retro look? She is a gorgeous number. And smart, according to her friend Verity Van Velde."

"I had no idea my brother hung out with witches." Ed mocked a shiver. "You do get around."

"If I can't go near another werewolf, then I'm open to any and all friendships offered. As you should be open to having a relationship with the witch. You have had bad luck with women."

"One witch in particular. So what makes me think this one could be different?"

"You won't know until you try."

"Your happy vibes are annoying, wolf. I can see why your wife kicked you out this evening."

"I'm heading home soon. With ice cream in hand, she'll be happy to see me. The baby will be sleeping. Do you know that faeries prefer going skyclad?"

Ed raised a brow.

"Isn't often I come home to a fully clothed faery."

"Nice. I thought witches did the skyclad thing, too?"

"See? You've so much to look forward to when dating a witch."

"I wouldn't call a binding something to look forward to."

"Well, if you're not into her, then dump her."

"I can't do that."

"Course not." Kir finished his whiskey. "Because you like her," he teased as he stood. "I gotta go. You need any help with whatever this zombie-witch situation is?"

"Not yet. But I'll call if I need you. Thanks, Kir. It was good to talk."

"Yeah, we're cool." He nodded and headed out.

That "we're cool" meant a lot to Ed. Their camaraderie, while still weak, would grow. Maybe someday they could do brotherly things like—who knew—golf or fishing? He could get into a little outdoor adventuring, though he suspected Kir's form of fishing may be in wolf shape. Ha!

So maybe he shouldn't be so worried about a relationship with a witch. He shouldn't look at it that way. It was a relationship with Tamatha. Didn't matter what she was—witch, demon or otherwise—he liked the woman and how she made him feel.

Yeah, things could be good for him.

So long as he avoided attracting the attention of twelve zombie witches.

Chapter 12

Something nudged Tamatha's elbow. She startled and looked up from the open book her cheek had been smashed against.

"Morning, sleepyhead."

"Huh?" Peeling strands of hair from her face, she straightened and winced at the muscles that pulled in her neck. She'd fallen asleep last night while reading about the local covens. "Is it morning?"

"That it is. Is my husband such a cruel boss that he makes you work all night?"

A tall, red-haired witch, who wore the corseted black Victorian dress as if she'd invented the goth style, winked at Tamatha.

"No, I was doing some research. I want to advance my knowledge on diabology."

And now, apparently, witches. Had her mother returned her text? She glanced about but didn't spy her phone in the scatter of books neatly arranged before her.

"Wow. That's a lot to study. But interesting?"

"It is."

"You find much on demons in a witch's grimoire?" Vika tapped the book cover.

"My interest wandered. What is that delightful smell?"

"CJ is brewing tea in the office. Oh, but, sweetie, you've a Post-it note stuck to your forehead."

Tamatha slapped a palm over her forehead and claimed the pink slip of sticky paper. A spell for night terrors had been noted on it. Why that had caught her attention she had no clue.

She sighed and pushed the compendium on witch families away from her. No luck with tracking her family back further than what she already knew. And she'd thought to look into Ed's family, but Thrash wasn't listed in any of the genealogical lists. It had to be a false name or moniker.

The scent of lemon and thyme drew closer, but Tamatha again sighed. She really liked Ed. As a friend. As a lover. But what he'd asked her to do was not something with which she felt comfortable. To kill her grandmother? Again? She didn't want to offend him or lose the chance to learn more about his breed. And if witches were killing demons, then someone had to do something about it.

Right?

"What's up with that?" Vika asked as she pointed to Tamatha's face.

"What do you mean? Have I more office supplies stuck somewhere?"

"No, that melancholy sigh. Ah…" The witch sat across the ancient table from Tamatha and spread her hands over the assorted grimoires, lists and compendiums. Her black fingernail polish glinted under the flickering fluorescent lights. "You're heartsick."

"What? No."

"Then it's a new love?"

"Why does it have to be love?"

"Because I can read it in your irises."

Tamatha touched the corner of her eye, wondering if that could be true. Iridology was the practice of reading fortunes in irises. And Vika was a talented witch, but she'd always thought her main focus water magic. Of course, most witches had many other practices besides their principal magics.

"Tea!" CJ entered carrying a wooden tray replete with pot and cups. The dark witch's long black hair was teased back into a leather binder behind his neck, and he was barefoot. The lack of footwear wasn't odd; Tamatha had come to learn the man was more comfortable without shoes on.

"I see you shook her awake, Oh Dark Queen of Mine," he said to his wife, and then to Tamatha he said, "We wondered about you earlier."

"Earlier?" She cast Vika a wondering gape. "How long did you two stare at me before you decided to wake me?"

"I figured you needed the rest. We've only been in the office an hour. You see it in her?" she asked her husband, who handed her a cup of tea with an extremely tattooed hand.

CJ offered a cup to Tamatha and then peered into her eyes. His dark ponytail fell forward over his black shirt. The twosome were goth defined, and never had Tamatha met a more perfectly paired couple. "Oh, yes, a new love, eh?"

"Seriously?" Tamatha sipped the tea. She shouldn't be surprised that two witches who were madly in love could see something like that in her. But she wasn't in love with Ed. Far from it. They were friends. Who liked to kiss. And fool around. And the sex the other night had been off the charts. "He's just a guy I know."

"Ooo, tell me more." Vika winked from over a sip of tea.

"It's not important. Not related to my work here. I shouldn't bother either of you."

"Bother me all you like," Vika said. "I love some salacious gossip."

Wrapping her fingers about the comforting warmth of the teacup, Tamatha offered, "It's not salacious." Because she'd keep the naughty parts to herself. "Ed is a demon I ran into one night, and he's agreed to answer some questions to further my knowledge about the species."

Vika raised a brow, accompanied by her thin but knowing smile. The expression said so much Tamatha blushed. CJ, thank the goddess, had made his way to the door, and she hoped he'd leave because the last person she wanted to discuss her love life with was her boss. Only when he did quietly wander out did she lean forward across the table.

"His name is Edamite Thrash, and he's so handsome," she said. "He's got all these demonic sigils on his skin that look like tattoos. And he's got this *manner* about him. So virile. Very sexy."

Vika squealed.

And CJ dashed back into the room, toppling his cup and spilling tea onto the concrete floor in the process. "Edamite Thrash? Oh, no, not him. You can't date him."

"Wha—why?" she cautiously asked the dark witch.

"Do you know who he is? *What* he is?"

"Yes. He's demon. And he has an office not far from here—that's how I ran into him," she said to Vika. "I was walking to the Métro one night after work. And he's kind. And smart. He says he heads an organization dedicated to keeping the peace and it's true."

CJ blew out an angry breath. "Tamatha, that man is reprehensible. Thrash heads a demon mafia."

"Mafia?" she spit out unbelievably.

"CJ, what do you mean?" Vika asked. "I haven't heard of a demon mafia in Paris."

"It's discreet, but Edamite heads it and rules over Paris. If any demons want to get in or out of this realm, he'll know about it. And he'll stop whomever he doesn't want here. No matter what it takes. He used to deal drugs to his own sister."

Sister? He hadn't mentioned a sister to Tamatha, only the father who was a werewolf. A drug dealer? Reprehensible?

"He's a nasty piece of work. Tamatha, you need to be careful around that demon," CJ insisted. "Better yet, I don't want you seeing him again."

She stood up from the chair and closed the book before her. "I don't think you get to tell me who I can and can't date. You may be my boss but you're not my father."

Vika cast a stern glance toward her husband. "Tamatha is smart and she's a big girl. She knows what she's doing." But the look she then cast Tamatha was filled with question and concern.

Actually, now that she'd heard about the mafia thing— and a drug dealer?—Tamatha wasn't at all sure what she was doing, but she wasn't going to let anyone know that. "I do know what I'm doing. And I always wear a white light around him."

"Seems to me if you trust a man you shouldn't have to go to such measures." CJ crossed his arms tightly. "I'm concerned for you, Tamatha. Just, please, be careful?"

"I always am. Thanks for the tea. I put in an all-nighter, so I should be leaving."

As she passed CJ she saw him sweep his arm out in

her peripheral vision. Tamatha spun quickly and put up a blocking spell with her palm. His magic bounced off the invisible shield and moved the air in tangible waves.

"What in seven mercies?" she asked, affronted. "Were you going to cast a spell on me?"

"I wanted to put a protection spell on you."

Vika stood and clasped her husband's hand. "Leave her, lover. It's not wise to mess in another woman's love life. Only bad things can come of it for both you and her."

Thoroughly admonished, CJ crossed his arms, yet he maintained his stern gaze.

"Have a good day, Tamatha," Vika said. "Call me if you want to talk!"

Tamatha waved at the twosome and quickly exited. Really? He'd thought to put a spell on her without even asking? Well, the man was a dark witch. She supposed he was accustomed to doing as he wished.

"Mafia?" she muttered. "What does that mean?"

Could the man truly be the evil overlord he'd confessed to?

Instead of heading to the Métro, Tamatha veered toward Ed's office building. Along the way she stopped at a café. The shop had begun selling to-go drinks à la American style, and she ordered a foamy cup of decaf chai with extra cinnamon. Her vita could use the warming spice.

With her bag of books slung over one shoulder and cup in the other hand, she paused before the glossy black marble wall of Ed's building and leaned against it. The cool stone surface against her shoulders felt good on her muscles, which had kinked from sleeping with her head on a table.

The sun was not out, but she didn't feel imminent rain. Of course, Paris was a bitch when it came to the weather, and one minute it could be high sun, the next pouring kittens. She really should invest in an umbrella and carry that in her bag. Because she couldn't always whip out the air magic to form a protective shield against the rain when around humans.

Man, these books were heavy. She set down the bag and sipped the chai, one arm crossed before her as she watched people across the street filing in and out of a *boulangerie*. A fresh baguette sounded like carb heaven. She hadn't eaten more than a few tea biscuits today.

But fore in her busy brain was CJ's voice saying that word: *mafia*. And then: *drug dealer*. She turned and stared up the side of the building. Six stories up, Ed's office occupied the top floor. She wondered if he appreciated the newly cleansed office, and then that wonder startled her.

Had the bad vibrations been created by him? Had *he* taken lives in that office? He'd said he did not kill, but he'd said it in such a manner that left it open for interpretation. There was a difference between murder and killing. And he was the demon in charge of all other demons in Paris? She knew nothing about his work. While his appearance appealed to her, dark and tattooed, she reasoned that others may look at him and easily pin such style as nefarious. A drug dealer? Possible. Even worse? Maybe.

She hated to think such things about him, but CJ had upset her. And she'd never reason to doubt CJ. He was an honest man, a good witch and a kind boss.

So who or what was Edamite Thrash? He *had* kidnapped her. Could his sudden turnaround and seductions be related to an ulterior motive?

Her phone rang and she tugged it from her skirt pocket. Ed was calling her? She glanced up again as she answered.

"I can see you standing down there," he said. "Saw you walk across the street from the café."

Shoot. She hadn't wanted to be so obvious. But then, she was out of sorts this morning. And the next thing she said proved it. "I heard something about you today."

"Gossip? Was it good, bad or—?"

"Ugly."

"I see. Are you going to give me a chance to defend myself against mere words?"

"Do you kill people?"

"What?"

"It's a fair question, Ed."

"I thought we had—" He exhaled heavily. "Do you think because I'm demon I'm a killer? I thought much more highly of you, Tamatha—"

"Don't make this about me. Certainly Jones told me you head a demon mafia and that you're a drug dealer."

"The dark witch is accusing me? And has he told you how many vampires he's killed lately?"

"Ed, I just…" She squeezed the to-go cup too hard and chai spilled out the top. "Oh!" Milky brown liquid spattered her shoes. "I can't do this right now. I have to go."

"Come up, Tamatha, please. Apparently, things have gone extremely south since I held you in my arms yesterday morning. We need to talk."

Arm held out with the dripping cup in hand, she tilted back her head. She couldn't see him in the window for the glare from the clouded sun. But she could feel his anticipation and anxiety. They did need to talk.

"Please?" she heard through the phone that she no longer held to her ear.

He did deserve to defend himself. And she did want to see him again. Because remembering how great it felt to lie in his arms went a long way in smothering any misgivings she had about him.

"Very well. I'll be right up."

But as she bent to pick up her book bag, she had a thought. Standing close to the building, so he couldn't see her, Tamatha pulled a white light over her body.

"Now I'm ready. For good or for ill," she muttered.

Ed paced the floor before Tamatha, who had refused to sit after he'd offered. She clutched the shoulder-bag handle before her, the book-laden bag hanging heavily before her knees. Her hair was tousled and she had apologized for her appearance because she'd slept in the Archives overnight. She looked a disheveled schoolgirl in her short tight skirt, high heels and white blouse that did not hide the perky nipples beneath.

And that turned him on.

Yet, the vibes flowing from her were anything but attractive or welcoming. In fact, he could feel the repellent electricity skitter across his skin from her white light.

"The day before yesterday we sat in a bathtub sharing confidences. Later, you traced my body with your tongue. And we had amazing sex," he said, stopping before her with hands splayed. "What's happened since then?"

She squeezed her eyes as tightly as her tiny fists.

"Tamatha—"

"Just answer the question I asked when I was standing outside," she insisted.

"I..." So she wasn't going to drop that one. An honest answer wasn't going to win him any brownie points. And the definition he had of drug dealer was much different than hers could be.

"Tamatha, there are some things about me you are better off not knowing. I do what I must. The organization I head is focused on keeping the peace. This mortal realm is not always an easy place to exist for my sort. Nor can peace and anonymity be achieved with mere talk or passivity. Sometimes more persuasive methods must be employed."

"So you have killed? And if you say 'only those deserving' I am so out of here."

He didn't know how to win against this woman. Not that he had to win. *Did* he have to win? He shouldn't look at things that way. He didn't want to spoil what felt so right to him.

So he nodded. "I trust details will not serve your curiosity. It is merely my confession that you seek. But it won't change how I feel about you, Tamatha."

"How you feel—Ed, you brought me into your life because you needed a witch. You didn't seek me because you were interested in me or found me attractive or even—"

"And yet every time I am near you I am compelled closer. I forget the important thing, such as tracking zombie witches, and can only wonder how I allowed myself to become so bewitched."

"Agg!" She dropped the bag and fisted her hands before her, shaking them. He couldn't figure the source of her rage. But it was a beautiful rage. "Every time you say that, that you can only believe your attraction to me is because of some spell I've worked against you, feels like a slap in the face. Don't you know how much it hurts me?"

"Tamatha, I would never hurt you."

"And yet the only reason you can possibly be interested in me is because witchcraft made you do it?"

"No, I—" It did sound horrible when he put it that way. And he didn't believe she'd employed a spell to attract him. "It's a figure of speech."

"That you should know better than to use with me. Oh! Do you have a sister? CJ said—"

"I'll thank you not to rely on the dark witch's information. Rumor is often distorted."

"So you don't have a sister?"

"I do have a half sister, as well as a half brother," he said, but it came out more defensive than he wished. She was forcing it from him, and he didn't like that. But he cautioned his anger. Horns were the last thing they needed in this conversation. "Blyss and Kir are blood siblings. They are werewolves in the same pack. Or they were in pack Valoir. They've both been banished. Blyss doesn't know about me. Kir doesn't think it's such a good idea to tell her about her demon half brother. And I did provide her with some pills, but I'm far from a drug dealer."

Tamatha's mouth dropped open. So much information, and all of it so damning on his part. She'd wanted his truth. A lie would have only hurt her, and he'd meant it when he'd said he would never harm her.

"My half sister didn't want to be a werewolf," he provided in the quiet pause that filled the room. "I have a manner of putting my hands to strange and curious elixirs. I sometimes fancy myself a purveyor of essentials."

Tamatha lifted a brow.

"A stupid title I toss out because it— Ah, never mind. I was able to obtain pills that could repress Blyss's wolf. But she's fallen in love recently and has gotten over that demented need to deny her heritage."

"That's…weird," Tamatha said on a gasp. "Both the need to not be a werewolf and the part about purveying drugs."

"Essentials," he corrected her. Then he mentally kicked himself for the stupid assertion to be right. It was all about control. And he didn't have the control with this witch. And…that suited him fine. He splayed his hands before him. "What else do you need to have verified about me that the dark witch has claimed makes me some mafia king? We might as well get it all out while you're here. Not like

I shouldn't have expected this. Women never stick around me for long. If it's not the horns, it's something else. I knew I couldn't trust a witch."

"What?" Tamatha stepped around the book bag. "That's not fair. You can trust me. But in order for me to trust you, I need to ask the hard questions. To get answers from you so I can then make up my mind about how I feel about you."

He bowed. "Mafia king at your service, witch."

"Don't call me that in that tone. You're mean today, Ed. And what happened to evil overlord? Are you a mafia king or the other?"

He shrugged. "Beauty is in the eye of the beholder. Or in this case, ugliness."

She slammed her arms across her chest, then splayed them out and grabbed the bag. "I need to get away from you and think about this. About everything. About us."

"There can never be an us," he said, following her to the door.

"Is that what you want?"

No. But he wasn't about to bow down to her standards of what was acceptable in a mate and how he should live his life. "Of course it's what I want. Better to nip this romance in the bud while I'm still standing. Not that you haven't attempted to knock me down."

"You're being defensive."

"Coming from the witch wearing a white light."

She bristled, but didn't say anything.

"I'm being truthful," Ed said. "But apparently, you can't accept my truths."

She started to reply but stopped, checking herself. "I'm in no mood. I spent the night paging through books looking for answers to the dilemma you posed to me. I'm trying to help you, Ed! I woke an hour ago with my cheek smashed against a night-terrors spell. That's just wrong. And then you are some mafia kingpin. And you think you can only be interested in me because I bespelled you. I want to go home and—"

"Then leave!"

"Really?" Her bottom lip wobbled. Was that a tear glistening at the corner of her eye? One blink and it would spill over that soft, pale cheek. Damn, she was pulling out the big guns.

And he couldn't resist.

Ed pulled her close and, despite the horrible electricity zapping at his veins, kissed her. Because he didn't know what else to do. Because he was one step away from falling apart and confessing his need for her. Because...

He hadn't meant any of those things he'd said to her. He didn't want this to end. But he didn't want to feel the pain of another woman's rejection. He'd been trying to waylay that, but he was too damned stupid when it came to emotions and relationships.

He did know he needed this intimate contact. And falling into her was a cure for any madness, even lack of sleep, betrayal and the weird mix of witchcraft and demonic magic that seemed to keep drawing them together.

She didn't relax in his embrace, but she didn't stop kissing him. He held her against him, wanting her to know he would always be gentle with her and ever respect her. And he might never get her from his heart now that she had etched a place into it.

But saying those things was too hard. He hadn't the right words for actions best performed in a moment of panic.

When their mouths parted, she said, "I will never bewitch you. Never will I use magic to win you. But if that's the way you feel about me..." She sighed and picked up her things. "Your amazing kisses are not going to change my state of mind. I have to mentally sort through everything I dug up while researching. I'm going to call you later, whether or not you like it."

He nodded, unwilling to refuse that contact and so desperately wanting to be in the kiss again. What was his problem? He'd given her good reason to turn and never want to speak to him again. Hadn't he been harsh enough with her?

But he couldn't be. The witch's rede was something like Do No Harm, and he agreed with that completely.

He held the door open as she passed through. Much as his heart twisted and his fingers ached to run through her hair while he whispered to her how much he wanted her to stay, he resisted that fall to weakness. "I can have Inego give you a ride home?"

The look she cast him told him what she thought of that idea.

"Or not," he said. "The Métro is always good transport. I've things to do. Zombie witches to track. Mafia-kingpin things to, er…sort out."

She didn't reply. He caught a palm over his heart and watched her walk away. He didn't want to lose the best thing that had entered his life in…ever. But he'd never had a good thing before, so he wasn't sure how to keep said good thing.

He touched his lips. She'd accepted his kiss even after he'd fired cruel words at her. Could she possibly care about him as much as he did her?

And that was it, wasn't it? He cared about her.

Chapter 13

Tamatha's notes from last night's research in the Archives were scattered—neatly—on the living room table. Beside them sat chunks of amethyst and quartz for clear thinking. And she'd added a hint of rosemary to her usual lemon perfume this morning for awareness. But after a few hours bent over the notes and not getting anywhere, she'd decided to distract herself from the project. A watched pot never boiled, and a brain forced to come up with a solution did best when it didn't know it was needed.

The vacuum glided over the dark-stained hardwood floors in the apartment. She glanced in the bathroom mirror as she passed by. The green face mask she'd slapped on needed to sit twenty minutes. That was about how long it took to get into all the nooks and crannies with the brush attachment.

Dancing her way down the hallway, she vacuumed up scattered lavender petals as well as rose, saffron and thyme. She hung her herbs and flowers from a double row of hemp twine strung along the hallway ceiling because it was drier there in the inner part of the building, and also, she loved the scents that infused the very walls and floor when walking through the front door.

Cleaning always put her in a good mood for reasons she would never admit to anyone else. Perhaps she'd share that detail with the witch Vika Saint-Charles, CJ's wife. Vika was a clean freak, and she also owned a business that cleaned up dead paranormals from crime scenes.

Tamatha decided she could go forever without viewing anything dead, but that thought switched her brain back to the looming elephant crowding her forebrain. A whole pack of elephants, actually. The demon Edamite Thrash, who could be more evil than she'd ever suspected. And her grandmother and her zombie coven.

She had tried to call her mother again, but she still wasn't answering. Petrina Bellerose would know what to do about this situation.

She hoped.

And after baking a chocolate cake earlier—and then eating a quarter of it—she'd finally banished the heavy dread she felt and had started to look at the situation rationally. Something did have to be done about zombie witches. And with the right information she would utilize her magic to help instead of hinder.

But what to do about Edamite Thrash and the possibility that, despite his dangerous and very mysterious lifestyle, she may be falling for him? Vika had recognized it in her, and so had CJ.

But did Ed feel the same toward her or was it as he suspected? Mere bewitchment. *Could* she enact a love spell without knowing it? Had she attracted him to her by crafty means even she hadn't been aware of? Could a love spell work as her OCD magic did—reactionary?

He had been mean to her in his office earlier in an attempt to get her to leave. And then he'd kissed her! The man had to sort out his feelings for her because he was cold one minute and hot the next.

She wouldn't let him go. She wasn't ready to do that yet. She was only just getting to know him.

"Love often," she whispered. "I could so love the crap out of you, Edamite Thrash."

Even if he were a dangerous drug dealer? Or rather, a "purveyor of essentials." He'd explained that had been about some pills he'd got for his half sister. A werewolf who didn't want to be a werewolf? So strange.

Shaking her head to sweep away the negative thoughts, she spent extra time running the vacuum along the living room ceiling to get at any cobwebs that may be forming. She had nothing against spiders, but sometimes their webs could trap negative energy.

Even over the vacuum she heard the door buzzer, and without clicking off the machine, she grabbed the doorknob and opened it to Ed. His calm expression moved into a curious head tilt. The last person she wanted to talk to right now was him. Yet also, she really wanted to see him. He'd come for her! So maybe he wasn't as ready to give up on the two of them as he'd thought he was.

And then she remembered.

"Oh!" Tamatha slammed the door shut and clicked off the vacuum. She touched her chin and the slimy green face mask slid off on her fingertip. "Oh, bother."

"Come on, Tamatha. Open the door," he teased from the other side.

"You shouldn't see me like this. I completely forgot about it!"

"What's wrong? I happen to like avocados."

Seriously? In the two seconds he'd got a look at her he'd

determined as much? Oh, mercy, a woman was not supposed to let her man see her *en déshabillé* with a vacuum in hand. Or with muck on her face.

"The door isn't locked," he said.

No, it wasn't. Her fingers hovered over the lock. One twist was all it required. Too bad she hadn't a spell for vanishing face cream.

"I can simply walk in," the man on the other side of the door suggested.

Why didn't she keep this place warded against demons? Then again, she'd have to take the ward down every time she did want him to cross her threshold. Like now.

Did she really?

Oh, mercy, yes. They needed to talk. And she needed another kiss from him. To know if he was really as interested in her as she wanted him to be.

Tamatha opened the door an inch. "Let me go wash my face first."

"I'm coming in," he announced.

She stepped back from the door as it opened. Resigned to accept that there was no reversing this situation, she shrugged and offered a weak smile. Hey, at least the man was here. That was twenty times more promising than when she'd left him. When he sniffed her face, then dashed a finger over her cheek and licked it, she could have died of embarrassment.

"Avocado and honey," he said. "I like it."

"And I am mortified. Now can I go wash my face?"

He kissed her then, so quickly she hadn't time to think. The heady falling into him swept away her worries, and then when he pulled away a few bits of green were on his mouth, which he licked. "Go for it. But first, I'm sorry. I spoke irrationally in the office earlier."

"You don't want us to end?"

"I…don't. Much as we'd both be better off if we did end this thing we've started. But no, I'm not ready to give up on us yet. Or rather, I'm willing to give it a try. It's not something I've ever done with a woman before. I mean, a relationship built around trust and truth. I want to be with you, Tamatha. To be near you."

"Even with a green face?"

"Don't some witches have green faces?"

"You've been watching too many movies. I don't think green skin is a witch thing. It's more for nixies and the sidhe. I'll wash it off."

He caught her hand before she could flee. "To be totally honest, I came here with an ulterior motive. It's about the situation. I want to bring you somewhere. Show you something. Maybe then you'll understand how much I need your help."

"All right. But first things first." She rushed into the bathroom, leaving the door open behind her. Bending over the sink and splashing water on her face, she lifted her head and called, "Where do you want to bring me? It's ten in the evening."

"I thought you were a night owl?" He leaned a shoulder against the frame in the bathroom doorway.

"I am." She patted her face with a towel. Okay, fine, so she had survived that embarrassing moment and the man was still there. He hadn't fled. Nor had he laughed. And now he was looking at her sans makeup. Another brave feat on her part. She deserved some kind of award for allowing him to see her like that. "Will I need walking shoes?"

"Yes—comfortable shoes and a sweater. It's cool this evening."

She touched up her hair with a few tucks of curls here and there and patted her face with some powder while Ed curiously observed. A dash of blush and some lip balm.

When she turned to him he caught her around the waist. "I liked the green-face look. It was tasty."

Rolling her eyes, she then confessed, "You have now witnessed the process."

"The process?"

"What all women go through to try and look their best for you men. Well, and we do it for ourselves. Mostly for ourselves."

He pressed a hand over his heart. "I solemnly promise to keep the process a secret from all other males. Are you still mad at me?"

"Don't I have a right?"

"Yes. No. I wish you weren't, but I understand. I was downright mean to you."

"You were being defensive until you kissed me. But then you let me go. You run hot and then cold with the snap of fingers. You are a hard man to figure out."

"Yes, well, *mafia* is one of those words that implies evil. I'm not, Tamatha. I am good. Mostly. I do try. Call me an evil overlord with a twist." He winked and that set her heart racing. "*Upstanding* probably isn't a word you'd ever see captioned below my picture. But I'm not as CJ makes me out to be. Can we call a truce for our walk?"

"We can. And don't worry—I like to form my own opinion of people. I do still like you."

"Because you need me."

"For research, of course," she teased.

She kissed him quickly, then scampered into her bedroom. A truce wasn't necessary. She liked being with Ed. And she did trust him. She just had to learn what he was all about and then decide if she could live with the kind of person he was or if that would go against her values. Because one man's opinion—that of Certainly Jones—could be clouded.

"Is your name real?" she called as she snagged a pair of purple suede knee-high boots from the closet. She wore a pink wrap dress, and the boots went nicely with it.

"Real?"

She stuck her head out of the bedroom. "Thrash. It didn't appear on any of the genealogical records when I was researching."

"Right. No. My mother purposely never gave me a surname. Something about protecting me from witches and their spells." He winked at her. "Deeply inbred, that fear of witches."

"I get that. So it's a made-up name?"

"Don't you think it suits me? I mean, it does have a rather evil ring to it."

Putting on her bloodstone ring, she then grabbed a blue cardigan and swung it over her shoulders and headed out to meet Ed at the door. "You like that it has an evil connotation to it?"

"It can be a necessity when I need to be imposing."

"Okay. I don't get that, but as part of the truce I'll let it slide. I won't be able to trace your family line without a surname. Did your mother have one?"

"Nope." He held the front door open. "But I'll give her a call and ask after Grandfather's information if you think that will help."

"Anything might help right now. Where are we going? Does it involve pineapple gelato?"

"Actually, there will be tombstones."

Chapter 14

The Montparnasse cemetery was the second largest in Paris proper, in ranking behind Père Lachaise. Many more cemeteries once existed centuries earlier, but as the city grew—and plague spread—burial sites were moved, covered over and forgotten in favor of urban beautification and outright fear of disease. The catacombs held proof of the rampant rise of dead to the ratio of available burial grounds.

Ed held Tamatha's hand and led her through the gate that he had opened with a wave of his hand. Then he quickly closed it behind them, taking a precautionary moment to scan the street for the police. They dashed down an aisle canopied by the *shush* of ash and lime tree leaves.

He'd expected revulsion or even fear from her when he'd suggested they visit a cemetery in the dark of night. But instead she'd squealed in delight, and even now, she had taken the lead and eagerly trekked down the cobblestone pathway in those sexy purple boots. He could love a woman such as that adventurous, quirky witch.

If he knew how to love. Which he did not.

But she wasn't going to like why he'd brought her here. Why did he feel compelled to add to her already growing list of reasons to hate him? That she had a list didn't surprise him.

So he liked to keep his MO mysterious, which led to others suspecting the worst of him. It was best for the things he needed to accomplish that most did not consider him a goody-goody. One could hardly banish a murderous wraith demon from this realm if he was known to help little old ladies cross the street. So, evil overlord he must remain.

And more good work must be done. Quickly. Because if he didn't take action soon, there would be another demon death. And he couldn't live with that when the city's demons were on his watch. Mafia king? More like Keeper of Demonic Nations. The keeping-the-peace thing included looking out for his own. Most of them, anyway. Those demons who hailed from Daemonia could stay there or go back—*don't let the portal door hit you on the ass, buddy*. Which was why he employed an exorcist specifically trained for expulsions to the Place of All Demons.

He had no idea how to begin explaining this whole mess to Tamatha, so showing her had seemed the best way.

Dropping her leather shoulder bag, which she'd grabbed to bring along after he'd announced their destination, she pulled out an empty mason jar and tweezers. "You don't mind if I get some grave dirt while I'm here, do you? I'm fresh out."

He leaned against a stone sarcophagus and gestured she go right ahead. "So this is like a shopping trip for you?"

"It is!" She skipped ahead and, when she sighted something in the shadows, ducked between two stone monuments so Ed could see only her backside swaying with her movement in a slash of moonlight.

Now, that was a sight. Her ass was nicely curved and a perfect handful. And he wanted to touch it right now. Because after the sex they'd shared, he could only think to do it again. And again. And... Well, then she'd got some bad information about him, and he needed to now resurrect her positive feelings toward him and bury the suspicions so she could trust him enough to share her body with him again.

He filed down the narrow aisle between tombstones and glided his hand over her derriere. Made his horns tingle to imagine her bare skin beneath his stroking fingers. And he moaned in approval.

"Don't tell me," the witch said as she scraped moss from the base of a tombstone. "Graveyards make you horny?"

"Not particularly. But your ass in this clingy dress does it for me." She stood, her back to him, and he glided his hand around and up her stomach to hold her against him. His erection nudged her backside. "Want to make out?" He nuzzled his mouth against the base of her ear and dashed out his tongue to taste lemons.

"I thought you brought me here to show me something?"

And like that, his erection softened. Right. Straight to the bad stuff, then. Well, he wasn't going to regain his good standing in her eyes until he revealed the reasons for her to hate him. And that made so little sense he'd just go with it.

"I did want to show you something."

"We can make out, too," she offered gleefully as she screwed on the jar lid.

He quirked a hopeful brow. A make-out session with a witch gathering grave dirt under the full moon? There were some things a man could never plan for but must always be prepared for.

"Later." She tucked her find into the bag. "After we've talked."

He winced. Yeah, talking. As if that was going to make matters better?

"You probably won't be interested in kissing me after what I have to show you. Which makes this damned difficult for me. But, for good or for ill, it's got to be done. Come on, witch."

He grasped her hand and led her down the twisting aisles, following the scent he could never lose. The scent of a darkly familiar death. Toward the back of the graveyard, close to a stone wall where the crooked tombstones were small yet close and blackened with mold and time, he suddenly stopped because the scent overwhelmed him. Evil and wretched, the musty odor tainted with blood and dust instilled a burning shiver on the sigil at the base of his spine. That one was a sort of "fellow demon recognizing" mark. When he was around others of his kind it tingled. Dead ones? The burn always startled him.

"Oh my goddess, what happened here?" Tamatha stepped right onto the spot where Ed had witnessed the death. "It's fresh, not ancient as the other morbid vibrations I get as I pass through." She looked to him over a shoulder.

"This is where the friend of mine—Laurent—was slain by *Les Douze*."

She pressed her fingers to her mouth and swung away from him, backing slowly from the spot that must harbor the violent imprint of the death. He knew she'd notice it, as she had sensed the lingering remnants in his office.

"I wanted you to feel it," he said. "To know that what I've told you is real."

"There was never a moment I didn't believe you."

That gave him much more relief than it should. She believed in him. The feeling was overwhelmingly of acceptance. And he wasn't sure what to do with that. Especially coming from a witch. His witch ward didn't tingle, not even a twitch.

"I thought if I brought you here you might get a sense of the sort of magic used?"

She shook her head. "Same as what I felt in your home, only tenfold. This is vile. Malefic. It runs over my skin like corpse worms. I don't want to be here anymore."

He caught her as she tried to pass him, hugging her gently but firmly. "Please, Tamatha. It's important to me."

"I haven't told you I would help you."

Now the witch ward on his arm did shiver. "I know that."

"And you've told me nothing about this demon mafia. And besides, there is another circumstance that may keep me from helping you. Please, I need to get away from this horror."

He exhaled and released her. The witch rushed down the cobblestone path. Another circumstance? Why Certainly Jones had put into her head that he was so evil was beyond him.

And then he could understand. Witch Number Two? She must have gone crying to CJ after Ed had managed to break free from her. Had probably told the dark witch all kinds of crazy lies about Ed. Of course, an assumption of guilt, of menace, would be made before a belief of beneficence. Not that he was so good. He had done things. Things he was not proud of. And things he knew had to be done, no matter the evil. But all he'd ever offered Witch Number Two was trust and an attempt at romance.

He had assumed the worst of Tamatha initially. So he deserved her reluctance at best. At worst, her downright refusal to help.

The click of her boot heels had stopped and he could

smell lemons wafting over the must and loamy scent of dying tree bark and mold. She waited for him. She'd not run away.

"Please," he said softly.

"But," he heard her whisper plainly. "My grandmother…"

"What?" He strolled up behind her. She wrung her hands together nervously. "Your grandmother?"

Her jewel gaze found his and he swallowed at sight of the tears that glistened there. His heart ached when he suspected she was hurting emotionally.

"It's something I learned going over the list of the twelve witches. I found all their names." She inhaled. "Lysia Bellerose was one of *Les Douze*. Ed, you're asking me to help you destroy my grandmother."

"I had no idea. Ah hell."

How he had managed to choose the one witch in the world who was actually related to one of The Twelve floored him. On the other hand, everything happened for a reason. And that wasn't destiny; that was the way the universe operated.

He took her in his arms and kissed her hair, her eyelids and her mouth. If he could make things better, he'd try, but he felt he had not the capacity or the magic required to do so. Who was he but an evil mafia king? A lowly demon who took great risk in even being in this beautiful witch's presence. If only he could be worthy of her.

"I'm sorry," he said. "I had no idea. I just wanted you to feel it. And now you have. Let me take you home. Sounds like we've a lot to discuss."

"We do. But take me to your home," she said and slid her hand into his. "I want to lie on your sheets and feel you on my skin. Together, we'll figure this out."

His fear of rejection was wiped out with that sweet entreaty. How had he got so lucky to meet this wondrous witch?

* * *

Tamatha preceded Ed into his apartment and dropped her things on the floor. She had told him about her grandmother, but right now, she didn't want to talk about it. His cedar scent had got into her senses, and all she wanted to do was lick him. Touch him. Press her skin against his.

He started to ask her something but she stopped him with a kiss. Running her hands down the front of his shirt, she unbuttoned it as she dropped lower. At his pants she unbuttoned and unzipped him and slid her hand inside to grip his thick erection. She rubbed the ribs with her thumb.

"I guess we'll save the talk for later," he said and lifted her in his arms and ran up the stairs with her. Tossing her gently onto the bed, he tugged off his shirt, revealing the dark array of sigils and tattoos. "Sometimes I can't figure you out, witch. You're angry with me and then you can't seem to get enough of me."

"Same with you. We're hot and cold for one another. I want all of you," she said, gesturing with a crook of her finger for him to approach the bed. "All of this darkly interesting stuff." She tapped his chest and traced a finger over a curve. Ink or a natural mark, she didn't care. "But this one looks so faint. It's as if it's disappearing."

He eyed the pale curved lines she touched over his chest. "Not disappearing. Might be a new one. I never know what they're about until they are fully formed."

"Maybe it's to do with *Les Douze*?"

"You never know." He kissed her, pushing her back on the bed and pinning down her wrists. "You're the one who started this. No talk of that now. I've got something for you." He rubbed his erection, which had escaped his pants, against her thigh. "Want it?"

She twisted out of his grip and shimmied down alongside him to lick the head of his thickness. Grasping the sturdy column and squeezing, she tugged him onto the bed to kneel while she sucked and licked and teased him with her tongue. Ed's fingers ran through her hair and pulled it from the pins she'd used to put it up. She wasn't undressed, but that didn't matter. Her nipples were so tight every slip of her dress over them increased the crazy-sexy need to let go.

There was something about taking a man in her mouth that satisfied her need for control. Because he was completely at her mercy and would say and do anything to make her continue. The skim of his gloved hand over her shoulder and down to clasp her breast through her dress warranted a wardrobe adjustment.

Kneeling, she untied her dress at the waist and unwrapped it. Ed pulled the bra straps down, and before she could spin it around to unclasp, he sucked her breast into his hot, wet mouth. His tongue teased her firmly and his fingers crept lower, parting her legs.

She wanted him inside her now. And always. He was like a new drug she couldn't get enough of. She didn't do drugs, but she could do Ed over and over.

Directing his exquisitely ribbed penis inside her, she lowered herself slowly onto his length and grasped him at the back of the neck and with her other hand ran her fingers through his hair. He continued to lick her breasts as she rocked slowly, deeply, indulging in his unique design and thickness. Every movement tugged at her apex, teasing the climax to the fore.

Ed swore and gripped her at the hips. His body tensed, the muscles at the back of his neck tightening. He felt alive in her hands and at her skin. Electric with imminent orgasm.

With a gentle stroke of his finger over her clit, she was coaxed into a rousing orgasm that matched his shudders, and they came together. She wrapped her arms about his shoulders and nuzzled her face into his hair as she panted and gasped in elation.

The thunder of his heartbeats against her chest matched the fierce pounding of hers. And she clutched him tightly, driving in her fingernails at his shoulders, wanting to push him in deeper, to own him, claim him. To make sure he knew that he was hers.

"This isn't bewitchery," she said on a gasp.

"Yes, I know. It's real."

And with that declaration, the two of them shuddered again, coming softly, fiercely.

Chapter 15

Ed lay on his back, his eyes closed, but Tamatha knew he was awake. Exhausted from great sex, as was she. She trailed her fingertips down his neck, tracing the feather that rippled gently, and then along his shoulder where curls and x's and what looked like maroon flame darkened his skin. Across his dark-haired chest and over his heart she studied the faint markings she'd noticed earlier.

"How will you know what this one means?" she asked, tapping above his nipple where the dark hairs barely disguised the tracing.

"I'm never sure what they mean until they are complete. Sometimes I have to have a demonologist interpret them for me."

"Isn't that someone who studies demons? Like me?" she asked sweetly.

"Yes, but can you interpret demonic sigils?"

"No, but perhaps with more study. Would you oblige me?"

"Study all you like, witch."

She was bothered less and less by his propensity to label her witch. It was no longer the accusatory epithet he'd once spit at her, but rather an endearment.

She slid her fingers over the ridged muscles on his abdomen, and there beneath the dark curls about his penis were faint lines. No sigils on his penis or testicles. The ridges were interesting enough as it was. Man, did she appreciate those ridges.

Kissing the crown of his semierect penis, she then ventured her discovery trail down a thigh. On the thigh closest to her, the dark markings looked similar to the tribal tattoos she had seen on human biker types, though she felt sure this meant something different than "it looks cool" or "it makes me look tough."

"You don't want to know about those," he said. "Ah hell. Tamatha, I've killed when it was necessary to save lives. And when I make a kill, the remnants of that kill are blackened into my skin. I feel the mark burn into me as if I were experiencing a six-hour tattoo session in seconds. Hurts like fuck."

Those were some thick lines, and…a lot of them. She wasn't going to overthink it. And then she couldn't help but think only of it. He had killed. Necessary kills? Was killing *ever* necessary? She didn't think so.

"To save the lives of others?" she quietly wondered.

"Yes." He didn't seem to want to elaborate.

What about killing zombie witches who were killing demons? That was different. Maybe. She had nothing to compare to the instances that had marked Ed's thigh. And she wasn't sure she wanted the full explanation or even details. Her curiosity could only take her so far before she drowned in fascination or fled from revulsion.

And yet if she agreed to help him, she would also be

killing. Twelve witches. But was it considered killing if they were already dead?

Ed sat up and slid off the bed. Standing before her, his hands to his hips, he looked like a tattooed god, a rockabilly hero, a motorcycle gangster, perhaps even an evil overlord. Sexy in his dark and dangerous skin. She couldn't get enough of him.

So she was attracted to a man who would kill? Who was she?

"It's apparent there are things about me that disturb you," he said.

She started to protest, but then couldn't force herself to make up a lie to soften the fact that, indeed, he was right about her being disturbed.

"I thought I was jumping in full circle when I took you to the cemetery. But that was outside of me. The real truth, what I really am? I want to show you," he said. "It's probably the stupidest thing I've ever done, but I feel as though I can trust you."

"Ed, whatever you want to say to me, I'll listen with an open mind and heart. The thing about you killing? Yes, it disturbs me, but give me some time to process it. I believe you only act for the good of others."

"You do?"

She nodded and that sexy smile of his lured her forward to kiss him.

"Call me crazy, but I have to do this. This is me." He stood back and spread out his arms. "Full demon."

"Oh." She sat up, crossing her legs and pushing her hair over her shoulder. "Yes, I'd like to see that."

"Not for your fascination or study," he cautioned, "but because I want to be open with you. To not have secrets."

"I understand."

"Really? Because this is not like me showing up at your door to find you with avocado on your face."

She grasped his hand, offering him a reassuring squeeze. "I do understand. But allow me some fascination. I am studying your species." She let her eyes wander to his erection. "There's so much about you that I like to admire."

He chuckled. "All right, then. But you have to know I'm doing this because I need you to trust me. And... I want you to see the real me, horns and all. Here goes all the marbles." He tugged off the fingerless gloves she had come to accept as a part of him. "Be careful you don't touch my hands when my thorns are out."

She nodded dutifully. And though she was eager and felt like clasping her hands before her in expectant glee, she did her best to contain that giddy curiosity and so shoved her hands under her thighs to watch as her lover transformed before her.

Horns grew from the nubs at his temples, thickening and gleaming as if hematite. They curled slightly over his ears and then abruptly curled back toward his face and upward in about a two-foot stretch. They looked heavy and deadly, like something a matador must fear.

A shrug of his shoulders sifted a darkness over his skin. The diluted, inky coloring spilled down his arms and the sides of his torso and from hips to midthigh. All the sigils and tattoos seemed to darken even more, becoming fathomless, like entries into his very being. The dark pigment hardened and must have been of the same material as his horns. His shoulders shifted slightly, pointing up in smaller versions of horns, as did his hips.

At his knuckles the thorns he had warned her about zinged out like tiny claws. And as Tamatha drew her gaze over his figure, noting the hardened leatherlike skin and horns—even his erection looked thicker and tougher—she picked up the scent of sulfur. And it wasn't offensive, but rather sweet, almost cloying.

Red eyes looked upon her. He was mostly human in form, save for horns and leathery skin, though his center and torso and front and back were yet merely skin sans the dark hairs she loved to run her fingers through. She peeked over the edge of the bed. Regular feet; no hooves. But they were blackened and thorned on the toes, as well.

"This is me." His voice was the same but not. Huskier, deeper and perhaps a little hollow. "Horns and all."

She sat up on her knees and inched closer to the edge of the bed. "Can I touch?"

"I would expect nothing less from you."

He held his hands back and away from his body as she moved forward and— The first thing she wanted to touch was the horns at his temples, but she remembered his warning about how that would make him horny. She'd save that for last, because this form did not offend her or make her want to run from him. He was beautiful.

The hard skin on his shoulders felt cool under her touch, like armor, yet it was pliable and moved like skin. From the border where that armor ended and formed into skin, black veins traced under the surface and tangled with the demonic sigils, giving his unarmored skin a virtual armor appearance.

Down his belly she stroked then grasped his penis. He gasped. And she wondered, "A little bigger?"

"Never measured in this form."

"I think it is. Almost as big as these."

Now she dared reach up and touched the base of one horn. It was slick and glossy, and ribbed as his penis. The black horn curved gracefully before dipping and jutting abruptly forward and up. She glided her fingers about and around and up.

Ed sighed against her cheek. "You know what that does to me?"

"Makes you horny." She kissed him quickly, then stepped onto the floor and gave his backside a once-over. "You've a tail!"

The tail waggled, though it was very un-demon-like. And it had black fur on it.

"I did tell you my father was werewolf," he said. "That's about all I got from him."

"It's so cute!"

"Tamatha."

"Sorry. Not cute. Nothing about your demonic form is remotely adorable." She slid back onto the bed and tapped his muscled stomach. "You are powerful and deadly and look very, very dangerous. So manly."

"Then why do you say that as if it's a tease? Do I not strike fear in your quivering witchy heart?"

"Should you?"

He shook his head. "No. I'm glad you didn't scream at sight of me." He slid a knee onto the bed and, with an exhalation and shake of his body, shed his demonic form, coming back to his human shape in but two breaths. "This is much better, yes?" He kissed her. "Thanks for not freaking."

"Horns and a tail don't scare me." She reached for his hand, but he shook his head. The thorns were yet visible. "Hmm…" She tapped her lower lip. "There must be an antidote to the poison contained in your thorns, yes?"

"Maybe?"

"I'll have to do some research. An antidote might be something to have handy if we are dating."

"Are we dating?"

"Yes, we are, like it or not."

"I adore you, witch." He pulled her closer and nuzzled his face into her hair, kissing the lemony warmth. "You really don't mind the horns?"

"They're sexy, actually. Do you think we could have sex with you in that form? Would it be dangerous to me?"

"Only my thorns," he said. "You just want to take my demon dick for a test drive."

"There is that."

"So that's why you like me, eh? I've got a big package."

"It's sizable no matter what form you're in." She reached for the package in question. "But I like your mind, too. And your quest to keep the peace. That is honorable. And you are handsome as sin. Now, I have a secret to reveal to you."

"Something more devastating than your horribly sweet avocado face?"

"You're never going to let that one go, are you?"

"It's all I've got. You're perfect in every other way."

"Maybe not so powerful as you think." She worried her lip a moment, then blurted, "Ed, I'm not the most powerful witch in Paris."

"Yes. So?"

He acted as though he'd known it all along. Tamatha eyed him curiously. "I mean, I'm probably not even top ten, if you want to get technical. That day you had me brought to your office I wanted to do anything to get to see you again, so I lied and hoped you'd never find out."

"Sweetness, I knew from the moment you stood before me."

"Then why did you let me work for you?"

"Because I felt the same way. Despite my initial reluctance to work with a witch, I didn't want to let you walk away from me."

"What did a witch do to you?"

"Why do you think it's that?"

"Because you're a strong, smart man. A healthy caution for witches is one thing, but you got it bad. So that makes me suspect a bad romance."

Ed exhaled.

"Please tell me? You've shown me your outsides. Let me have a peek inside. Promise I will listen with an open mind."

He kissed her and hugged her but was careful not to touch her with his thorns. "I did date a witch two years ago. I didn't know she was a witch and thought my demonic nature was secret from her. I use the excuse of birth defects for my horn nubs."

"And that works?"

"Human women are much quicker to believe that than the possibility that real demons exist."

"I suppose."

"One once actually made the guess that they were body modifications. Implanted. You know, some humans have things implanted beneath their skin to create art or because they're stupid?"

"That creeps me out. So the witch you dated didn't know you were demon? I find that hard to believe."

"She did. But I didn't know she knew until she'd drugged me and let the magic fly. She tried to enslave me." He sat beside her, exhaling heavily as he ran a hand through his hair. "For three days she worked her magic on me. It was torture, literally. I think her magic finally gave out and I managed to break free. It was hell."

"Oh, Ed. I didn't know. That's terrible. So you, uh…"

"What? You think I killed her?"

"I suppose the torture would have justified it."

"Never. Nothing justifies murder, Tamatha. A killing made to stop evil to prevent more deaths? That's doable.

It can be argued it was a means to save others. But still…" He stroked the dark tribal mark on his thigh. "Impossible to justify. But someone's got to do it, so I guess that means it's me."

She tilted her head onto his shoulder.

"Anyway, after her magic failed, I got out of there. Left her. I haven't heard from her since, though I suspect she might have given Certainly Jones an earful. So you see? Not a big fan of your kind." He turned his back toward her. "One of the feathers is chained still, yes?"

She looked closely, and yes, a feather was wrapped in chain. "Oh, Ed." She held him. "That's because she tried to enslave you? I'm so sorry. This whole situation with the zombie witches killing demons. You've lived such horrors. I can't imagine how hard this must be for you."

"You know something?" he asked softly.

"What?"

"You holding me like this makes up for it all. I don't know how to love another person, but you make me feel like I could learn."

"Everyone is capable of love. And it will come when you least expect it."

"That's the same thing my brother said to me the other night. What about you and your Love Often? It must come to you all the time."

"It does, because I am open to love." She spread her hand over his chest where the faint sigil had begun to form. "Open yourself to the possibility."

"I think I can do that." With a heavy exhalation he tilted up her chin and studied her gaze before speaking. "I understand I'm asking a lot of you to go after *Les Douze* if one of them could be your grandmother."

"There's no doubt, Ed. One of the twelve was Lysia Bellerose."

"Do all the women in your family have the same last name?"

"Yes." She stood and toed the dress on the floor. "And should we marry, we keep the family name. We're not so keen on giving a man so much power as to take his name." She shuddered, and Ed caught the minute movement.

Yes, a powerful witch, he reiterated mentally. Perhaps more powerful than she believed herself. And he honored that strength. Now to use it without tainting their fragile bond. A bond trust may have grown closer when he had revealed himself to her, outside and in. He hadn't planned to tell her about that experience. It had simply felt necessary. Now that he had, he was feeling unguarded, not exactly standing square and confident as he should be.

Open to the possibility of love? It still seemed out of his grasp.

Yet he could only imagine what Tamatha must be feeling now he knew the witch was her grandmother.

"Do you think your grandmother likes wandering around a zombie?" he asked.

She looked up from gathering her abandoned clothes that were neatly folded near the bed (OCD magic at its best). "I never thought of it like that. I haven't seen these zombie witches. How can you be sure they are dead?"

"They were burned in the eighteenth century. I'd call that dead."

"Right. Sorry. It's hard to grasp, you know? I wish my mother would return my call." She pulled on her bra and panties. "There could be implications."

"You think if you cast a spell against your grandmother…?"

"Yeah, I'm not sure. I might have to ask Certainly about this one. That is, *if* I agree to help you on this. I'm not going to commit until I talk to Mom. Is that okay?"

"I am thankful you are considering it. I don't know who

else I can ask. There are other witches in Paris, but—I don't want to work with any witch. I want you."

She shimmied her shoulders. "Good answer. I'd be jealous if you asked someone else. And so you know, Ed, I promise you—" she crossed her heart "—I will never enslave you as that witch did."

She'd crossed her heart. That meant so much. He nodded. "Sounds good to me. Back to the plan."

"Do we have a plan? I need to find out who is behind this," she said as she pulled on her wrap dress and searched the bedroom floor for her boots. She picked up his gloves and tossed them to him. "Like I said when I was in the cemetery, I suspected the magic was malefic. Not even dark witches will go there."

"Then who would do such a thing as to raise a coven of long-dead witches?" he asked, pulling on the gloves.

"And why?" she added.

"Well, we know the why," he said, slipping on a shirt. "If they are going after the demons who accused them."

"Yes, but the one who raised them must have that goal, yes?" She began to button up his business shirt, a crisp white number, and he allowed her. "So someone—living—wants revenge against demons in general or just those who accused the witches. That would probably make the someone an offspring of one of the dozen. Or possibly a contemporary, seeing as how long witches can live."

"Do you have a list of those who accused *Les Douze*?" he asked.

"Yes. I found one in the Archives yesterday. What is the name of your relative you mentioned was in the denizen that is being targeted? Because Thrash was not on the list."

"That is a moniker I have used since forever. We demons sometimes take different names for anonymity and—"

"Drama?"

"Nothing wrong with a little evil-overlord drama, is there?"

"Edamite Thrash. That's drama, all right. Is your first name even Edamite?"

"It is. My mother has always been simply Sophie. And since she never married my father, neither she nor I felt compelled to use his surname."

"So there are no family names in the demon species?"

"There are. I'm just not sure what ours is or was." Ed nodded. "I'll give Sophie a call and ask her. Though I'm not sure she'll answer. She and my father are in hiding. She's been off my radar for over a year."

"You two aren't close?"

"We don't hate one another."

Which didn't particularly mean close, either. She sensed it was a sensitive subject for him.

"Probably the witch names are more important in this case," she said. "In order to track them to a possible summoner. Though if we want to nail down possible targets, then we should figure out the demons, as well. I think this could only be a spell cast by a warlock."

"Ian Grim?" Ed immediately posited, as he gestured she leave the top two buttons undone on his shirt. "That's the only warlock I'm aware of, and I know for a fact he's out of town."

"You and Grim are friends?"

"No, but I do know his woman, Dasha. I see her on occasion because I provide her with—er..."

"Essentials you have purveyed?"

"Exactly. But it's to keep her alive when Ian is not around. Trust me. Dasha mentioned something about Grim venturing through Russia for the summer."

"There are warlocks all over the place. You just have to know where to look."

"And you do?" He bowed his forehead to hers and kissed her nose.

"A lot of answers can be found in books. Sounds like I'll be perusing the pages again this afternoon."

"I wish I could help you, but I suspect the Archives are off-limits to anyone who does not work there. And even more so to one who heads a demon mafia."

"You have to have a badge to get past security," she said and then hugged him. "You're not an evil person. I think Certainly has some bad information. But it doesn't matter."

"It matters to me what you think of me."

"Then you're good, because I adore you. So what are your plans for today? What does an evil overlord do all day?"

He chuckled and picked up his suit coat, and they strolled down to the kitchen, where Tamatha collected her shoulder bag. She intended to go straight to the Archives.

"I've got scouts at the cemetery, keeping an eye out for the witches. And I've a little snafu I'm tidying up over in the Bois de Boulogne. Has to do with humans and Ouija boards and some particularly mischievous incorporeal demons. Sometimes those damned boards really work."

"Oh, I know that. You need any help?"

"No, got it covered. But you'll keep me updated on your list making?"

"I will. And you'll call me after you talk to your mother?"

"Right. So here are the names of the two demons who have died." Ed pulled a notepad from a kitchen drawer and scribbled on it. "I don't know if they are the first two the witches have killed. I could have missed others." He tore off the page and handed it to her. "I'll be thinking of you all day."

"Me, too." Tamatha kissed him, then placed her palm over his chest. "And remember—stay open to the possibilities."

"With you I believe all things are possible."

Chapter 16

Tamatha looked over the list of twelve witches who had been burned alive on August 25, 1753. Lysia Belle-rose was the third on the list. It was not alphabetical, nor could it possibly be in order of rank. Or so she assumed. She'd called her mother again and left a message, hoping Petrina could shed some light on her grandmother's life. And death.

But with the list she could trace offspring and perhaps even lovers. Whoever had raised the coven from the dead could be anyone associated with *Les Douze*. Though they must possess powerful magic.

"The most powerful witch in Paris," she whispered as she sat back in the velvet chair, kicked off her heels to let them straighten on the floor below the table and pulled up her legs. "Certainly not me. But who? A warlock? How many warlocks currently live in Paris?"

She had heard of Ian Grim. And Zoe Guillebeaux's

father was a warlock. She couldn't recall his name. That could be an excellent next step. Narrow it down to warlocks and then match that list to the list of relations and friends associated with *Les Douze*.

She glanced to the maplewood cuckoo clock that CJ kept wound and dusted. The woodwork was stained black and two ravens carved above the timepiece cawed over their shoulders. One looked directly at her. Which reminded her of Ed and his ravens. His feather sigils on his skin had moved as if real under her touch. And when he'd been fully demon she could only admire him. She'd thought that first night she'd run into Ed that a full moon would bring family and challenge. And had it ever.

Tapping her lip, she sighed and then remembered… She pulled the list of the two dead demons he'd given her from her purse. More names to help in her research quest.

"It's only been two hours," she muttered. "I'm going to need lots more tea."

But first, she texted Ed that she was researching warlocks. She wondered how he was faring, and then her mind drifted again to last night. How trusting for him to have shifted before her. And fascinating. Truly, she found Ed in demon shape sexy. And not at all frightening. Save for those thorns he always warned her about. The ones on his toes must completely recede when in human form because he'd not been worried about hurting her with those when they had sex.

"An antidote," she said suddenly and got up to head into the demon room. "A foray into something else," she decided, knowing when she focused on something too intensely it never came to her. Distraction was always the best cure for finding anything. As well, having an antidote to Ed's thorns could be something she would like to keep handy.

On the way to the demon room CJ waylaid her. He carried a metal bat and wore a catcher's glove. "Want to help?" he asked.

"What's up?"

"Something got out in the demon room last night. An imp."

"Yes, I want to help. Do I need something like a baseball cap?"

"This will do." He tugged a long steel shaker of salt from his back pocket and slapped it into her hand. "I'll distract and attempt to catch the critter. You salt and exorcise. Can you do that?"

"Depends on where I'm sending it. I've not the skill to expel to Daemonia."

"Nothing so demanding. Just back in the book from which it escaped."

A half hour later, CJ closed the book *Lesser Imps* and called teatime. Tamatha sat on the floor near a scatter of books that had been disheveled when CJ had leaped to catch the naked and giggling teddy bear–sized imp. The books on the floor snapped to attention and found positions on their respective shelves.

Blowing away a strand of hair and setting the saltshaker aside, she let her eyes wander over the book spines and gasped when she saw the title *Demonic Breeds and Their Attributes*. Perfect.

Ten minutes later, she had found the section that detailed the corax demon. The text had been written in the sixteenth century and used *f*'s for the *s*'s and had a lot of *thyne*s and *thee*s. Ancient texts gave her a giggle. A very detailed drawing looked only a little like Ed's demon form. But it did get his ribbed penis and thorns right.

And it included an antidote to counteract the poison from the demon's thorns.

She tugged out her phone and typed in the list of ingredients. There were only three, but one of them would prove difficult to obtain.

"Oh, I can't make that." She slumped back against the bookshelves.

The main ingredient in the antidote? A ground corax demon's thorn.

This time the frenzied call from Inego led Ed to the rue Clotilde behind the Pantheon. Not in a cemetery. And too damn close to public houses and streets. Even set back from the boulevard Saint-Michel, the mausoleum attracted lines of tourists, who filed in and out to peer at the lackluster tombs of famous past Parisians. Ed avoided the crowds and tracked the scent of dead witch down a narrow alley that wended into a courtyard lined on both sides by tall hornbeam.

A calico cat mewled and scampered out of his way. Cats never did seem to like him much. He hissed at the retreating feline and then sniffed the air. The scent of death had suddenly vanished.

Ed spun and tracked the retreating cat. Could it have been...?

"A familiar?"

He rushed after the cat, but it dodged under the hornbeam. Making a leap, Ed landed the side of the shrub, grabbing the end of the cat's tail. Wild hisses and claws went at him as he pulled the critter out from under the scratchy shrubbery. Claws cut into his skin, drawing blood.

"You mangy beast!" He let the thing go and it scrambled under the hedge.

Ed turned and sat against the wall of thick, glossy hornbeam, inspecting the cuts that had gone through his shirt. The white linen was stained black with his blood. Never a drop of red. He'd always been cautious not to fight or do anything that might result in his own bloodshed when near humans.

He sensed the skin healing, but nothing would save this shirt.

"They're damned dead witches!" came a hiss from the other side of the hedge.

"What?" Ed turned but couldn't see through the thick shrubbery. "Who's that?"

"I'm the cat, you asshole. You gotta watch it. Almost broke my tail with your grabby hands. Idiot demon."

"Are you a familiar?"

"Well, *duh*. Ouch. This hedge is scratchy."

"Come to this side and we'll talk."

"Really? 'Cause you know the only reason I've a human voice is because I've shifted from cat form."

"Right, but— Oh." Which meant the guy was naked. Familiars shifted much differently than he did. They never retained their clothing because, well, cats didn't wear clothing. One demonic bonus he should be thankful for. "You stay on that side. I'm Edamite Thrash."

"I know who you are, asshole. I've tracked you through the city before. It's what I do. Prowl and observe. Name is Thomas. And you are after dead witches, right?"

"Right. Do you work for them?"

"Hell no. I don't allow witches to use me for the demon-summoning thing. That's crass. And messy. But I can smell those damned witches a league away. Nasty!"

"Were you following one? Until now I've assumed they were contained in the Montparnasse cemetery."

"Yeah? Well, one got out. But I lost her. One minute she was there, the next…poof."

"She just disappeared?"

"Like Houdini. Why are you after those smelly witches?"

"They're killing demons."

"Nothing wrong with that."

If demons hated witches, familiars hated demons on an equal level.

"If they are able to escape what I had assumed were the bounds of the cemetery, that can't be good for anyone. You know what will happen when humans see a zombie witch?"

"Chaos," the cat said. "I'd offer help, but I don't have a clue, man. You need to talk to Ian Grim."

"He's out of town. You know any other warlocks in the area?"

"Pierre Guillebeaux, but he's off-kilter in the head most of the time. Working on some whacked time-travel nonsense. There's Arius, but that warlock is one nasty case. Walks around in one of those stupid frock coats from another time."

A warlock wearing clothing from another time period? Generally that was the case if they had hailed from such a time. Which would make the warlock old enough to have worn frock coats. Perhaps around the eighteenth century, when the witches had burned. That could be his witch. "Who is it?"

"What's in it for me?"

Ed couldn't imagine what to offer a cat shifter. "I'm fresh out of catnip. Sorry."

"Asshole." The shrub shuffled and Thomas huffed in resignation. "Name's Arius Pumpelché. But I don't know where to find that one. Rather, I do, but I value my fur. Talk later, asshole."

And with a disturbance in the hornbeam, and an abrupt meow, the cat scampered off.

Ed pulled out his phone and saw the text from Tamatha. She was researching warlocks and an antidote. In reply, he texted the warlock's name.

* * *

"'Arius Pumpelché'?" Tamatha read Ed's text. "Never heard of him. Or her. With a pompous name like that, must be a man."

The scent of cinnamon tea preceded CJ's entrance into the witch room, where Tamatha had returned to her desk neatly covered with her notes. He set down the tray and poured two cups. She looked up to see he was eyeing her fiercely.

"No," she said in reply to his unspoken but duly felt question. "I have not broken it off with Ed."

"Didn't ask."

"I felt your burning question," she said, sipping the perfect brew. If the man hadn't such a talent with tea, she would—well, she would nothing. He was her boss and she did like CJ. And chasing down imps? It did not get cooler than that. "Sit down, will you?"

CJ landed in the chair opposite her. He poured his own tea and sipped, waiting for her to speak. The man had once been possessed by a war demon, as well as other hideous sorts, including grief, pain and chaos. But one would never guess he was so strong as to endure such a trial from his gentle demeanor. Though she knew he could take out a tribe of vampires with a simple tap of his left finger against one of the powerful spell tattoos on his body.

Tamatha pushed her phone aside, on which she'd been taking down notes, and leaned her elbows onto the table. "Did you know there is a coven of dead witches roaming the streets of Paris?"

"Dead witches?" The man's dark brow arched.

"Zombie witches, to be exact. At least that's what Ed calls them. He's been following them and is determined to ensure they don't harm any more demons."

"Any *more*? That would imply— What's going on, Tamatha? And do I need to bring this before the Council?"

"Oh, no, CJ, you can't. This is something Ed is handling." He being the mafia king or evil overlord, which was a moniker she felt sure he used for street cred. "I don't think he'd like it if I brought in the Council. Besides, you know them. They never get involved."

"Yes, they observe." He sipped his tea. "Is this dangerous?"

"The tea or the witches?"

He smirked.

"I suspect so. They are *Les Douze*."

The dark witch placed both hands, palms down, on the table. His look was so serious, again, Tamatha felt his question.

"I have to help him," she replied. "My grandmother was one of The Twelve. It's a weird coincidence that when Ed was looking for a witch to help him, it happened to be me, someone related to one of the dead witches."

"Coincidence? Not with Thrash."

"CJ, you're going to have to put aside your obvious distrust for the man so I can discuss this with you. He's not like most demons."

"And what are most demons like?"

Her shoulders dropped and she blew out a breath. "I don't know. My studies are so new. I know very few. Cinder is the only other demon I know, and he's not even demon anymore. He transformed to vampire years ago, thanks to Parish. But I do believe demons have gotten a bad rap. Not all are evil."

"I know that. But do allow me my prejudices against demons after having had a dozen trapped within me for months after returning from Daemonia."

He'd been on a spell-collecting adventure and shouldn't

have been there in the first place. "Yes, well, you did go there of your free will. Not like Daemonia is a recommended travel destination."

"Sometimes a man's gotta do—" he waved a dismissive hand between them "—whatever. I'd never try to justify my stupid acts of indiscretion."

"Did a witch tell you things about Ed? Is that why you've such a bad opinion of him?"

"You mean Paisley Burns?"

She nodded. Ed hadn't given her a name, but she could assume that was the witch who had tortured him.

"She was a victim, Tamatha. Thrash had almost killed her."

"Really?" Tamatha placed her hand on his. "Was that before or after she enslaved and tortured him for three days?"

"Oh?"

"She didn't tell you that part?"

The dark witch shook his head and took a sip of tea. She couldn't blame him for forming an opinion based on the witch's story. Which, apparently, had been a story altered to make her appear the victim when really Ed could have died at her hands.

"Doesn't matter," Tamatha offered. "I trust him. Your opinion, while I value it, isn't necessary."

"I had only Paisley's story on which to base my opinion. You believe she really did try to enslave him? Then I will reserve my judgment on the man." CJ stretched his hand across the table and tapped her phone. "What's that name?"

"Arius Pumpelché. Warlock. You know of him?"

"I do. Do you want to hear my opinion on her, or would you prefer to ignore that, as well?"

Certainly was certainly laying it on thick. But she could handle him. "Her?"

"You've heard of Ian Grim, I'm sure."

She nodded. "That warlock has been around since the seventeenth century. But he didn't go warlock until he decided to keep his current girlfriend, Dasha, alive after she'd been beheaded by the guillotine during the French Revolution."

"Yes. Keeping dead things alive is a grave crime against both the Light and the Dark. Arius Pumpelché puts Grim to shame on the scale of Bad Things Warlocks Do. She was banished from the mortal realm after an altercation with demons and witches. Necromancy, actually. She'd tried to bring dead witches back to life."

Tamatha straightened. That sounded like the warlock in question.

"Fortunately, she failed and was exiled to Daemonia. I didn't realize she was back in Paris. How did she get out of Daemonia? Is she in the city?"

"I don't know. It's a name Ed sent me. I don't know how he got it, but we both suspect it must be a warlock who summoned *Les Douze*. Who else could summon a dozen witches who were burned at the stake three centuries ago? And if she's attempted it once before?"

"Yes." He rapped his fingers on the table. "But if someone had summoned dead witches, the warlock would need to be in the city, near the place where he or she summoned the witches. And if Arius is in town, the Council needs to be made aware. You're sure I can't help you with this?"

"I'm not even sure what this is yet. I'm still researching. I know that the demons *Les Douze* once enslaved were the ones who accused them, and now it seems those witches are going after those demons' family. Which might explain how Arius fits in. I just got his—er, her—name, so I'm going to do some more research."

"Is Ed's family involved with *Les Douze*?"

"Why do you ask?"

CJ shrugged. "It's no coincidence you and Ed have been brought together. Your grandmother is one of *Les Douze*. That would lead me to suspect one of Ed's relatives could have been one of the accusing demons."

"Really?"

"It makes weird sense on the greater scale of the universal explanation of things. You two were drawn together for a reason. Maybe the universe is pushing you toward that. I have a bad feeling about this, Tamatha. Sounds like you and Ed might be tied together in a manner that's not necessarily going to result in good news for the two of you. One of you is not going to make it out of this alive."

"That's quite a feeling."

"It's extreme. I'm sorry—I shouldn't guess at things. I am not psychic, nor do I portend futures. But I maintain my belief that Ed is not good for you."

"He's not a mafia king. And you said you were going to reserve judgment."

"Does it matter? I'm only concerned what your involvement with him could bring. Tamatha, I care about you. Both Vika and I do. We don't want you to get hurt."

"I'm a big girl and a powerful witch."

"You are. On the same level as I am."

"Oh, I wouldn't say that."

"I would. You're too humble about your skills. You sent that imp back into the book *like that*."

"It was just an imp."

"Not many witches would have an expulsion spell to hand and be able to react so quickly. If you won't accept my help, you must at the very least keep me apprised of the situation."

"Trust me, I will. And it's not that I don't want your

help, CJ. I'm just not sure yet what help I require. And if you did help, that would require you work alongside Ed, so there is that."

"There is that," he agreed. "But if this gets out of hand, innocents could be harmed."

"We both understand that, which is why I've been ignoring my work today and focusing on this."

"Consider this your work," he said. "Organizing dusty old grimoires can wait. I had better put on another pot of tea. You drink whiskey at all?"

She shook her head and laughed. "I'm not much for alcohol, only the occasional glass of wine. Though I wouldn't refuse croissants if the doorman heads out on break later."

"You got it. So can I ask? How did you and Thrash get together in the first place?"

"We bumped into one another in the alley and I bound him with a spell. Then he sent his minions after me because he thought I was the most powerful witch in Paris."

Certainly's brow rose measurably.

"I know. And he knew. But...you know."

He smirked again. "I guess I do. Talk to you later. Uh, the warlock stuff is down there." He pointed to a particularly dark corner of the room. "Do protect yourself with a white light before touching any of the volumes. And if you can turn off the OCD magic, that would be wise."

"Thanks, CJ."

"Promise me you won't try to contact Arius without my coming along?"

She shrugged. "If she's in Paris, I'll let you know."

Finishing her tea first, Tamatha then approached the dark corner and knelt before the lowest shelf. The books smelled musty and of something rotted. Shadows and fear, perhaps.

Shaking out her shoulders, she closed her eyes and drew up a white light, imagining it spread from the crown of her head and down over her body until it tucked under her toes. There was no way to control her OCD magic. She'd hope for the best.

When she opened her eyes a pulsing green glow had manifested around the shelf of books. She tapped the spine of a red leather volume, but it stopped glowing. She moved on to the next. The blue-bound volume didn't inspire her and it also stopped glowing. The third spine of scuffed brown leather sent a chill up her arm when she touched it. The glow burst so that she cringed back to avoid any residual magic.

"This is the one."

She tugged it out and carried it back to the table, opening it to a random page. The page revealed a sketch of a smiling woman with black hair tugged back in a bun and a prominent nose. She looked positively puritan. In elaborate calligraphy, the name scribed beneath the sketch was Arius Pumpelché.

A green glow again emanated from within the pages and a faint scent of smoke teased the air. The image turned up its head and looked at Tamatha. She quickly slammed the volume shut.

"Shit."

A scurry of shivers raced over her skin and she rubbed her upper arms. Muttering a reinforcement spell, she hardened the white light and formed a virtual shell about her body. It was invisible and she could easily move, but she felt the heavy weight of it against her skin.

Better encumbered by protection than not.

Pacing before the table, she summoned her courage and again opened the book. A drop of black ink that she hadn't previously noticed dribbled across the page of tiny scrawls…and began to write.

That wasn't unusual for the magical volumes she had seen in the Archives. But what was unusual was the message: "You've found me. And now I have found you."

Chapter 17

Ed's mother, Sophie, was always elated to hear from him. They talked perhaps three or four times a year. Last year she had disappeared with her lover Colin Sauveterre, who was Ed and Kir's father. There had been a big stink in pack Valoir right around the time Colin had hooked up with Sophie (before Ed had been born). Kir had grown up believing his father had left the pack because of another woman. A demoness. So Kir had always hated demons.

But that wasn't the real story.

Kir had only recently learned that Colin had been forced to leave the pack after Kir and Blyss's mother, Madeline, had an affair with the pack principal. All Colin had wanted was love. And he had found it with Sophie months *after* leaving the pack and his wife.

"So there," Ed had wanted to say to his brother. But he had not because he valued what little relationship he had with Kir.

And he valued the connection he had with his mother. Sophie had become addicted to V—drinking vampire blood straight from their veins to get a high from the human blood rushing within—and had over the years grown distant. Now she reassured Ed she was clean and she and Colin were starting anew. But she needed to stay out of Paris. Sophie was a wanted demon. The enforcement team Kir had formerly headed while in pack Valoir had wanted to deport Sophie to Daemonia for her crimes against vampires, but Kir had helped her to escape that fate before he himself had been banished. Should she return to Paris? Pack Valoir would go after her and exile her immediately.

"Your grandfather?" Sophie said, after he'd explained to her about the twelve zombie witches and the deaths of the demons he suspected were related to their enslaved ancestors. "His name was Rascon."

"And a surname?"

"That was just it, Ed. I'm sorry. But I do recall some of the others in the Libre denizen that accused The Twelve. Let me think a bit and give you a call back, yes?"

"That would be helpful, Mom. If I can track down their relations, I might be able to prevent more deaths."

"You're always so good, Ed. You get a bad rap from your werewolf brother. But I know, in my heart, you do nothing for yourself and everything for others."

He smirked and tapped the back of the phone with a finger. Good ole Mom. He did try. But sometimes it felt as though he were pushing against a wall of hot lava. Impossible to stop.

"How are you, son? You mentioned a witch was helping you with this. Is she someone special to you?"

"Mom," he drawled.

"Oh, so she is." A teasingly accusatory tone, if there

ever was one. He'd not told her about Witch Number Two attempting to enslave him. Some things a man shouldn't tell his mother.

"I should go," he said. "I've got this mess to deal with."

"Of course. You don't like to talk about yourself. So humble. But you watch out for yourself, son. If zombie witches are going after Rascon's relations, then you are a target."

He hadn't considered that until now. But if he was a target, then so was his mom. It seemed *Les Douze* were operating strictly in Paris. With hope, they would stay contained to the cemeteries and their peripheries and away from his mother.

"I will, Mom. Tell Colin I said hello. You two take care of one another. *Au revoir.*"

He hung up as a knock at his door sounded. He eyed the door, unable to see through it, but certainly he detected that luscious lemon scent on the other side. He rushed to open the door and pulled Tamatha in to give her a hug and kiss her deeply.

"Wow, someone's happy to see me."

"You are a bright beacon, witch. You change the air when you're near me, you know that?"

She splayed both hands open near her shoulders. "No magic, I promise."

"You've bewitched me with your beauty, kindness and heart. That's a special magic."

"You are a charmer, Edamite Thrash."

She tapped his chest—he wore no shirt—and kissed him over the heart. "This design is growing darker. Maybe it's related to the demon killings?"

"I won't know until it's fully formed. You hungry? I ordered in. Got vichyssoise warming on the stove."

"I'll get the wine!"

* * *

After the supper dishes had been tucked in the dishwasher, Ed led Tamatha to the couch with a fresh bottle of wine in hand and two goblets. He sat next to her, kissing her first before testing the Zinfandel. "That's bitter."

"I like it," she offered. "It's dark and mysterious. Like you."

"I feel my mysteries have been revealed to you in the course of the days we've gotten to know one another. I have nothing left to hide."

"Nor do I. Oh, but, Ed." She set the goblet on the coffee table. "I was talking to Certainly this afternoon. He suggested that the two of us may have been brought together for a reason. He thinks it could be one of your relatives who was one of the accusing demons."

"We are on the same page. My grandfather may have been one of the accusers. I didn't mention it to you because I wasn't sure. But if you've the list of the witches' accusers?"

"I do, but I assume these were the human aliases the demons used." She tugged out her cell phone and brought up the list she had copied from the textbook. "Check it out."

He took the phone and scrolled through the list. "Rascon." He handed her the phone. "They're not aliases. That was my grandfather's name. I confirmed it with my mom before you arrived. This is weird." He ran his hands over his temples, resting his palms over his horn nubs. "I don't get it. How could we have possibly been drawn together?"

"I think Arius is very powerful. I'm not sure she was capable of placing the two of us in that alley the first night we met, or if she is even aware of our association, but…"

He twisted a look at her. "She?" he insisted.

"Yes, the warlock is a she. And…she knows about me. She left me a message in one of the books I was looking through for answers."

He turned a gaping question on her.

"It was written in ink as I watched. Something like 'I've found you now.'"

"Hell. Maybe she's the one I've sensed trying to spy on me?"

"It could be. I've been reinforcing my white light to superstrong ever since. Oh, and I've to reinforce your protective wards, as well. I brought supplies today."

"Great. But really? A *female* warlock?"

Tamatha shrugged. "Not so uncommon. But I didn't learn much about her. There was only a short entry about her. Warlock since 1754 because of necromancy. Banished from the mortal realm. No family history. Not even a skills-and-magics list. CJ said she was banished to Daemonia and should still be there. So if she's here in the mortal realm, that means she's escaped exile, which should be impossible for the average witch. But for a warlock, well, I'm sure it's very close to impossible. Even CJ wasn't able to leave Daemonia on his own. His brother, TJ, had to rescue him."

She rubbed her palms up and down her arms. "I'm worried, Ed. I'm not sure my magic will be enough to protect me against a warlock. Or to protect you."

"You don't need to protect me, sweetness." He hugged her against his chest and kissed the crown of her head. "I won't let her hurt you. And you've got your white light."

"Right, but to protect myself from a warlock? I'm not sure. So I've called in backups. Actually, it just occurred to me to do so on the way here."

"Certainly Jones?"

"I'll bring him in if and when we learn it is actually Arius who is behind all this. For now I think I can get the help I need from Verity Van Velde and Libby Saint-Charles. They're equally as skilled as I am. As a threesome we should be able to track Arius, figure out where she is. They should be here soon."

"Here?" Ed stood and looked about nervously. "Why did you invite them to my place?"

"Well, it's where I am, and it's bigger than my *pied-à-terre*, and— Are you upset?"

"No, I just…" He exhaled, his shoulders dropping. "I'm not sure."

"Are you afraid of getting girl cooties in your man cave?"

"I don't think it's so much the girl cooties as—"

"Witch cooties?"

He shrugged and winced, offering his assent to her assumption.

She stood before him and stroked his jaw. "Aw, poor alpha demon is going to have his cave invaded by a bunch of witches and he's not sure he can handle it. You are so precious."

"Tamatha."

"Sorry. I shouldn't tease. But I promise none of them will cause you harm."

"I can look after myself."

"I know you can. But allowing a semicoven of witches into your home has got to be difficult."

"I haven't had much time to process—"

In the kitchen a phone rang. Tamatha rushed to get her purse. "That's mine!"

She said hello to her mother. "It's not late. Only ten. I'm glad you called. There's a situation here in Paris. Yes. Er… I'm going to put you on speaker, Mom. I want Ed to hear this, too." She set the phone on the counter, and Ed sidled up onto a stool next to her.

"Ed?" her mother said. "A new lover, darling?"

"Yes. Ed, this is my mother, Petrina Bellerose. Mom, say hi to Ed."

"*Bonjour*, Ed. Are you taking care of my daughter?"

Tamatha fluttered him a wink and she was pretty sure he blushed.

"Uh, yes?"

"He doesn't sound very sure of himself. How long have you been dating this one, Tam?"

"Not long. We're still discovering one another." She clasped his hand and he pulled it up to kiss. "But he's great. I want him to listen because what I have to tell you involves the both of us in a weird twist of fate."

"Oh, I adore twists of fate. Especially the weird ones. Go on."

Her mother was entirely too cheerful. Tamatha did not want to tell her what she had to, but she could use Petrina's advice. "It's about Grandma Lysia."

"How so, Tam?"

"Do you remember anything about Grandma right before she was burned? Like her friends and allies. Was she associated with any demons?"

"Her lover was a demon. I don't recall his name, but I know it's scribbled somewhere in one of Mom's diaries. Why do you ask?"

"Her lover was a demon? So, could he have been one of the demons who accused her?"

"No, the accusers were humans. I was there. I saw them standing at the fore before the vicious crowd. Utterly common humans."

"Mom, I believe they were demons who had taken corporeal form in human bodies. You know it can be difficult to spot such demons unless you know what you are looking for. And even then."

"Yes, that's true. Hmm… I was quite young at the time.

And in such a state. My mother was to be burned as entertainment for those stupid humans."

Tamatha sometimes forgot the horrors her mother had experienced. She couldn't imagine watching Petrina being marched to the fagots. "Could Grandma's lover have turned against her?"

"Oh, Tam, I don't know. Again, I was young and wasn't overly interested in my mother's love affairs. If it were true, such betrayal would have created a terrible curse—Oh."

Tamatha got the same thought as her mother. She slapped a palm over the tattoo on her biceps. The Bellerose women had been cursed in love since the time of Lysia Bellerose. Could it have been because her lover had sent her to the pyre to be burned alive?

"Are you sure he was a demon?" Petrina pressed.

"No, not until I can get her lover's name and check to see if it's on the list. I've traced the records in some books in the Archives and have a list of the accusers. Do you think the Bellerose curse could have resulted because of Grandma and her lover?"

"If he was demon? I'm sure of it. The witches in our family have a sort of organic pull to magics that are most needed. Much like your OCD magic, Tam. It naturally developed because you're such a stickler for order."

Ed tilted his head curiously. It was one of those questioning looks that told her she might have some explaining to do after the conversation with her mother. She squeezed his hand and shrugged.

"It's very likely," Petrina continued, "that the curse could have formed as a result of your grandma's lover accusing her of witchcraft. Oh, how awful. I had no idea. How does your Ed figure into all this?"

"He's a demon," Tamatha said. "And he's been pulled

into the murders of demons by—" now he was the one to squeeze her hand "—witches raised from the dead. I haven't seen them. Ed has. He suspects they are *Les Douze*."

Silence hummed loudly on the phone.

"Mom?"

"But Mom is… Your grandmother… She's *dead*, Tamatha."

"Not exactly," Ed offered. "I'm sorry to speak so frankly, Madame Bellerose, but I was able to speak to a demon friend before he died—er, due to witches who attacked him. He said *Les Douze* was responsible."

"So Mom is…undead? Someone raised her from the grave? Tamatha, she was ash. I stood there for a whole day following the burning, watching as they shoveled away the ashes and dumped them in the Seine. I was barely able to save some of her ash in a vial. I don't understand."

"I suspect a warlock is involved. Why she would have reason to raise *Les Douze* is beyond me. But these witches seem to be going after demons who are related to the very demons who accused them. Sounds like revenge."

"Over two centuries later?" Petrina asked. "That makes little sense."

"I know." Tamatha sighed. "I'm sorry, Mom. This is weird. But we can't let it continue. The witches have to be sent back to their place of rest or they will murder again."

"I suppose you are right. If they are revenants…" The woman's shudder was heard over the phone line. "Ed's a demon? How did you two meet?"

"She ran into me one dark night," Ed offered, "and before I could introduce myself, she bound me with a spell."

"Good girl," Petrina said. "Your diabology studies are coming along nicely. But the two of you have apparently kissed and made up. Is he good for you, Tam?"

"Yes." She leaned over and kissed Ed on the cheek.

"Did you tell him the family motto?"

"Yes—Love Often," she said quickly.

"Right. Hmm…" Petrina said. "Aristo died yesterday."

"Oh, Mom, I'm so sorry."

"It's fine. We knew it was coming for weeks. The cancer was aggressive. I've his funeral arrangements to deal with and then I'm returning to Paris for a few days. I can't let you deal with this alone. This is my mother, after all. She's… What does she look like, Tam?"

"I haven't seen her, Mom. Ed has. She's not in a good way."

"Of course not. If some warlock has commanded her and the others to her bidding, she can't want that. She would welcome her destruction. I'm sure of it. You have to put her to rest, Tamatha."

"I will. I just needed to hear it from you."

"And maybe you can break the family curse?"

"How so?"

"Well, the ideas are swirling in my brain right now. If Grandma could be reunited with her demon lover, and he apologized…"

Ed gaped at Tamatha.

"If you can get us the name of her lover, that would put us on the path to such a reunion. It could work."

"Yes, I'll have to look for it when I return to Paris. I've her things stuffed away in storage. The two of you were drawn together by Mom's magic," she stated.

"You think so?"

"There are no coincidences, darling. If she's in pain, if she wants free of the malefic magic controlling her, she may have very well summoned the two of you. Is Ed's family related to one of her accusers?"

"Yes."

"That makes sense. Oh dear, if it was his relative who

was your grandma's lover, then the two of you are reliving that union. Ed may bring your death."

"No, Mom. That's…" Yet Tamatha's heart pounded. Her mother never speculated. She spoke from intuition. And her intuition was never wrong.

"I would never harm your daughter, Madame Bellerose," Ed said. "I swear it."

"Perhaps, but that matters little when family magic is involved. Tamatha, must you work with him on this?"

"Yes. We're woven into this together. I trust Ed. He trusts me."

"Then you'd better tell him the complete family motto. Oh, there's the coroner's car. I invited him over to discuss the arrangements. I'm not sure I can keep a tear from my eye knowing what I now know about Mom. Tamatha, please be careful. And, Ed."

"I have your daughter's back. Nothing will harm her."

Petrina sighed. "I'll try to get to Paris tomorrow evening. The next morning at the latest. Love you, Tam."

"I love you, too, Mom. I'll be okay with Ed. Call me as soon as you get to town."

They said goodbye and Tamatha clicked off the phone. Ed caught his head against his palm and watched as she paced the kitchen floor. "Your mother had no idea your grandmother's lover was demon?"

"She was twelve when Grandma was burned."

"Right. Again, I'm sorry. This has to be difficult."

"It is, but like Mom said, if Grandma is being controlled, she must be desperate for her freedom. I have to give it to her. We need to contact *Les Douze* and hope that leads us to the warlock. I hope the others get here soon."

"The coven about to invade my home." He clasped his hands before his chin and offered a wincing smile to her.

She knew this was hard for him. Perhaps she should

have done this at her place, but she felt comfortable here. And she wanted him to be a part of all magics involved. He had revealed himself to her. She would do the same.

"So what's this about the *complete* family motto?" he asked.

Thinking of revealing secrets… Her mother had meant well to bring that up, but could she really tell him? On the other hand, if Petrina suspected Ed could bring her death, wasn't it only fair to explain the dangers to him?

"Love Often," she said. "That's the part the Bellerose women always tell their friends and lovers."

"But there's another part?"

She nodded and kissed him. It was a slow, lingering kiss that didn't need to deepen because the press of their mouths together was enough. A binding that went beyond bewitchery and seemed to combine their very molecules in a giddy bouncing bonding.

"Love often," she offered against his mouth, "because they never last for long."

Ed's right eyebrow arched sharply.

"The curse my mom was talking about is that the Bellerose women's lovers never last long. They either can't handle dating a witch and storm off—those are the lucky ones—or they fall desperately in love and literally go mad with love. They have to be locked up. Or there's the third option."

"I'm not going to like the third option very much, am I?"

"Death," she said. "Usually accidental. Sometimes we bring it on because we just want the man gone. It's that organic magic Mom mentioned, like my OCD magic. It just…occurs. It can be natural, as well. Aristo, Mom's current lover, had cancer. He developed it while dating her. When she said it was aggressive, she meant it. They've only known each other a month and a half. Again, part of the curse."

"You believe cancer can be attributed to a curse?"

"He was healthy when she met him."

He rubbed his chin. "So you hadn't intention of telling me I might develop an expiration date the longer we are together?"

"I was kind of hoping the curse would avoid you. You're cute. I like you," she said in an attempt to lighten the mood. "I'd like to keep you around awhile."

"I'd like to stay awhile. Besides the routine evil-overlord tasks to keep me busy, I do enjoy being with you. A lot. I'd have to be alive to continue to enjoy it."

"Most definitely."

"You don't believe what your mother said about my bringing your death, do you?"

Tamatha sighed. At that moment the door buzzer rang. "My mother's intuition is never wrong," she said as she went to answer.

Verity tossed her deep violet hair over a shoulder and smiled a huge, warm welcome. "Tamatha, it's been too long!" She lunged over the threshold and the witches hugged. Verity was much shorter than Tamatha, so it was a good thing she hadn't put on her heels yet.

"It has been a few years. You are pretty as always. Come inside and tell me all the details of your life. Oh, this is Verity Van Velde, Ed." She skipped over to him and clasped his hand. "And this is Edamite Thrash, corax demon."

"Is that so?" The witch's amethyst eyes performed a once-over of the man. "Pretty."

Tamatha could feel Ed's blush, so she kissed him quickly on the cheek. "Libby will be here soon. And I told her to bring along Vika."

"I thought you said you only needed three witches," he protested.

"Well, I could hardly have invited Libby without her sister. You won't even notice we're here."

Chapter 18

Trying to ignore the presence of four witches sitting in his living room, drinking wine, laughing, giggling and gossiping, was an exercise in never-going-to-happen. Not even notice they were there? Yeah right.

Sitting in the kitchen, nursing a whiskey, Ed picked up that Verity was dating Rook, one of the founders of The Order of the Stake. He knew that man—a vampire hunter—and respected him. So the purple-haired witch checked out. One of the redheads, Vika, was married to Certainly Jones, who was a dark witch who also ranked respectably on Ed's radar. Save for when it came to telling Tamatha bad things about him. Apparently, Jones had not the return respect, but Ed wouldn't hold it against him.

It was the other witch, the curvaceous redhead with a booming voice and a tendency to dance as she talked, who he determined was married to a former soul bringer, who before that was a former angel. Those bastards were all-powerful. And he couldn't ascertain if the dude was merely human now or just resting his abilities. Either way, he'd keep an eye on Libby Saint-Charles, at least, to make sure her husband wasn't nearby.

The conversation had grown quiet, and Ed picked up a few Latin terms tossed about. They were talking about herbs and spells. And Tamatha pulled out the amethyst-hilted athame that she always carried in her book bag. When a clink of metal sounded in the living room, he suddenly felt a curious power fill the entire loft.

He spun on the kitchen stool to see all four witches had pressed the tips of their athames together. A brilliant white light surrounded them in a bubble and then it burst and it blasted him from the stool to land on the floor in a sprawl. His whiskey glass went skittering across the marble floor, leaving a dribble of golden liquid in its wake.

"What the—?"

Tamatha's face appeared above him. "We've supercharged our collective magic. We're ready to go to the Montparnasse cemetery to do a seek-and-find. Together, the four of us should be able to contact The Twelve. You coming along?"

"What about the warlock?"

"If she is involved, we'll try to find out from *Les Douze*, but we want to avoid contact with her until we can be sure. Maybe it would be best if you stayed here." She grabbed his hand and helped him jump to his feet.

Libby sidled over and eyed Ed up and down with a cheeky summation that ended in a smirk of her bright pink lips. "No, let's bring him along," she said. "He'll make good bait."

"Good idea," Vika chimed in. She wore a long black gown and appeared most witchlike to Ed. Add a pointy hat and broomstick? Happy Halloween! "We'll send him in first to lure out *Les Douze.*"

Ed stood there with an open mouth and a strange wonder as the foursome debated his value of serving as the worm on the hook. Tamatha was against it while the other three were perfectly willing to shove him to the vanguard to stand before the crew of zombie witches.

And so was he.

"I'm in," he said. He clapped his hands together resolutely. "Let's do this. You ladies going to transport yourselves to the cemetery? Should I shift?"

"We can do you one better."

Tamatha grabbed his hand, and the witches all clasped hands, Vika finally taking his other hand. He didn't have time to ascertain what their next move was but suspected it involved transport—

Landing unsteadily on dew-moistened cobblestones in the middle of a shadow-darkened graveyard, Ed's next thought was that the witches were nowhere nearby. And he was glad he hadn't needed to shift and fly there on his own. He didn't feel at all drained. Now, if Tamatha could teach him that spell, he could get some good use out of it traversing across the city.

He cast a glance about. "Tamatha?" They must have landed elsewhere during transport.

He stood near a mausoleum that featured columns of stacked skulls around the stone entrance. An icy chill skittered over his arms and up his neck. His feather sigils shivered. The dark felt like ink, liquid yet staining. He could see shapes of tombstones and winged stone angels. Nearby traffic sounds were muffled. A raven cawed, sending a familiar vibration through his bones. It was a warning cry.

And then he heard the growl.

* * *

Tamatha could feel malefic magic thicken the air. Shadows of tombstones and mausoleums were barely visible in the fog that hung like steam about them. She clasped Libby's hand, and she in turn took Verity's hand. All four witches joined hands as the distinct scent of sulfur mingled with a rotting miasma.

"Ed?" Tamatha called.

"Over here. Where are you? I can't see much— Ah hell. They're here."

Heartbeats thundering, Tamatha fought the urge to rush forward to protect him. Instinct settled her. He was a big boy. He could take care of himself. And she would lose her protection if she dropped the others' hands. Together their magic was a force.

"I can't see them yet," she said aloud to the witches. "Let's focus. Call out their master."

Libby began a low humming tone and her sister Vika matched it with a harmony a few octaves higher. Verity whispered Latin for a channeling spell. It would connect them to *Les Douze* if the creatures were open.

And Tamatha finally caught a glimpse of Ed. He ducked a sweeping hand that clawed for his face. The hand was connected to something. She couldn't make it out, but it didn't look human.

While the witches appeared to be reciting Sunday afternoon chants, Ed fought for his life. *Les Douze*, minus at least two, that he counted, came at him full force.

With a sweep of his hand, he repelled the vanguard with a dusting of black sulfurous smoke that should cause most to gag and tear up or even go blind for a few minutes.

Apparently these dead things were not most.

While a few dropped back and began their zombie shuffle toward a tombstone to the left, the others roared toward him. Ed tried a flick of his fingers to repel them. Half went tumbling backward, a few spilling over the remaining who stood.

One particularly aggressive creature flung herself at him, grabbing him by the shoulders. Metallic black gunk leaked from her gaping mouth. It looked like melted hematite, but smelled like the worst rotting fish. He gagged and struggled. Claws cut into his skin. The witch ward burned to his bone. Shoving at the thing didn't manage to push it from him, but it did disconnect one of its arms, which then dangled, caught in his assailant's tattered clothing.

"Bait," he muttered. "What was I thinking?"

Anger suffused his veins.

Tamatha chanted the warlock's name, entreating her to show if she indeed mastered *Les Douze*. Her fellow witches' powers bolstered her own and made her voice clear and strong. She felt the air change and sensed the malefic presence, but she couldn't know if it was from the zombie witches attacking her boyfriend or if indeed the warlock was nearby.

And then she felt the burn on her wrist and saw the dark line tracking her veins. She shook her arm, even while still clasping Libby's hand. The red-haired witch saw the black tracing up Tamatha's arm and swore.

"She's here," Vika said, and the witches silenced. "Show yourself, warlock!"

The zombie witches howled and cawed like banshees. Ed yelped. A furious wind ribboned through the cemetery, redirecting some witches who had gone off course of the demon toward him. Yet they hissed as if they'd been stung by the wind, which had to be the warlock.

Verity dropped hands with Vika and Tamatha and slapped

at her palms, which flamed blue. Her fire magic had activated against her will. She couldn't control the flames.
Vika, a master of water magic, doused Verity's hands with
a shower that instantly steamed to nothing, leaving the fire
lesser but still amber flames.

The warlock was here, and her power was too strong.
Perhaps she even tapped into the combined witches' powers. While the remainder of *Les Douze* retreated behind
tombstones and some into the dark maw of an open mausoleum, Tamatha felt her magic drain. She tapped her first
fingers together, but instead of earth—which she hoped
to use to smother Verity's flames—a sputter of smoke
hissed out.

Libby cried out. Red claw marks cut through the witch's
neck. And Vika clasped her shoulder as blood oozed through
the serrated fabric at her hip. Verity fell to her knees clutching her stomach with smoking hands. She spit out a beetle
and cursed.

The icy pain of talons cut across Tamatha's cheek. Losing strength in her legs, she was the final one to drop. Their
magic dissipated and the graveyard fell silent.

Ed, who lay sprawled behind a grave, twitched. And
then his entire body quaked and she smelled the sulfur.
Shifting, the demon slapped a thorned hand onto a nearby
tombstone and pulled himself up, ebony horns cutting the
midnight air. He growled and clenched his fists. Red eyes
searched the darkness.

"The warlock is strong," Vika said as she inspected her
sister's wounds. "We'll need stronger magic if we're going
to stop that bitch, Tamatha."

"Yes," she said absently, because her focus was on the
demon who marched toward her. He did not look happy.
"Ed?"

"Witch!"

He gripped her by the wrist. Verity cast a sputtering flame at him, but the demon merely shrugged it off.

"I'm sorry—we tried!" Tamatha said, resisting his strong hold, and she was able to pull free, though in doing so she twisted her wrist painfully and something cut her skin. "Calm down, Ed!"

"They would have ripped me limb from limb," he snarled at her in that hollow demonic tone that was far from sexy now. The horns at his temples cut the air with a tilt of his head. "Not so powerful after all," he assessed of her.

"Leave her alone!" Libby grabbed Tamatha by the shoulders and pulled her away from Ed. "Shift back, asshole. You're doing no one any good in that form and someone could see you."

"Witches!" the demon growled. And with a roar that echoed over the cemetery, he then shifted into a conspiracy of ravens and soared up into the sky.

"That was freakin' cool," Libby commented. "Didn't know the guy could do that."

Tamatha shot her a glare.

"Hey, it was. Is he flying away, then? Nice guy. Not."

"Libby," Verity chastised as she checked Tamatha's injuries. She held a palm over the cut on her wrist and closed her eyes.

"Sorry," Libby said. "Ah, the ravens are circling around and swooping back down. So maybe he's not going to abandon you. But maybe he should. No man has a right to grab a woman like he did you."

"He was frightened," Tamatha defended him. "You would be, too, if a dozen zombie witches came after you."

"Point taken. But I only counted ten. Either they've lost two or a couple were hiding." Libby turned to check on her sister.

The ravens flocked close to the ground, but before talons

could touch the cold cemetery pathway, they transformed and coalesced into the dark figure of Edamite Thrash. He shivered, as if a bird shaking out its wings, then let out a moan as the final remnants of the shift left him.

He'd shifted to demon form without volition, and when that happened, it was because he was angry. Angry that he'd been so ineffectual facing a coven of dead witches. They were zombies. Bags of bones and rotting meat. They should have been easy to defeat. Instead, they'd nearly torn him apart.

And the quartet of live witches who had attempted to stave off the zombie-witch attack had served much less than he'd expected from "combined magic." Which had made him even angrier. Not directly at Tamatha, but again, simply because—what the hell? They. Were. Zombies. They shouldn't be that hard to put down.

And once shifted, with the anger racing through his system, he'd gone after the first person he'd seen—Tamatha.

Ed swiped a hand over his head, reactively checking that his horns had completely receded. He touched his knuckles. No gloves to cover the thorn nubs. He hadn't time to put them on at his home before the witches had whisked him away to Montparnasse. What was that? A trace of red blood on the back of his hand? Wasn't his. And the zombies bled weird metallic stuff.

Had he cut someone?

"No, that's impossible. That would poison—"

He rushed for Tamatha but the witch Vika put up a palm, repulsing him as if with an invisible shield. He stumbled backward against a tombstone, catching an arm across the top to keep from going down.

"No, it's okay," Tamatha said as she pushed away from

her friends. "He was out of it. Didn't know what he was doing. Are you okay, Ed? They didn't hurt you?"

That she was more worried about him than herself killed him. She had talon marks across her cheek. Ed nodded but didn't try to approach her again. He could have hurt her with his thorns.

"Let me take care of you, sweetie." Verity pressed her palms against Tamatha's cheek and closed her eyes.

Meanwhile, Libby eyed Ed with an admonishing glare.

"Your bait worked," he spit at the curvaceous witch.

"Yeah, but the warlock's magic was too strong. We're going to have to go at this another way. If we don't have guns big enough to blow her away, we'll have to combine our powers."

"I thought that's what you just did," Ed protested.

"So did I. Back to the drawing board, as they say. We should all head home and search our grimoires for effective magic. I sensed something beyond malefic."

"It was demonic," Vika said, joining her sister's side and smoothing at the torn dress fabric at her hip. "I recognize the feel of it from when CJ was infested with demons."

"Demonic?" Ed asked. "That doesn't make sense. They are killing demons. You think a *demon* is controlling *Les Douze*?"

Vika shrugged. "I honestly don't know. It was witch magic, for sure. Mixed in with the demonic. Weird. Maybe CJ will have some answers. Verity, you want to take Tamatha home with you tonight?"

"No," Tamatha said, though Verity still worked her healing magic on her cheek. "I'm good. I'll go home with Ed."

All three of her friends glanced to Ed. More admonishing witch vibes. He felt them as a cold shiver in his veins. Duly taken. He should have never gone after Tamatha. She did not deserve his anger.

"Your friends don't trust me," he said. "I don't blame them."

"I'll be fine," she said and gasped as her friend pulled her hands from her cheek to reveal smooth, healed skin. "Thanks, Verity. I need to rest. This night has taken a lot out of all of us. Not to mention you, Ed." She tucked a hand against her stomach and wandered toward him. "Will you take me home?"

"Yes." He kissed her forehead and stroked the hair from her cheek. Verity's magic had healed her completely; not a sign of damage on her pale skin. As were the others healed. "We'll be in touch," he said, and then he lifted Tamatha into his arms and walked past the witches.

"Dude, we will be keeping an eye on you," Libby called after him.

"I don't doubt that!" he returned.

And then thinking he had had enough of witches for the evening, and that he only wanted to be home as quickly as possible, he considered flying out of the cemetery with Tamatha in his arms. She would be carried aloft by his conspiracy, but even considering another shift gave him a headache. He was too drained. And he shouldn't risk anyone spying a witch flying through the air on the back of ravens' wings.

He landed the sidewalk outside the cemetery and set Tamatha down. Pulling out his phone, he called for a ride. Twenty minutes later, Inego dropped them both off before his building. He scooped his tired witch into his arms and carried her inside.

He laid Tamatha on the couch and only then did he notice her wrist when her hand fell away from her stomach. "You're cut here. The purple witch didn't heal it?"

"Oh, it's nothing." She grasped her wrist and winced. "Must have gotten it when I…"

She hadn't been involved in hand-to-hand combat with the zombie witches. The only wound she had taken from the warlock had been across the cheek.

Ah hell. No.

Ed slapped a palm over the back of his hand. His thorns were retracted, but the cool, hard thorn nubs were always sharp. He had struggled with her in his demonic form. Had he accidentally cut her?

"Tamatha, is that cut from my thorns?"

She shook her head and closed her eyes, suddenly seeming as if she could drop into the sleep of the dead. The poison from his thorn would infect her and not stop until she was dead.

He shook her by the shoulders. "Tamatha? Tell me!"

"Maybe," she said softly.

"No!"

If his poison were coursing through her system— He hadn't time to consider the horrible reality. He had to act. Fast.

"The antidote. I've got to make it."

"No," she said lazily, and her head dropped to the side. "I'll be…"

He remembered the antidote she had explained to him. Some of it. It involved crushing the demon's thorn and mixing it with salt and…something.

"How much salt?" he asked, shaking her again. She shrugged out of his grasp and he grabbed her by the chin. "Tamatha, listen to me. We don't have much time. The poison will kill you. I need to do this now."

"Will hurt you," she whispered.

"Hurt?" Yes, removing his thorn could have a dire effect. Much worse than a simple hurt. "Fuck that. I'm not going to watch you die."

"But my mother's intuition—"

About him dying? "Is not going to be accurate today. Now help me. How much salt?"

She sighed. Her hand flopped lifelessly over the edge of the couch. "Equal parts."

"Salt. Ground thorn. And…?"

"Whiskey."

"Whiskey?" That sounded random, but he wasn't going to doubt. Not when time was crucial.

He didn't own a single crystal of salt. He had plenty of whiskey. And the thorn. That was going to hurt like a mother, and had irreversible consequences, but that mattered little.

"I knew from the get-go when a demon gets involved with a witch he never survives to the end of the story." Good ole Mom and her faery tales.

Ed dashed into the kitchen and picked up his phone. He called the building concierge and told him he had an urgent need for salt. Any kind. Borrow some from a resident and bring it up. The concierge promised he'd be up in ten minutes.

"Make it five," Ed said and then dashed to the liquor cabinet. He yanked out a bottle of twenty-year-old whiskey and unscrewed the cap. Pulling down a stainless steel mixing bowl from the cupboard, he almost dumped all the whiskey into it, then remembered, "Equal parts."

He'd start with the most precious ingredient. Opening a drawer by the stone, he pulled out a bowie knife.

He called out, "How you doing, Tamatha?"

No reply. Shit. He dashed into the living room and found her lifeless, her hair spilling to the floor like a Sleeping Beauty in wait of the prince's kiss.

Ed rubbed his lips. He was the furthest thing from a prince. Why was this happening? She wasn't supposed to be the one hurt. He was. A shake of her shoulder forced her to mutter drowsily.

"I love you, Tamatha. I'm going to save you." Fuck. He was the one who may very well kill her. "I'm so sorry."

The door buzzer rang. He retrieved the glass jar of salt and shoved a ten-euro bill into the concierge's hand. Door slammed behind him, he knelt and partially shifted so his horns grew out on his skull and his thorns popped up on his knuckles.

Placing the knife blade to the hard base of the thorn behind his forefinger, he dug into flesh and thorn.

Chapter 19

Ed blinked through the pain. Black blood gushed from the wound on the back of his hand. He'd cut through cartilage and what had seemed like bone for the tremendous effort it required to remove a thorn from his knuckle. The thorn landed on the marble floor. He bent forward, clenching his jaw and pressing his fist to his gut. Tears formed in his eyes. He felt sure he'd never experienced anything so painful. And he had taken battle wounds from demons, werewolves, vampires and even zombie witches.

No time to lament the agony. He'd suffer his skin flailed from his body if it would save Tamatha. Even more? He'd give his life for hers.

Grasping the thorn, he dashed into the kitchen, grabbed the mortar and pestle—no idea why or how he owned one, but he was glad he did—and began to grind the ingredient.

Blood spilled from his knuckle, so he switched hands and used his right to crush. No sound from the couch, but he could see the top of Tamatha's head, her goddess hair spilling to the floor. Not moving. He crushed harder, finding it a difficult task, but soon enough, he had reduced the thorn to a black powder.

Grabbing the jar of salt, he cautiously removed the screw-on lid. He could touch salt, but the instant it hit his bloodstream he'd be a goner. He should wrap his hand to cover the wound but he hadn't time. So with his good hand, he carefully sifted into the mortar an equal amount of salt over the crushed thorn.

Whiskey to hand, he tilted back a swallow. It scoured down his throat, but it distracted from the pulsing burn at his knuckles. He poured what he thought was an equal amount into the mortar then mixed it together with a spoon from the drawer. The instant the silver spoon hit the mix it began to steam. He whipped it into the sink.

"Can't use metal, apparently." A burn on the back of his wrist began to sizzle into his skin. "Shit!" He thrust his bloodied hand under the faucet and turned on the water. Must have got a drop of the mixture on his skin when he flicked away the spoon.

Finally, skin cleaned, but his knuckle still bleeding, Ed slammed his palms to the marble counter. A new sigil veined its way about his wrist where he'd been burned by the salt, forming a black, thorned chain. That meant only one thing in the demonic realm: death.

Well, wasn't as if that surprised him.

"I can do this. I have to save her. Then it doesn't matter what happens to me."

But how to administer the antidote?

Clasping the heavy stone mortar to his gut, he dashed over to the couch and knelt. "Tamatha?" She was unresponsive, yet when he laid his fingers against her neck, he felt a strong pulse. "I'll have to wing it for this part."

Turning over her wrist, he saw the cuts made by his thorns, which had not healed. And would not, he guessed, for he had seen the purple-haired witch place a healing touch there. The cuts were thin. If he laid the antidote on them, it wasn't as though they would suck it in. Maybe?

"I don't know what to do next," he muttered. "Shit! What do I do? I need those witches back here."

Maybe there was a way to reach them. Pulling out Tamatha's cell phone from her purse, he was thankful the Contacts listed Libby Saint-Charles. When the witch answered she sounded frantic. "It's Tamatha?"

"She's been poisoned by my thorns," he said. "I've got the antidote mixed up. How do I administer it?"

"Injection."

"I...don't know how to do that. I don't have a syringe." Why was he so damned ineffectual? He could keep the demons in Paris under thumb but he couldn't save one witch? "Libby, she can't die. She means too much to me. She's the only— I love her."

"Chill out, demon boy. Close your eyes and concentrate on me."

"What?"

"Just do what I tell you, or I will hunt you down."

"Yes, I'm listening." Ed closed his eyes and pictured the sassy redheaded witch. An angel lover? Wonders never ceased. Something clattered onto the floor near his knee. He opened his eyes and saw the plastic syringe lying there.

"You get it?" she asked.

"Witch, you do good magic. Okay, I gotta go. I have to do this."

"Listen to me, lover boy. Inject it into her heart. It's the best way to initiate the antidote through her system fast."

"Her heart? But—?"

"Do as I say."

"Yes. Okay. Thanks, Libby."

He tossed the phone aside and picked up the syringe. He tried to grab the mortar with his other hand, but his bloodied fingers slipped over the marble bowl. His hand had gone numb. And a black streak ran up the back of his hand from the severed thorn to his wrist. It felt icy and at the same time burned as if he'd stuck his hand into a bee skep.

Managing the syringe with his right hand, he suctioned up the antidote into the device then leaned over Tamatha. She looked too peaceful, her pale pink lips parted and her skin like milk. Her hair even looked softer, like silk. He kissed her eyebrow and inhaled her lemon skin. Fresh and bright. A witch like no other.

A woman like no other.

He didn't deserve her. But he wanted to be worthy of her.

Positioning the syringe over her heart, he shook his head. What if he didn't do this right? His ineptitude could kill her faster than the poison might. Then her witch friends would come after him and—if that happened he deserved whatever they served him.

"I love you," he said and pierced her chest with the needle. He squeezed in the antidote, then tossed the syringe aside and lay across her stomach, hugging her. "Please don't die. We are good together. My world is brighter when you're in it. Tamatha…"

Her body remained cold and immobile, yet he could hear her heart beating beneath his ear. He grabbed her wrist. The wounds had blackened much like the wound on his knuckles. Something was wrong. Shouldn't she jolt back to life? At the very least, gasp in a healing breath?

A knock at his door startled him. If the concierge had returned he could just leave. "Busy!"

The knock came again, fierce and insistent.

"Go away!"

A mist of red smoke sifted under the doorway and floated into the living room at the end of the couch. It swirled like a tornado contained within a human-sized space, and then a woman formed, sitting on the couch arm near Tamatha's shoes.

"Who are you?" Had to be a shifter. Or a witch. Or— He didn't have time to make friends right now. "Get the hell out of here!"

The woman, with bloodred hair and blue eyes, crossed her arms and closed her eyes. Intent on staying put. She wore a deep green frock coat over a revealing black bustier, tight black leather leggings and laced-up combat boots. A white triangle was etched onto her forehead, and on her chin, vertical white lines flowed down her neck. The symbols looked demonic to Ed.

Who was she? She had broached the wards Tamatha had put on this place, so...

And then he suddenly knew. "Arius Pumpelché. Warlock!"

The woman put up a staying hand when he lunged toward her. "Your rage will kill her, demon."

"And your rage has conjured foul witch zombies. What do you want?"

The warlock pointed to Tamatha, so still, and her lips were turning blue. "You neglected the most important part to making the antidote work."

Ed gasped, his chest heaving. He didn't want to take help from a warlock. But he wasn't a fool. "What is it?"

"The spell."

"Spell?" The bleeding thorn removed from his knuckles had weakened him, and yet his anger threatened to bring on the shift to demon form. His wounded hand tightened and the remaining thorns *shinged* out from his knuckles. The horns at his temples grew halfway. "What is the spell?"

"Touchy, touchy, demon. You watch your anger." The warlock held up her open palm to reveal another sigil painted in white. Ed felt an intense sting in his horns, as painful as it had felt when he'd sliced off his thorn.

"Tell me!"

"For a trade."

"Anything!"

Arius opened her eyes and looked directly at him. "I'll speak the spell and you will bring to me the progeny of those who accused *Les Douze*."

So the warlock could set her zombie witches on them and kill them. "Why are you doing this? Why do you need the revenge? How are you connected to *Les Douze*?"

Arius folded her hands in her lap and looked over Tamatha. "She doesn't have long."

"Just tell me!"

"My husband, Martine, was one of *Les Douze*. Your kind killed him, demon. Now I'll take my revenge."

"Why wait so long?"

"I've been…preoccupied."

Tamatha had said something about Arius being exiled to Daemonia for necromancy. "How did you get out of Daemonia? Witches aren't capable."

"Does it matter? I'm here. And I am an impatient woman. You want her to live?"

Ed spread his fingers before him. The severed thorn was drawing out his vita, stiffening his entire arm. The demonic sigils on his skin were on fire, most especially the one that had been forming over his heart for days.

Over his heart? Could it be? Did the new sigil signify

Tamatha making a mark on his life? He felt the most pain there right now. He couldn't lose her.

He slapped a hand over his heart.

"You take the deal," Arius said, "and you will live to love your witch."

"But I am one of the denizen's progeny."

Arius smiled a slimy curve. "I didn't say how long you would live."

"You don't need my help to bring in the others."

"I will to bring in Sophie. She's gone off radar. Even my demonic magic can't track her."

Ed bowed his head. An arm's reach away his lover lay dying. The warlock wanted his mother? He couldn't sacrifice her life for another...

He glanced to Tamatha. Could he?

"You a mama's boy, Edamite?" The warlock's eyes were cold blue shards. Ed shivered. Or maybe it was his life slipping away. He shook his head. And made his choice.

"Speak the spell," he uttered. "And you have my word I will locate my mother."

"Excellent." Arius began to chant.

And Ed clutched his arms about himself. He hadn't promised he would bring in the denizen, only that he would find his mother. But he had no idea where she was. Thankfully.

Chapter 20

Tamatha gasped in a breath. Her back arched and she shot upright to sitting position on Ed's couch. As she looked over her hands, a residual shimmer of something she recognized as magic escaped her pores and twinkled into nothing as if faery dust. Inhaling, she assessed her physicality. She felt energized, as if ready to go jogging or run a marathon.

Her lover fell to his knees before her and bowed his forehead to her leg. "Thank the heavens Above," he said. "I thought I'd lost you."

And why was that? She couldn't recall... Yes, she could. She'd been cut by his thorns while in the cemetery summoning *Les Douze*. She hadn't wanted to make a fuss about it—to give him any reason to feel responsible—until she had started to fade, and then when she'd begun to panic that something might really be wrong, the poison had quickly taken her breath and knocked her out.

"Oh, Ed." She bowed over him, and he abruptly jerked away, stepping back.

"You can't touch me. Not like this."

It was then she noticed his arm was streaked with black, as hers had been in the cemetery. As well, his hand was coated in black blood.

"The antidote," she whispered, checking her arm and wrist. The black lines she'd seen climbing her arm in the cemetery were gone. "You made it yourself?"

He nodded, clutching his arm. His hand hung there, bloodied and seemingly lifeless.

"Thank you," she said on a grateful hush. "But the antidote required— Oh, Ed, you removed one of your thorns?"

He nodded again. "Don't worry about it. I'm fine. I want to hold you but I don't want to poison you again. It was my fault. I'm not good for you. I could have killed you."

He'd cut off his thorn for her? That was so unselfish, so…loving. "You are in me now."

"You say that like it's a good thing. I don't understand."

"So it worked? Just the antidote? I'm sure there was a spell I was supposed to speak…"

"Nope. Everything's cool. Injected the antidote into your heart. Thanks to Libby, I knew to do that." He winced. "I don't ever want to hurt you, Tamatha, but that killed me to plunge the needle into your heart."

She felt over her chest but everything about her was invigorated and hummed with energy. "I'm good. Please, go wash off so I can hold you. I need to get lost in your arms."

He rushed toward the bathroom, and Tamatha picked up the syringe from the floor. "Thorns, salt and whiskey." She thought of the black veins running up his arm. "What horror has he incurred to save me? Oh, Ed."

Did he really love her? Maybe it had been a reaction, seeing her near death. He was an honorable man. Of course he would sacrifice himself for her. For anyone. It was his nature to care about others and not himself. But what would result from removing his thorn?

Dropping the syringe, she ran upstairs into the bedroom. The shower was running. She spun into the bathroom and sorted through the cabinet above the towel closet, finding some medical gauze and tape. When he stepped out of the shower, wrapping a towel around his waist, she motioned he sit on the toilet seat.

"My healing magic isn't as practiced as Verity's. I need to prepare an altar and speak a spell to heal, but I can do the human thing and bandage you up and send good vibes your way."

He held out his hand and they both inspected the damage. He no longer bled, though he cautioned her against touching the severed base of his thorn for fear that it could still contain poison. After he'd pressed a wad of gauze to his knuckles, only then would he allow her to wrap his hand and tape it.

She traced a finger up his arm. His veins showed in black vines that looked hard and felt cold under her touch. He confessed he hadn't feeling in his hand and could shift his fingers only minutely. Bending his arm at his elbow took effort. And there at his wrist was a dark chain of what looked like thorns. Was it a new sigil or had she missed that one, him wearing the gloves all the time?

"Don't worry about me, sweetness."

Always sacrificing, she thought. He didn't even realize how kind his heart truly was.

"I don't know what to say," she confessed. She knew what she wanted to hear from him. Maybe. She wouldn't force it. She mustn't. He'd shown her how he felt about her. Words should mean little now.

"Come here," he said.

Tamatha wrapped her arms about his neck and melted against him. He shivered and clutched her tightly as he buried his face against her neck and hair. He smelled like soap and cedar and ice, and everything she never wanted to let go of.

"I don't know what I'd do without you," he said. "You've become a part of me. See." He tilted back a shoulder and tapped the sigil over his heart. It was fully formed but not as dark as the rest of his sigils and tattoos, which she took to mean it could darken yet. "That's you. You've imprinted on me."

It did look like the Bellerose family crest. "Wow. It's a rose." She kissed the sigil and it briefly glowed red. "Is that good or bad?"

"Felt great," he said with a smile she really needed after the night they'd had. "Makes me forget the pain in my arm and hand."

"You sacrificed so much for me."

"Sacrifice? Please," he said with a grimace that tried to be joking. "It was very little to save your life." He kissed her and the soft touch lured her deeper into his arms. "Let's not argue. I have you safe in my arms. And I never want to let you go. You tired?"

She nodded. "Immensely."

"Let's fall asleep together. But *after* I put on my gloves."

"I'll get them for you. You crawl into bed. The night has been long and trying. You need the rest more than I do."

She rushed down to the kitchen, where he always kept his gloves on the counter by the door. She grabbed them and then paused. An unfamiliar scent lingered by the door. It wasn't Ed's sulfur or anything remotely familiar. From the zombie witches? No, that had been more a rotting stench.

They'd barely escaped with their lives after the warlock's presence had arrived in the cemetery. She hadn't seen her but had felt her there and had known it was the one she'd read about in the book.

"The warlock?" She tilted her head, drawing in the scent again. Dry, metallic, maybe a hint of sulfur?

Could Arius have been here? But she had put up wards to protect Ed from an intrusion. Wards that, admittedly, she hadn't thought would hold up for long against malefic magic.

Embraced from behind by a man in a towel, she turned and helped him put the glove on over the bandages. "You smell that?" she asked.

"What? Lemons and sex?" He nuzzled into her hair and hugged her against his bare chest. "Come to bed with me, lover. I want to hold you so I know that you are alive."

She ran her fingers down his arm that felt colder than the rest of him, and when she threaded her fingers through his, he didn't clasp them. But he managed to sweep her from her feet and toss her over a shoulder with his other arm. And she forgot about the disturbing scent and hoped he had enough energy for a good-night kiss and snuggle.

Morning shimmered a bright blue beam across Ed's partially opened eyes. He put up a hand to block the light streaming through the stained glass window and noted it was from a section of Jesus's eye. If he hadn't burned to hell living in this place, he certainly could survive a little thing like removing one of his thorns.

Though when he lifted his other arm to try to flex his wounded hand, it felt leaden and he couldn't move the fingers. And the chained thorns had thickened. That was not good. But so long as it didn't travel farther than above his elbow, he could deal. He'd have to deal.

What was foremost on today's must-deal menu was the

warlock's bargain. He'd agreed to bring his mom to the witches in the cemetery. He always kept his bargains. But he hadn't let on that he had no clue where Sophie was. It could take a while to find her. And in that while, surely he and Tamatha could come up with a means to defeat the warlock.

He should probably explain his deal with the near-devil to Tamatha, but then she'd want to make it better. And there was nothing she could do. The bargain was his cross to bear. And apparently, old blue eyes glaring at him from the stained glass was intent on seeing him bear it.

He'd have to call his mother. But he wasn't about to give her up to the warlock. He'd tell her to go deeper, to cease all contact with him. Which meant he needed a distraction for the warlock. Perhaps the others in the denizen?

No, he wouldn't sacrifice one for another. He'd have to hope that Tamatha and her witch brigade could find a way to defeat Arius before it came to that. But really, he wasn't about to rely on anyone but himself to make this right. It was his mess. He'd dig his way out of it.

He got up and decided to dress before Tamatha woke. He didn't want her to see him struggling with his gimp arm. He recalled his mother telling him to take care of his horns and thorns. If one were damaged it may never heal and could seriously weaken him. And to lose a horn or thorn? Death was almost assured.

"Let me stop the warlock before that happens," he muttered as he strolled into the closet and plucked out a black dress shirt.

Tamatha was aware of Ed kissing her and telling her he had work to do at the office. She could stay as long as she liked, but he wanted her to call him later. In response, she squiggled beneath the sheets and wasn't compelled to open her eyes. She was so tired.

But when the sound of the front door closing downstairs clicked in her brain, she couldn't sleep anymore. She was exhausted because she had almost died last night. But worse? Ed could have been torn apart by demons.

"I can't lie around." She slid out of bed and pulled on her clothes. "You want a war, Arius? I'll bring you one. There's got to be a way to stop a warlock. And I'm going to find it."

Before Tamatha could begin to search for more information on Arius, she went directly to the demon room in the archives and pulled out the volume that detailed information about the corax demon. Sliding her finger down the inked text, she passed over the first few pages and tapped the word *thorns*.

"Deadly poison," she muttered as she read the details. "Four on the back of each hand. Thorns grow to full length with anger."

The antidote to the poison was listed, as well. Crushed thorn, salt, whiskey. The words to the spell. And as a footnote in very tiny writing that she had to put on her glasses to read, she learned this: "Thorns regenerate if removed, as do horns. Slow process. Improper healing may cause death."

"Hmm...that's good to know. So if he takes care of the wounds, he won't die from it. Good. I wouldn't have wanted him to sacrifice himself to save me."

But still, it must have hurt tremendously. And it crushed her heart to know he'd gone through such pain for her.

She set the book aside and her phone rang. Her mother announced she'd arrived late last evening and had gone directly to the storage chest in the attic and pulled out her grandmother's things.

"I've been reading Lysia's diary since I got in town. I'm so tired. But, Tamatha, I had to call you before I fall asleep."

"What did you find?"

"Lysia's lover's name was Rascon. She doesn't detail that he was a demon, but there is a notation about the Libre denizen here. Could that possibly be his denizen?"

"Ah, goddess. Rascon is Ed's grandfather's name. And yes, he was a demon."

"So it's as I suspected. You two are living your ancestors' love affair. I'm not sure what to think about that." Petrina yawned over the connection. "I'm coming over after I take a nap."

"I'm at the Archives right now, and I'm on to Ed's when I'm done here. I'll call you later, okay?"

"Be careful, Tam."

She stroked her wrist where the cut from Ed's thorns had healed, yet a dark line remained, as if his ink had imprinted under the layers of epidermis. And then she remembered the crest forming over his heart. From her? It had to be because she'd recognized the design. How wondrous was that?

"I will be careful, Mom. Get some sleep."

Half an hour later, Tamatha returned to the witch room. Certainly had delivered a fresh pot of tea, and she poured her second cup. Ginger cardamom today. It was warm and a little spicy. Perfect to keep her anxiety level reined in.

After much digging, and more than a few failed locator spells, she uncovered the *Book of All Spells* under a pile of warding texts, which made sense because they had completely shielded the book from discovery.

This *Book of All Spells* was a copy of the original, of which a witch who currently lived in America, Desideriel Merovech, was the keeper. Whenever a new spell was created, cast or devised, it was written in the pages. All spells were recorded there. The book was a living thing, a sort of automated Xerox that took down everything the original recorded.

As Tamatha turned the pages, images moved and text rearranged. Whispers of chants, Latin and simple magics were quiet, but she felt them viscerally move through her veins. Scents of must, oil, earth and even the ocean rose.

She found the section on raising the dead. The pages were stale and fragile. Touching it gave her a shiver.

To her, death was fresh, vital and brief. Following death, the bones were returned to the ground or returned to ash. But even before burial, the soul left the body and became a part of the greater consciousness. But zombies? They were vile, wretched doppelgängers of death. Nothing final or fresh about them.

There were quite a few spells for raising the dead. Dead vampires mostly. But as well, dead humans and a few species of paranormals. When she turned to the page that detailed "lifting thyne witches from thee ashy remains," the words briefly lit up in a blink. As if to say, *Stop here, you've found it, this is the page.*

"This has to be the spell that Arius used."

Careful not to touch the paper, for the ink could leach into her skin and impart the malefic magic, Tamatha silently read the spell, being careful not to whisper a word lest it be transformed into something real. The overall spell was simple, but could be enacted only with blood magic. Meaning, in order to raise the dead, one needed the potential zombie's blood or the blood from a close relative of that zombie. As well, a demonic hex was required, which could be performed by only a demon.

"Hmm…" She sat back in her chair, pondering. "Is the

warlock working with a demon? Doesn't make sense if she's destroying demons."

On the other hand, alliances could be twisted. The demon could be the warlock's familiar. Or to really stretch, it was possible Arius could have picked up some demon magic while exiled in Daemonia. That made the most sense.

As well, the warlock needed blood.

Tamatha and her mother were directly blood-related to Lysia Bellerose, but she knew Arius had not access to their blood. So it must be another relative of *Les Douze* she had used to summon the entire dozen. Who? It had to be a relation to Arius. She could have used her own blood then. And if not, she had to have the blood of one of the witches or their relatives.

Tamatha spent the remainder of the afternoon going through the list of *Les Douze*, searching their genealogy and comparing names in their family histories, and when she reached number nine, she let out a hoot.

"He was her husband."

The witch, Martine Chevalier, had married Arius Pumpelché in 1750. Naturally, Tamatha had not picked up on that because female witches tended to not take their husbands' surnames. A few years later Martine was burned at the stake with *Les Douze*. Also noted was that his wife, a fellow witch, went mad with vengeance. She was made warlock but a week after her husband's death and not a year later was bound and exiled to Daemonia as punishment for her crimes.

Tamatha tapped her lower lip. "Arius tried to bring Martine back from the dead. Did she have his blood?"

Daemonia was the Place of All Demons. A horrible place for demons. Likely a literal hell for a witch. She couldn't imagine what the warlock must have endured.

But she was here in the mortal realm now. Or was she?

Tamatha hadn't actually seen her yet. She tapped the line on her wrist. Though no witch could access earth magics from Daemonia. Could Arius?

Could a witch escape from Daemonia? Perhaps a powerful warlock…

"Deep thoughts?"

Startled thoroughly, Tamatha let out a chirp and straightened her spine. Compulsively, she spread her hands over the page in the genealogy book. CJ stood in the doorway, a stack of papers held against his chest.

"Sorry," he offered with a curious lift of his brow. "Have you figured things out?"

"You went to Daemonia," she prompted. "How did you get there and how did you get out?"

"It was a foolish venture. Many vampires were sacrificed to open a portal and gain access. I was trapped there, unable to utilize my magics to get out. If it hadn't been for my brother, TJ, coming in to rescue me, I might still be rotting in that bedamned place."

"Arius Pumpelché was exiled to Daemonia," she said.

"Yes, I told you that."

She turned the book on witch genealogies toward him. CJ studied the opened pages. "She's the one behind raising *Les Douze*," she said. "I know it because I felt her in the cemetery last night."

"You tried to conjure her?"

"We called up *Les Douze* and she came along with them. Not in the flesh, though, so I don't know if she's here in the mortal realm or somehow operating from Daemonia."

"She wouldn't be able to work magic in this realm from Daemonia. Which means she's here. But I can't believe we didn't know about her escape. I should check with Cinder. He keeps the tech stuff in order for the Council. See when it happened or how."

"Yes, please do that. Any information will be helpful."

"We'll have to report this. Which will include your name and Thrash's since you two are working on capturing the warlock."

"I'm cool with that. The Council won't stop us, will it?"

"I'm sure not. You are trying to stop evil, not encourage it."

"Though capture wasn't exactly my plan. I'm hoping to…" Tamatha sighed and pushed the book forward on the table. "I don't know what the plan is. I found the spell for raising dead witches. It requires a demonic hex. Do you think Arius would be capable after spending so long in Daemonia?"

"I'm sure of it. Can you handle this, Tamatha?"

She nodded. "With Ed's help? Yes. Can you handle standing back and allowing me to handle it?"

He considered it a moment, then smiled. "Yes. As I've said, you are very skilled. And if you trust Thrash, then I'm of a mind to see if the demon can redeem himself to me. What's this?" He grabbed her gently by the hand and turned it over to expose the mark left behind from Ed's thorns. He stroked it and flinched, hissing. "That's demonic."

"Really?" She rubbed the skin. It didn't hurt. And she entirely expected it to fade completely. "Ed's thorn cut me last night."

"But that's— Well, you are alive, so that must mean someone had an antidote. Tamatha, this is not what I had in mind regarding him redeeming himself."

"It was an accident. We were battling zombie witches and fighting the warlock's magic. It just…happened." She didn't need to tell him the nefarious details; that Ed had come after her in a rage. "Ed was the one who mixed up the antidote and was able to save me. He cut off his own thorn to do it, CJ. Wasn't that heroic?"

The dark witch didn't show any sign he was pleased. Instead he leaned closer and met her gaze. "How did he get the spell? Did you teach it to him?"

"Well, no. He said he injected me with the antidote and that worked."

"Inject—no. All antidotes require a spoken spell. You know that, Tamatha."

Yes, she did. And what she'd just read about the antidote had remarked a spoken spell. "He did mention Libby helped. Maybe she gave it to him."

"Libby Saint-Charles is involved?"

Tamatha nodded. She wasn't about to tell him his wife, Vika, had been involved, as well. He wouldn't like that. Maybe. She couldn't get a read on CJ. Was he angry or being protective?

Again, he tapped her wrist over the healed wound. "The demon is in you now. Forever."

She'd said much the same to Ed last night. Didn't sound so awful to her. In fact, it felt awesome, as if they'd taken a step further with one another.

"Do you know what happens when a demon bonds with a witch, Tamatha?"

"I, well— We didn't bond, CJ. That's a sexual thing, isn't it?"

"It's this." He tapped her wrist again. "His blood exchange with yours."

"It wasn't exactly blood. It was his crushed thorn, along with salt and whiskey."

"He could have gotten your blood on his thorn when he cut you. And then in turn he injected you with his very essence."

She hadn't considered that. It sounded so not like a

party. "Am I going to turn into a demon?" she asked, feeling a little frightened now.

"Worse," CJ said. "You've given the demon control over you. None of your magic will be able to stop him. If he wants to control you in any manner, he can."

"Ed would never do that."

"If he even thinks it, it will happen. You might learn exactly how much the man cares for you now. I wish there was a spell to reverse this, but he's marked you and you are his now." CJ blew out a breath. "I feel terrible just saying that. I'm so sorry. Perhaps I should request the Council put someone else on this matter with the cemetery zombies."

"No, CJ, I can handle this. You said so yourself. Please, give me a chance," she pleaded. "I trust Ed. Besides, I've made my mark on him, as well."

"How so?"

"The corax demon is marked through life with major events and magics."

"Yes, with sigils on his skin that look much like tattoos."

"My family crest is forming over Ed's heart. It's my mark on him, I know it is."

"You mean that bell-shaped flower you've tattooed on your arm? Interesting."

"What do you think it means?"

"Such a significant symbol that represents your family?" CJ's brow lifted. "My first guess would be that he's in love with you."

Tamatha beamed at that knowledge. Ed hadn't said as much to her, but yes, she liked to think that they had grown that close. Close enough for love? She wanted it from him. But she remained cautious because of the family motto.

"But a more learned guess," CJ added, "would be a death mark. You and that family-curse thing. Don't most of the men you women love eventually die? I'd guess the demon is not long for this world."

"I'm going to go with your first guess."

"You do that. It's no skin off me if the demon dies. Then I won't have to worry about you being controlled by him."

"That's very rude of you. And surprisingly unsympathetic."

"Tamatha, be smart. I know you want the romance and roses, but really? Have you *ever* had a relationship with a man that did not end with his death or him leaving you while he was carted off in a straitjacket?"

She sighed and shook her head.

And then she remembered what her mom had suggested. "But I might have a chance to break the curse. If we can reunite my zombie grandmother with the demon lover who sent her to the stake, then maybe the curse will be lifted."

CJ whistled and shook his head. "Mercy, you need to fill me in on everything."

Chapter 21

Ed greeted Tamatha with a half hug. He wanted to crush her into his embrace but his left arm wasn't cooperating. And still he felt weak and drained. Not up to par. As if he'd shifted to a conspiracy a dozen times in one day.

Would the Bellerose death curse get him, too? He didn't want to think about it.

She noticed his lackluster hug and grabbed his hand. He hissed, but then remembered he was wearing gloves and she wouldn't be harmed.

"Still hurt?" she asked.

"Not so much hurt as…numb. I can't seem to move my arm. Don't worry about it." He kissed her. "I'll recover."

But he wasn't so sure. He'd never heard about a corax demon coming back after removal of his thorns and horns. He was up on all demon activity in the city, but…well, just…but. He didn't know. He didn't want to know, either.

"I wonder if I could whip up a recovery spell?" she said

as she glided into the living room, dropping her purse on the counter as she went by it.

"I'm fine, sweetness."

She turned and displayed the inside of her wrist where he had originally cut her. "CJ tells me we're bonded now," she said. "Maybe I've got some of your demon mojo I can tap into."

He took her hand and studied her wrist. A dark gray line showed where the cut had healed. His heart actually constricted as he looked at it. He'd harmed her. Almost killed her. And she was acting as if it were nothing more than a scratch.

"Bonded?" he asked. "Is that like when my werewolf brother bonded with his faery wife? It's for life?"

"Oh, I don't think so. I believe it's more on the lines that we're inside one another now. We might sense each other, maybe even tap into one another's magic."

"I don't want you trying to make this better. You could make it worse."

"You don't trust me?" She slipped her grasp into his and kissed his fingers. Green eyes peered up at him and those thick lashes dusted the air.

He was bewitched, and happy for it.

"I love you," he said and then swallowed because he hadn't expected to say that. But really? "I mean it, witch. I love you."

She hugged him and he tucked his head down and nuzzled into her hair. "I feel the same way," she said. "It feels fast. But right. You know? But also it feels like destiny."

"You mean like with *Les Douze* and the Libre denizen? I don't know about that."

"We were brought together for a reason, Ed. I believe that with all my heart."

"So we were brought together, meant to fall in love,

to ultimately slaughter your grandmother and see me die from the family curse?"

"Don't put it like that. I think we can break the curse!"

That bedamned curse. Something about him dying because he loved her. So he either died from a lost thorn or because of romance. Could he get a peek behind door number three? "The one where I'm supposed to die?"

"Yes, that one."

She was entirely too chipper about the whole thing, but as she led him to the couch, he dutifully followed. What else could he do? If her family curse didn't kill him, the missing thorn surely would.

He sat and she turned to place her hands on his knees. "My grandmother's lover was a demon named Rascon."

"Rascon? But I told you. He's my grandfather."

"I know! Isn't that oddly cool? Ed!" He loved her enthusiasm, but he was having trouble rising to her level. Because that implied nothing more than a sure death.

"How do you know that?" he asked.

"My mother returned to Paris last night and went through Lysia's things. She found some diary entries about her lover Rascon."

Blowing out a breath, he settled back against the couch. Now things were getting freaky. Maybe there was something to this destiny thing.

Tamatha curled up beside him. "What do you think of that for destiny?"

"It's freakin' weird, if you ask me. What makes you think the warlock didn't bring the two of us together as part of her plot to destroy the Libre denizen?"

"Well, I don't have proof she didn't. But I'm erring on the destiny side. It suits me better. Besides, how could she have known about your grandfather and my grandmother? Wait. Maybe she could have."

He should tell her about the warlock's visit and their bargain. *No.*

"I learned that Arius's husband, Martine, was one of *Les Douze*. He would have told Arius about Lysia's affair with Rascon. Which could explain how she's put the two of us together. But there's no worry. Now all we have to do is get Rascon here to apologize to Lysia and I think we can break the spell."

He gave her such an incredulous look that she actually flinched.

"He is still alive, yes?" she asked.

"He is. I've heard about him now and again, but have never actually met him. Not sure where he is, but my mom would know." And the last person he wanted to contact now was Sophie. "So you want my grandfather to apologize to his zombie lover for sending her to burn at the stake? I'm not sure that's going to go over too well."

"We have to try." She clasped his hand, and while she wasn't wielding the fluttery lashes for seduction, Ed's heart still performed a double beat. "Don't you want to avoid death?"

"At all costs. But there's a lot worse things in this strange realm that can kill me than loving you."

"No, there's not. The Bellerose curse is extremely accurate. If you don't die, at the very least, you'll go mad. I do love you, Ed. I want you to be alive and sane so I can continue to love you."

"Sanity and a heartbeat sound good to me. But you're overlooking the key point here. Even if Rascon did apologize and he and your grandmother kissed and made up, and the curse was broken, there's still the problem that zombie witches are destroying demons. They are controlled by Arius. No long-lost love reunion is going to change that."

"I know. But Arius's husband was one of *Les Douze*.

She's doing this for that reason. All for love. Don't you see? That's her weakness. Love."

"I sense love is the weakness in the hearts of most. I wonder why she waited two and a half centuries?"

"Because she was exiled to Daemonia and she's only recently escaped. CJ is checking the details of that. CJ also said Arius would need the blood of one of *Les Douze* to raise them from the dead. She must have some of her husband's blood. If she were to run out, I suspect the zombie spell would be broken."

Ed swore and stood, pacing toward the stained glass windows that curved about the living area. He recalled Arius's visit. The cherry-red hair. The demonic marks. Had she worn some kind of vial about her neck?

"This is nuts," he said. "This all seems to hinge on lovers and their broken hearts. Why do people do that? What is so special about love?"

Tamatha huffed out a breath, but shrugged. "Love can make a person do strange things."

He turned to her. "How many times have you been in love?"

"I, uh…" She stood and approached him. "Does it matter?"

"Not in the greater scheme of things, but I am curious. You tell me your lovers die or go mad. Did you love them all?"

"Oh, no. I can like a lover and enjoy sex with him, but that doesn't mean I love him. Though I can say I've loved from my heart twice in my lifetime. What about you?"

He shrugged and turned to face the window.

"You have loved?"

"Is it important that I have? Maybe I haven't found the right woman until… Saying 'I love you' means something to me." He glanced over his shoulder. "That's the first time I've said it to anyone."

Tamatha's jaw dropped open. "Your mother? Father? Half brother?"

He shook his head and looked away. So he wasn't one of those gushing emotional kind of guys who liked to hug the world and count daisies. His heart was hard and black. He was demon, for hell's sake. He'd never thought love was something he'd know or deserve.

But when he was with Tamatha he did know. And love? He stroked the back of his hand where the glove covered the bandage. He'd cut off his thorn for her. That meant something. Maybe he'd like to have love for more than the short time her family curse would offer him. If he didn't die from his lost thorn first.

The warmth of Tamatha's hands embracing him from behind settled into him like a sigh. Had he fallen in love only to stand before death's door? He couldn't move his fingers on his left hand to even touch her. What the hell was going on with him?

"I might not have much longer," he said. Because he had to. He wanted to be truthful with her. "I think it's because of the thorn. Removal brings death."

"What makes you believe that?"

"Things my mother told me when I was younger. Tamatha, I'm not right lately. And while the black streak has moved lower on my arm, I can't—"

"It's not the thorn," she said. "Your thorns and horns can regenerate. I read it in a book about demons. Unless the healing goes wrong. But you're keeping it clean, yes? If you feel like you're in pain or suffering, it's because of the curse. Oh, Ed." She moved around in front of him and hugged him tightly. "Call your mother and find your grandfather. We need to break this curse now."

"I can't."

"Why not?"

"I can't talk to Sophie now." Might he risk Arius tracking Sophie with a mere phone call? It was possible if she had tracked him in his own home.

"But that's the only thing that will break the curse, that will save our love."

He turned to her and saw such hurt in her expression. Hell, he had thought he would die to give her life. What was one more sacrifice to win her love?

But his mother? He'd known Tamatha a short time. Maybe it was lust? Which didn't explain the imprint over his heart.

Hell, he could not sacrifice his own flesh and blood for a fleeting romance. It felt wrong. And it felt like destiny.

And he didn't want to believe in destiny.

"I'm sorry," he said. "You should leave now."

Chapter 22

Tamatha wasn't sure if Ed would contact his mother. He'd flat-out refused and then told her to leave. She couldn't imagine that he was angry with her and only hoped it was residual effects from losing his thorn that was making him not nice. Because he had only just told her he loved her. He wasn't going to change his mind so quickly, was he?

Even if he had jumped the gun with his proclamation of love for her, she could deal. It was part of the curse. Men started to lose their minds the longer they were involved with her.

They needed Rascon to break the curse.

So Tamatha came around to thinking if she could heal Ed, then he could think clearly. And what she couldn't do without supplies was now possible with an altar and concentration.

Switching her focus to the spell before her, she closed her eyes and lured her inner senses toward her wrist where

Ed's vita connected her to him. She sat upon a velvet cushion before a small altar on the bedroom floor. Red and white candles were lit for healing. Myrrh burned in a pewter tray. And she was skyclad. She wanted to be as open as possible to anything she might tap into.

Whispering a prayer to all the men who had died or gone mad because they had deemed to love the Bellerose women through the ages, she then ended by saying Ed's full name three times. Her soul reached out to him and she drew on the invisible tendrils that wavered through the air and soared through the city.

And when the tendrils seemed to attach and she gulped in a breath, Tamatha smiled. "Feel me," she said. "And heal."

Pacing the marble floor in his office, Ed paused and glanced to the items on the shelves. The genie in the bottle was quiet, the glass dark. The angel dust had been a trade from one of The Wicked, half demon–half faeries who had escaped their exile in Faery. Their irises were pink and Ed had found an elixir administered by drops to change them to innocuous brown. Many of The Wicked had found asylum in the mortal realm, and thanks to his good relations with them, he needn't worry about policing them as well as the full-blooded demons.

And the alicorn. He paused from reaching for it. Tamatha had remarked the good vibes she felt from it and how sad that had made her. Why had he never considered that the creature might have experienced pain to give up such a thing? That it had very likely been stolen from the unicorn since, indeed, the beast was immortal.

He owned many items of magical nature and some were evil. It had never bothered him. Until now.

Tamatha made him see things differently. And that was a good thing.

He should not have been so brisk with her earlier, asking her to leave. But he'd not known what to do. To explain about his mother would have revealed his alliance with the warlock. Not really an alliance. He'd figure a way out of it. And when he did, Tamatha never had to know.

The alicorn sat upon the dusty shelf, seeming to beam out pink vibrations at him. Good, joy, all that was right. And he knew he should be honest with Tamatha. Completely.

"Damn it," he muttered and marched away from the annoying thing. "I'll tell her! I have to. I could be dead from that stupid family curse soon. She has to know I would do anything for her, even if it meant lying to the warlock."

On his way out, Ed paused before the door. An overwhelming warmth spread in his heart. He clasped his left hand over his chest, then unbuttoned his shirt to reveal the Bellerose sigil over his heart glowed. And his body... hummed subtly. As if sensing an intrusion.

"What the hell?"

Then he realized he was using his gimp hand. He flexed the fingers. Without pain. Complete use had been restored to his hand. He removed the glove and drew his thorns out—all four of them. The one he'd cut off had regenerated. Just as Tamatha had said it could happen.

"What kind of magic...?"

It was magic. Had to be. And it was her magic. He knew it as he knew she was inside him, flooding his veins, healing his thorn. It was a weird intrusion, and he didn't like it. He appreciated the healing, but he certainly didn't want the witch to control him like this. It reminded him of that horrible time he'd almost lost his soul to a witch's enslavement.

Reacting to that sudden anger, he thrust out his palm, as if to shove someone away from him.

Tamatha's body was thrust away from the altar by an invisible force. She landed on the end of the bed and tumbled off to sprawl on the floor. "Ouch!"

A silken spill of a sheer red shawl fell over her shoulders, which she clutched about her. Blowing aside the hair from her face, she saw the candles had ignited the altar. With a forceful breath of air magic, she extinguished the flames. Black ash sifted into the air and seemed to take flight...as if ravens.

"Did *he* do that?"

No. She considered the line on her wrist. They *were* bonded. If she could send him healing vibes, perhaps he could do the same. But he wasn't a healer, so instead what had he sent? It had felt violent.

"CJ was right." Ed *could* control her. And he'd been so rough with her. Had he felt her intrusion and shoved her away? If he loved her, why wouldn't he embrace her?

"I'm not going to make an assumption. I did just control him with the healing."

She'd try something else. Like a simple kiss. Something he should welcome...

This time Tamatha's body slid across the floor and crashed up against the window. The glass cracked but didn't break. Maybe she had tapped into the wrong demon?

When a flock of dark birds battered against the cracked window, she turned and stood, putting up her hands in defense. A little air magic would send them off—

"Ravens?" Was it Ed?

Unwilling to use repulsive magic against her lover, she rushed to the unbroken window and opened the sash. The conspiracy flooded in and flocked about her, their wings hitting her hair and forcing her to pull up the shawl as a shield in defense. When she stumbled and landed on the bed, the ravens shifted.

Ed formed over her, his hands pinning her wrists to the bed, trapping her. "What the hell, witch?"

Her demon lover loomed before her, his gray irises edged in red. He was angry? But she had only tried to heal him. How dare he react so cruelly?

"Get off me!"

Ed stood back, shifting his shoulders to stand tall and defiantly over her.

Tamatha almost cast a repulsion spell, but relented at the last moment. "I was testing the connection. And apparently, you can control me, as CJ said."

"Is that so? CJ told you this? You didn't mention it to me."

"Yes, I…" Didn't she?

"You were the one *inside* me, witch."

She cringed at the tone he used to call her witch.

"What were you trying to do? You have no right! This goes way beyond the whole boyfriend-girlfriend thing. I will not have you fucking around inside my head."

"I wasn't in your head," she argued as loudly as he did. Tugging the sheer red wrap about her did not alleviate her vulnerability. "I wanted to give our bond a try and thought you could use some tender care. I was healing your hand. And I see you've got control of it again." He wiggled his fingers, then curled them into a fist and punched his opposite palm. "You're welcome."

"If you would have let me know you were going to do this, maybe I wouldn't have been taken by surprise. But if you believe you have a right to just jump inside me, no matter the reason—" He swept his hand before her and his black smoky magic soared toward her.

Reacting to the threat, Tamatha repulsed it with air magic, following with a frill of fire on the end.

Ed dodged the fizzling flame. "Is that so?"

"You're forcing me to defend myself!"

"And with such flare. I'll see your flame." He snapped his fingers and a swarm of small black-winged creatures soared toward Tamatha. "And raise you an unkindness."

The miniature flock of ravens dive-bombed Tamatha's hair. She shouted, "*Expulsus!*" And the creatures misted to nothing. "Ed, stop!" She held up a palm to deflect his next move. "This argument is ridiculous. We should both be focused on the more important reason we are together right now."

He gripped her by the shoulders and squeezed not too gently. "You were the one freaked about my being able to possibly control you. And then you go ahead and do the same? Tamatha, I trusted you."

She exhaled. Yes, he had. And she hadn't thought of the implications when she'd prepared the altar to send her healing magic. She'd only wanted to help him. But he was right. She should have asked or, at the very least, let him know what she was doing.

"Sorry." She bowed her head. "I was wrong. You are right."

"No, I don't want to be—"

At that moment the cracked glass in the window cracked even more and fell inward. Ed grabbed her about the waist and charged into the living room to avoid the flying shards.

"What the hell?" he muttered against her hair. "What is going on?"

"You flung me against the window with your reactionary magic. It cracked."

"Shit. I'm sorry. I—I could have hurt you. You could have been cut by glass. I didn't want that. I wanted you out of me." He clutched her against him as if clinging would make her safe. "I love you. But that scares me. That's why I reacted so strongly. What are we doing to one another? I threw magic at you."

"I'll never do it again. I promise. I wanted to heal you."

"Thank you. It worked. I love you for that. I shouldn't have reacted."

"I should have told you what I wanted to do."

"Let's make a vow to never use our bond with one another."

"What if it can help the other?"

He shook his head. "Never. Please, Tamatha—it's wrong."

Much as she didn't agree, because if she could help him and vice versa, she would never neglect that power, she nodded. "Agreed."

With a gesture of her hand and a whispered "*Resolvo,*" the glass window re-formed and fitted back into the wood sill. "Was that our first fight?"

"I think so."

"Wait. That time you had me kidnapped—"

He kissed her. Because he didn't want to bring up the bad stuff. He was glad she was safe, not cut by glass, and hell—she'd attempted to heal him and had succeeded. Not a thing about the two of them warranted further argument. Only falling into this kiss mattered now.

His hands glided over the silky fabric draped about her shoulders. "You're not wearing much. What is it with witches and the whole skyclad thing?"

"It opens us to the full potential the universe is willing to offer. I needed it to reach you with my healing vibrations. Does it bother you?"

"Does this bother you?" He lashed his tongue over her nipple.

She arched her back, lifting her breast higher. "Nope. But maybe you should check the other one. See if that one bothers me."

His mouth closed over her ruched nipple and she clung to his shoulders, wanting to pull him into her, but not wanting to lose the delicious sensation at her breast. "Mmm, yes."

He lifted her onto the couch and licked down her stomach and didn't stop until his tongue found her clit. His hands glided down her thighs and hiked her legs up over his shoulders.

If fighting led to makeup sex like this, Tamatha could do with the occasional argument. What the man could do with his tongue. Her body shivered and she ran her hands through his hair, making a point of gliding slowly and circling his horn nubs.

He growled against her and the vibration of his voice teased her closer to climax. Gripping his hair, she pulled gently but insistently. Right there. Yes, he went deep and followed with his fingers.

"This is the only way I want to be inside you," he said and lashed his tongue over her skin. "You like that?"

"You've got a magical touch," she said on a rising note, and then she gasped out an exalted cry as the orgasm rocked her world.

In the morning, Ed sat up on the bed and grabbed his ringing cell phone. After his argument with Tamatha he'd rethought his priorities. He would do anything to protect his mother, but that meant he needed to keep her in the loop. He'd called Sophie last night and explained his need for her to stay out of sight and also for contact with his grandfather. His mother must have given Rascon his number.

"Uh, hey, Grandfather. This is a little weird, but there's a situation going on in town that needs your involvement."

"I'm delighted to help my grandson. Can we meet?"

"Yes, soon. But I'm afraid there's no time for getting to know one another."

"If what you need me for is so important, I understand. I'll take you out on the town after the problem has been solved. So what is going on?"

"Do you recall a witch lover from the eighteenth century?"

"I, uh… Why do you ask?"

"It seems that after the two of you parted ways, a curse was fashioned. That very curse is now affecting my lover and me. And a warlock has gotten involved, as well. The warlock has been killing the progeny of your former Libre denizen."

"That sounds like a mess. But why the interest in my lover?"

"You remember her?"

"Yes. The witch, Lysia Bellerose."

"You two were in love?"

"What do you need, Edamite? Tell me."

"I need you to apologize to Lysia for accusing her and sending her to the stake."

Silence reigned on the other end of the line. Ed assumed Rascon was sorting through memories. They must have loved fiercely. Surely he would want to make amends by explaining his reason for siding with his denizen and accusing her so cruelly.

"I'm afraid I can't help you with that one," Rascon said.

"I don't understand. You must have been forced to accuse *Les Douze* by your denizen."

"No. No force involved. You see, I was the one who led the denizen in accusing those heinous witches."

Chapter 23

The look Ed gave Tamatha made her sit upright on the bed and press a hand over the sigil on his chest. His heartbeats thundered beneath her touch. So much so that her heartbeats sped up. "What is it?"

"Rascon, please," he said to the caller. "Meet me and let's talk about this." He tossed the phone aside. "My grandfather hung up on me."

"Why? You didn't say a thing about Lysia being a zombie. I don't understand."

"We suspected that Rascon was forced to go along with his denizen in accusing the witches?"

She nodded.

"He was the one who led them in the accusation. He doesn't want anything to do with apologizing to Lysia. So I guess that's that with breaking the curse. At least we can still try to take out the warlock. Because you know, we're so powerful and have all the skills to do that."

His sarcasm set her back. Tamatha clutched the pillow to her chest and watched as he dressed. They had to break the curse. More than stopping *Les Douze*, she wanted the curse broken. So she could have Ed. For longer than most. And if that was being greedy, then sign her up for the trophy. She'd take the greed award and wave it proudly.

"What's the plan for the warlock?" he asked as he buttoned up his black shirt and tucked it in his pants. "Are you witchy foursome working on something?"

"Vika and Libby are digging deep into their family grimoire and Verity is trying to contact Ian Grim. Supposedly the warlock owes her one."

His manner was curt and she sensed he was ready to give up on it all. But he didn't seem like the kind of man who could do that. Otherwise he would be some witch's slave right now.

"What if we could get Arius's husband to somehow tell her to stop?" she asked. "He's one of *Les Douze*. It must be horrible for him to be controlled and to exist in such a condition. Surely he must want it to end."

"Doesn't sound like a party the warlock would like to attend. Or me, if you intend to dangle me as bait again."

"Never. I promise. But you did volunteer to it the first time."

"You don't have to beat me with the stupid stick more than once. I learned my lesson. Though, I'm not complaining. Just don't need to try a stupid thing more than once. What about your Certainly Jones? He's a dark witch. He must have a warlock-fighting trick or two up his sleeve."

"You don't think I can handle this?"

"You alone? No." He stood at the end of the bed, arms crossed over his chest. "Do you?"

"Thanks for the faith."

"We don't need faith, Tamatha. We need a bloody miracle."

"What about the two of us working together?"

"We've tried."

"But now that we're bonded?"

"I thought we'd made a promise not to—"

"To use our bond against one another. But combining forces and working as a team?"

He sat beside her and clasped her hand with his restored hand. Kissing the back of hers, he rubbed the back of it over his cheek, lingering, then said, "We do make a good team."

"Yes, and if Arius has some kind of demonic magic—which we suspect—she's mixed that with her witch magic. So can't we do the same?"

He kissed her. "I love you."

"Really? Because I had thought you might have changed your mind after our altercation last night."

"I was acting naughty. Reacting when I should have merely been grateful. But we kissed and made up, yes?"

"I do like your kisses. Especially the ones right here." She touched her crotch and smiled up sweetly at him.

He bent to kiss her there. "I love you. I love you. I love you. And I'm actually beginning to believe it's real the more I say it."

She stroked his cheek. "Why have you ever thought you were not worthy of love?"

"An evil-overlord thing, I guess."

She snickered, but she knew he was being too hard on himself. And if he'd always believed such, it was a real and tangible emotion that he couldn't simply erase because their relationship had opened up a vein to love. It would take time, and that was cool with her.

"I love that you are willing to love," she said. "Often?"

"Sure. But only you."

"Good answer. So have any more demons been killed since the last?"

"No. But I'm not hanging out in cemeteries keeping watch."

"I thought you'd posted guards?"

"No reports of foul deeds from Inego."

"What if the warlock has no choice but to show?"

"Still pretty sure she's not going to attend any party we decide to throw."

"Ed." She tossed aside the pillow and crawled to the end of the bed. Still naked, she knelt and pulled him to her by the front of his shirt. "If we kidnap her husband, then I think she'll show."

"Kidnapping a zombie witch? Eh. I'm not so sure about that one. Despite their decrepit appearance, those things were strong. I'm not sure I could fight them off if they came at me full force again."

"Have you a better idea?"

"You're serious?"

She nodded.

"Possibly with our combined magics." He shuddered and twisted a look over his shoulder.

"What?" she asked, but no sooner had she spoken than she felt a weird intrusion that shimmered over her shoulders. "Something's in here with us."

"It's the warlock," he said. "Put up wards!"

Tamatha dashed to her altar and scrambled to light the black candle. Her fingers slipped and she dropped her beryl wand. It broke in two. She gasped. She'd owned that wand for decades. It had teemed with the earth's energy and always enhanced her spells.

"Ah, shit."

Ed's utterance did not inspire hope in her. Turning

slowly, she saw the warlock standing in the center of her living room before her boyfriend. She wore skintight red leather, thigh-high boots and a rich emerald frock coat. Her face was marked with white sigils that didn't look like any kind of magical sigils with which Tamatha was familiar.

And in one hand she wielded a menacing ball of green flame.

"*Protegendum!*" Tamatha called up a protective shield before Ed and herself in a flash of white light. The warlock's flames bounced off the shield protecting Ed.

"Thanks," he said. "I needed that." To the warlock he asked, "Are you Arius Pumpelché?"

"You know I am, demon. You had one job to do and you failed."

"A job?" Tamatha asked. "Ed, what is she talking about?" The warlock's smirk crept over Tamatha's skin as if corpse worms. "Ed?"

His hands gripped in and out of fists at his sides. He winced, then tilted his head toward her and confessed, "She wanted me to bring my mother to her in exchange for providing the spell that accompanied the antidote that healed you."

"You broke that promise, demon."

"You said you didn't need a spell," Tamatha said. She'd forgotten CJ's concern that a spell had indeed been needed. "You've spoken with the warlock already?"

"I lied because I didn't want you to know I'd made a deal with this bitch. I was desperate. You were near death."

"Spare me your lovers' squabble," Arius said. "You are fated to die as it is, demon. You, Edamite Thrash—" she touched her throat and squeezed the two white lines together and Ed gasped for breath "—are the progeny of Rascon, who accused my husband of witchcraft. I watched him burn at the stake!"

"Yeah?" Tamatha said, stepping up behind Ed. "Well, wasn't your husband, Martine, one of the witches who kept the Libre denizen captive and controlled them?"

"He was." The warlock straightened, offended at that obvious question. Yet she lowered her head, aiming her gaze on Ed. "They should have been thankful for the entrance to this realm. The demons had no right to accuse the coven so. They gave them life on this realm."

"Life as a slave," Ed defied her through gasping breaths. "Witches have no right!"

Tamatha felt the pain of his suffering in that statement. He knew too well how a demon could suffer at the hands of a witch.

Arius pressed her fingers tighter at her neck. Ed choked.

Tamatha eyed her altar for something, anything she could use against the warlock, but she didn't think herbs and some rose water would help much. Ed was choking but he was strong. And he was still talking, so he was holding in there.

As long as they kept the warlock talking, maybe all she would do was talk. Then she noticed the faint shimmer over Arius's image. And she realized it was just an image.

"She's not here," she said to Ed. "It's a projection."

"Indeed." Arius turned to her. "Stay out of my business, witch, and I'll let your demon lover live."

"You made this my business when you decided to raise my grandmother from the dead. She doesn't want to be a zombie. And I'm going to help her have peace. As well as your husband. How can you do that to him?"

Arius dropped her hand from her neck and Ed sucked in a heaving inhalation.

"Martine knows it's for revenge. I've waited centuries for this. And I won't have two meddling nobodies screwing it up." The warlock thrust out a blast of fire that ricocheted off Ed's shield, as well as Tamatha's, but it ignited on the sheers hanging before the window.

Tamatha pressed her middle fingers together and recited a water spell. Rain spilled from the ceiling, soaking the entire room. It also wiped away Arius's image.

"You took the warlock out with water?" Ed scratched his head. "What next? Flying monkeys?"

"She's not defeated. That was just a message." She ceased the rain spell and pushed her wet hair over a shoulder. "A little air magic should dry things up nicely." With a few recited words and a sweep of her hand about the room, the water evaporated as quickly as it had formed.

Ed pulled her into his arms.

"You okay?" She touched his throat.

"Yes, but she was able to permeate your protection spell. I could feel the demonic magic in it. It was familiar."

"She's obviously studied while in Daemonia. I think if we want to defeat the warlock, we need to turn her revenant spell against her."

"And how do we do that?"

"We get my grandmother and the warlock's husband on our side."

"I've already said Rascon isn't going to help. And I do know the zombies would rather munch on me than listen to anything I've to say."

"Right." She took his hand and turned their palms up. Tracing across the gray line that marked her wrist, she said, "We should be strong together, yes?"

"I'll give anything a try once. Twice if it feels good."

She kissed him. "Then let's go talk to some zombie witches."

"Aw, and here I thought you'd understood what I'd said about doing things that feel good."

"We'll have sex later," she said. "Zombies first."

He followed her down the hallway. "I'm not sure I'm keen on how you prioritize, but okay, then."

They didn't get out of Tamatha's apartment because the front door opened to reveal Petrina holding a faded red leather-bound diary. Petrina's eyes brightened at the sight of her daughter, and she swept in to hug her while Ed stood back, observing. The mother looked as young as the daughter, yet she was decidedly bohemian in fashion. He took that cue from the flowers woven into her hair and the long flowery dress she wore. Beads wrapped both wrists nearly to her elbows, and rings competed with the tattooed sigils marking her fingers.

"Mom! This is Ed."

When Tamatha grasped his left hand, he was again thankful for having got back the feeling in that hand and arm. And when Petrina pulled him in for a hug, he had a moment of wonder when her hand slipped down and over his ass.

"Whoa." He stepped back and bowed, offering a *Namaste* to the touchy-feely mother. "Nice to meet you, Madame Bellerose."

"It's Mademoiselle," she stated with a wink as she breezed by him and into the living room. "Tamatha, I've brought your grandmother's diary— Oh." She paused in the center of the room, looking about. Her nostrils flared. "What was here?"

"The warlock sent a hologram of some sort to give us a warning that we've a battle ahead of us," Tamatha said as she took the diary her mother handed her and began to page through it. "She's a she."

"Really? A female warlock? Makes sense. No man could survive that long in Daemonia with such vengeance in his heart. He'd die after a few years. We women are strong."

"Unfortunate for the poor witches she has raised from

the dead," Ed felt it necessary to point out. "How to fight this warlock?"

"Oh, you are adorable." Petrina stroked his cheek and glided her fingers down to touch the feather sigil on his neck. "Nice. I do love a tattooed man. I taught my daughter well, I see. Are you sure you're happy with this one?" she asked Tamatha. "If not, I could take him off your hands."

"Yes, Mother, very sure," Tamatha offered absently. Her attention was deep in the pages of the diary. Much to Ed's peril.

Petrina circled him, eyeing him up and down. He'd never felt more like a piece of meat hanging in the charcuterie until now. And usually an assessing look like that from a woman should make any man feel great. If not propositioned.

"So you are living in Greece?" he managed when Petrina stopped her gaze at his mouth. "I've heard the water is as blue as a sapphire."

"Yes, sure." She dismissed the comment with a flip of her hand. "So. Fighting a warlock. Let's put our heads together, shall we? Ed, you can put your head against mine anytime."

Thoroughly embarrassed by her wink, he did catch Tamatha's teasing smile. If he survived the mother, he imagined he could stand against a gang of zombie witches and one pissed-off warlock.

Chapter 24

Petrina shivered and slid away from Ed on the couch where she had been sitting close enough to have babies with him. Tamatha overlooked her mother's behavior because she was who she was. Sensual, seductive and flirtatious. She'd never worried her mother would steal a boyfriend before, and she didn't now. What did worry her was the shiver.

"Mom?"

Petrina stood and paced to the window, pushing her fingers through her long blue-silver curls that spilled tiny queen's-lace blossoms in her wake. She was never without flowers, even in winter.

"I can sense your demon lover's death." She turned a sad eye on Ed and clasped her arms over her stomach, shivering once again. "Soon."

"You ladies and your weird family curse." Ed gestured dismissively as he got up and gathered the teacups from their afternoon brainstorming session over how to kill a warlock. "I'm good."

"You don't look it," Petrina commented. "You've gotten paler since I've arrived."

He made a doubting face. "Just some residual stuff from nearly being torn apart by zombie witches, I'm sure. I'm good. Let's get this show on the road. You said you needed some supplies from the graveyard? And that you wanted to try and contact one of the witches without the warlock's interference?"

"Yes, we should get going." Tamatha tucked her grandmother's diary in her book bag and ran into her bedroom to slip on some knee-high boots. She called out, "Mom, get the nightshade from the fridge!"

"Will do!" But when Petrina passed him by, allowing her gaze to slither up and down him, Ed felt as if she had walked over his freshly mounded grave.

He believed the Bellerose curse was real. And admittedly, he wasn't feeling top-notch. But he wasn't about to step back and allow the women to do all the work. They needed him. And he'd die to help Tamatha and her family.

Because he loved her and she was the best thing he never knew he wanted. Crazy maybe. But certainly worth the ride.

He flexed the fingers on his left hand. All functional. So what was making him feel as if he'd run a marathon and could use some oxygen?

The man waiting for them inside the cemetery gates appeared unremarkable to Ed. So much so that he wandered right past him. But Tamatha recognized him from the etching she'd seen in the demon genealogy book.

"Rascon?"

Ed spun around and walked back, putting an arm around Tamatha's waist. Petrina drew up her white light and whispered a demon protection spell.

"Grandfather?" Ed asked.

The man looked about seventy and had gray hair and olive skin. Not at all pale like Ed, but Tamatha had never met his mother, so he could have got his paleness from his werewolf father. Rascon wore boat shoes and a canvas hat and vest along with canvas pants and a gray T-shirt. Unremarkable. Almost had a tourist vibe. One would never pin him as demon. Especially not a vindictive demon who had once sent his witch lover to the stake to be burned alive.

"Yes, Grandson, I am Rascon." He didn't step forward, but Tamatha was well aware he'd taken in her and Petrina. The old man was sharp. "I couldn't let things go the way we left them, so I deduced you were on your way here when I saw the three of you leave the witch's apartment."

"How did you know when I—?"

He must have used demonic magic to trace his grandson from the phone call. Or GPS.

"You followed us?" Tamatha asked. "What do you want? If you're not going to help us—" Ed squeezed her hand, and she decided it wasn't her place to do the condemning. She felt her mother move up close beside her and leach her white light onto her. Thankful for that, she knew with her and Ed's new bond, that light would also protect him.

"If you've come to hinder us, you'll have to go through me," Ed said. "I'm just trying to keep the peace in this city. It's something I've always done."

"I know." Rascon shrugged. "Your mother told me you're a fine young man, what with you keeping a watchful eye over the city and keeping our species in line. You're someone to be proud of, Edamite. I'm sorry, but this one thing in my past won't go to rest, much as I'd like it to. I had to do it," he said to Tamatha. "*Les Douze* needed to be taught a lesson. We were not pets to control. We were *and are* thinking, breathing, living souls."

Tamatha nodded. "I agree. But weren't you in love with Lysia?"

"Eh. It was a ruse. So she would trust me and release me. I was the last one *Les Douze* released. We formed the Libre denizen with the intent of ensuring no witches ever controlled another demon again. It was a lofty goal. We hadn't the skill or the manpower to accomplish such a task. But we did take down a dozen of them. I'm sorry. I know you two are Bellerose women. I can feel it in my veins, the latent command that yet lingers and always will." He shivered. "Lysia was so powerful. But understand that I did it for my freedom. You've much worse to deal with now. Someone has conjured *Les Douze*?"

Ed stepped before Tamatha. "It's not your problem. And I'll have to ask you to leave. I'm sure you'll have nothing against us, once again, putting *Les Douze* to rest, so just… leave."

"Who raised the witches?" Rascon asked.

"Arius Pumpelché," Petrina provided. "Know her?"

Rascon hissed. "Crazy witch. Tried to raise her husband from the dead right after he was burned at the stake. It was a fine day when she was exiled to Daemonia. But she's here?"

Tamatha nodded.

"While in Daemonia," Rascon said, "she used the demons to learn their ways and gather their magics. She is reviled by us all. And she will be a force to fight unless you've demonic magic."

"Which I do," Ed offered.

"Not powerful enough," Rascon said. "Even if you should combine your magic with your witchy lover. Arius is warlock times ten with the added demonic knowledge. I remember her too well, and that was when she was not so powerful." Rascon sighed. "Perhaps you should simply let her complete her act of vengeance then let her slip away."

"So you're cool with her killing your daughter Sophie?" Ed offered. "And me?"

The demon met Ed's question with a startled moue. "Not my Sophie?"

"Arius is after *all* the relatives of the Libre denizen. I told Mom to go deeper into hiding, but unless we take care of the warlock, she'll never be safe." Ed tilted his head side to side, stretching his muscles and gearing up his fortitude. "Like I said, we've got this under control."

"One more demon on your team would only increase that control," Rascon suggested. He stepped forward. "If I can help you take out that bitch of a warlock, then you have me. You have my word I will give my all."

Ed glanced to Tamatha, who nodded. He didn't want the old man involved. He looked ineffectual and weak. And he hadn't wanted to help originally. What gave him hope to trust him?

"Let me protect my family," Rascon offered.

"Excellent," Petrina whispered and gestured to Rascon to follow her. "We're going to summon some zombies. Are you in?"

The elder demon followed the witch. "Zombies are new to me, but I'm always willing to give things a try. Twice if they feel good."

Tamatha glanced to Ed and smiled. She didn't have to say anything. So he'd inherited his grandfather's penchant for reckless adventure.

Rascon agreed to talk to Lysia if they could summon *Les Douze.* That might negate the curse and in doing so gain Lysia as an ally and perhaps even allow her to introduce them to Martine Chevalier. The key to defeating Arius.

Before Tamatha could enter the salt circle she and her

mother had poured onto the cobblestones before a massive family mausoleum, Ed tugged her aside into the shadows created by a mourning angel.

He kissed her slowly, savoring the feel of her mouth on his. Lemons overwhelmed and he smiled. "I love you."

"I love you, too, Edamite Thrash. That's why I'm doing this. I want to break the curse. And now that your grandfather is on board, it's very possible it could happen."

"I still don't trust him. He came to see me too eagerly. And then to return after I'd asked him to do the one thing he would never dream to do? Something doesn't feel right."

"It's love, Ed. Rascon has a love for his family. His daughter. And you. He wants to protect you. Believe in love, will you?"

"I believe I love you." He kissed her again.

"That's all that matters. So you two will need to stay outside the salt circle."

"I have no problem with that request."

"Right, but…" She tugged him back before he could walk toward the circle. "That means you'll be, uh…you know."

He didn't have to think about what she meant before it popped into his brain. "Really? Again? I'm starting to feel like a worm on a hook."

"Yes, but you're a sexy worm. And you're still wearing the white light my mother put over us, so that will help a little."

He shook his arms. "I don't feel it. But that's how it's supposed to be. Got it. Let me do this, then."

He gripped her hand and slid it up over her wrist. Tamatha could see the family crest on his chest glow through his shirt while she felt the heat on the healed wound on her wrist. Their bond was strong. And with a sudden puff of black smoke, she felt as though she'd been covered over with something intangible.

"My style of white light," he said with a smirk. "The double protection should be just what you need. Now come on, witch. Let's go play with zombies."

Nine members of *Les Douze* remained. Ed had taken out one during their altercation the other day, and the other two, well, Tamatha didn't know where they were. She'd asked her mother what Lysia looked like. She'd died before cameras had been invented and no one had ever sketched her.

Petrina had smiled and said how often people had remarked that she had looked so much like her mother. Save that Lysia's hair had been much darker.

Okay, so Lysia was her mother's twin. Zombified.

And which one was Martine? She could pick out at least two zombies that looked remotely male. It wasn't easy looking at any of them. Flesh hung off exposed bone. Metallic ooze stained their tattered clothing. Missing hair and teeth, also, some cheeks missing.

But there. That one. It had to be Lysia. She stood tallest and had most of her hair. It was bluish black, darker than Petrina's but definitely of the same shade. Interesting how as the generations had progressed their hair had got lighter. Tamatha cautioned herself not to slip into fascination.

The zombies shambled closer. Ed and Rascon stood behind the salt circle in which she and her mother stood.

Sprinkling ash from a velvet bag into her palm, Tamatha recited a ward against the dead. Holding up a hand and now reciting a spell, she called on the wind to prevent their approach.

"Lysia?" Petrina called out. And then on a gasp, she murmured, "Oh, *ma mère.*"

The zombie Tamatha had suspected was her grand-mother yanked her head up from its sideways tilt and eyed them both. She opened her mouth and metallic ooze drooled down her chin.

"Oh, Grandmother." Tears wet her eyes. She wanted to embrace the tattered remains of her grandmother and… change her. Bring back her life. But that was impossible. One could never return a person to their original flesh-and-blood mentally-stable state after death.

The warlock was nowhere to be seen. Tamatha must work quickly.

"Rascon," she said, signaling the demon step forward. "Talk to her!"

"Right." The demon's first steps were confident and sure, but after five or six he slowed and his fingers flexed by his sides.

Meanwhile, Ed stepped to the side of the circle beside Tamatha. He reached across the salt line and, with a gri-mace, grabbed her hand. The mark on her wrist blazed brightly and he nodded, teeth gritted. It hurt him like hell to cross the salt line, but he wasn't going to let her go.

Goddess, but she loved him.

The zombie in the lead studied the approaching demon, then snarled. "You lied to me!" Lysia yelled. Her voice was graveled and hollow but she was understandable. "You made me believe you loved me!"

Rascon removed his canvas hat, pressing it over his chest, and put up his hand placatingly. "It was a necessary evil, Lysia. You enslaved me."

The witch hissed at him.

Rascon turned to them and gave a shrug.

"Give it your best," Ed said.

His grandfather nodded and with a breath of bravery

turned back to the zombie. "Please, it's been centuries. Can you forgive me?"

"For doing this to me?"

"I did not bring you back from the dead, Lysia darling. That was—"

"Don't say the warlock's name," Tamatha said quickly. "We don't want to invite her to the party too early."

Rascon nodded. Then he dodged to avoid Lysia when she charged him, but she still caught him about the neck with a clawed hand. The other zombies began to mobilize and get antsy.

"I have to help him," Ed said as he let go of Tamatha's hand and rushed forward to help free his grandfather. A tangle of limbs and shouts ensued.

Tamatha stepped forward, but her mother caught her hand on her shoulder. "Stay safe in the circle, Tam."

But her lover was in danger. He couldn't realize the whole coven was closing in on him. She tried throwing more repellent magic. Flame burned only briefly on the zombies before quickly extinguishing. She was reluctant to use fire. How cruel to wield the killing fire against them once again? And her grandmother. While tugging at Rascon's hair, she flung Ed away into the groping arms of her dead cohorts.

Closing her eyes and spreading the fingers of both hands before her, Tamatha focused on Ed and their connection. "Strength," she commanded and felt the surge of power infuse her system.

"Whoa!" Ed called, and he cocked a grin at Tamatha. "I felt that." Turning, he sent out a wave of demonic magic toward the crowd of zombies. That separated them and sent a few flying.

Yet Lysia was still tearing at Rascon. Ed gestured to throw magic at the twosome. Then he appeared to think twice and instead reached for his grandfather, managing to pull him away from the threat. Fabric tore and Ed landed on the ground at Lysia's feet.

The witch growled and lunged for him. She'd torn his shirt away from his chest. The zombie stopped abruptly before plunging her clawed fingers in through his rib cage. She pressed her palm to the sigil over his chest. "The Belle-rosé crest?"

Wincing at the obvious painful connection, Ed offered, "It's your granddaughter. She's imprinted on me. We are in love."

Lysia jerked her gaze up to meet Petrina, who nodded and said, "This is Tamatha, Lysia. Your granddaughter. She was born over a century after your death."

"My granddaughter loves a nasty demon?"

"He's good, Grandmother," Tamatha said. "He thought he was sacrificing his life to save me a few days ago. Fortunately, his life was spared. But he's weak still because of the curse that was created when Rascon betrayed you. All men who love Bellerose women go mad or die. I want to love Ed forever, Lysia. Please. Help make that happen."

The witch righted in a spitting spray of metallic ooze. She wiped the stuff from her forearm, which showed more bone than flesh. "This was a foul punishment. Why?"

"A warlock brought you and your coven back to seek revenge against your accusers."

"Just so!" Lysia said, slapping a palm to her chest.

"But, Grandmother, the warlock is killing all the accusers' relations. Ed is Rascon's grandson. The warlock wants him dead, too."

"We're trying to break the spell cast by the warlock," Petrina said. "The one who was married to Martine Chevalier."

Lysia cast her gaze toward one of the males wearing tattered damask breeches. Torn lace hung around his neck, which exposed the thorax. One arm was missing. Had to be Martine.

"Exorcise me back to the grave," Lysia said decidedly. "And all will be well."

"All will be well if you can forgive Rascon."

Lysia jerked her gaze toward the demon, who struggled with two zombies, though they seemed to have lost steam and one merely gnawed on Rascon's wrist while he pushed against the other's forehead to keep it at chewing distance.

"A Bellerose woman never bows before a man," Lysia said. "Most especially a demon."

"I require no subservient gesture!" Rascon said as he shoved off the biting zombie. "Nor forgiveness. Simple understanding that I acted to protect those of my breed is all I ask of you. It is what my grandson Edamite does now. And I believe he loves your granddaughter with a true heart, Lysia. He can be trusted as I never could be."

Lysia dropped to her knees before Ed, who still lay sprawled in cautious submission. She placed her hand over the Bellerose crest and he gritted his teeth. When Tamatha made to move for him, he shook his head at her. "I can feel your grandmother's sorrow," he said. "She is in so much pain." He groaned as the intensity of his experience increased.

"Good." Lysia stood, breaking the bond. "Someone knows what I have endured. You, demon, will carry my pain. If you should think to harm my granddaughter, you will know my pain tenfold."

"That will never happen."

"Demons lie. But I hope you are an exception." Lysia nodded. "I release you from my hatred, Rascon, but I will never forgive you." She crossed her arms and wobbled. Once a zombie… "Now, send me back to the grave, if you will."

Not sure if the Bellerose curse had indeed been broken, Tamatha hadn't a chance to ask about it. Green lightning sparked the air around them, zapping a few of the zombies dead. And suddenly standing before them stood the warlock in full demonic tribal war paint. In one hand she held a staff that glowed red and in the other a misshapen creature's skull. Around her neck hung a red vial on a leather cord.

"Let's party," Arius said.

Chapter 25

"Martine!" the warlock called. One of the zombies moved forward from the pack, seeking the commanding voice. "Get behind me, husband."

The male zombie in the tattered damask breeches shambled over behind the warlock.

Ed joined Tamatha's side in the salt circle and clasped her hand. She in turn clasped her mother's hand. She wasn't sure where Rascon was, but he'd served his purpose. Only time would tell if the family curse had been broken.

Right now, she had a more dire problem with which to deal. The vial hanging from Arius's necklace must be blood. The blood of her dead husband? Had to be. It was key to sending the zombies back to the grave.

Petrina began to chant a reinforcement spell that would increase any magic they used. Ed cast up a black smoke that surrounded them in the salt circle. He'd stepped into the circle?

"How'd you do that?" she whispered, with a glance to the salt.

"Must be our bond. I can feel it prick at me, but since your grandmother took her hand off me, I feel a hell of a lot better than I have for days. Strong."

Maybe the curse *had* been broken?

Lysia spit and called out to her coven with a rangy howl that would have called werewolves had they been in the vicinity.

"Yes," Arius directed with her staff. "Gather, witches! There is one of my targets standing before us now. Search for the other! He was directly responsible for the flames that ate away your flesh and blood."

Two zombies shambled off in search of Rascon.

Arius put back her hand holding the staff and Martine grasped it. Tamatha thought he held the staff more for support since his head seemed dangerously close to falling off.

Fingers coved to bracket her head, Arius began to chant. It wasn't Latin, and her voice seemed to double and then break off into unison of horrific sounds.

"She's speaking in demonic tongues," Ed said. "Shit!" His entire body cringed and their bond allowed Tamatha to feel his pain wash through her system. Electric and sharp, it cut at her from within.

"Break your bond right now," Petrina demanded, "or you'll never have the strength to fight the warlock. Drop his hand!"

She did so, reluctantly shaking off Ed's hand, but when he responded by also pulling away, she knew that even though it hurt in her very soul, she had done the right thing.

"Gather flame," she recited and began to draw up her magic.

Arius laughed odd, wicked laughter that crackled like

ice. But when Lysia suddenly turned and began to stalk toward her, the warlock silenced. "Mind your place, witch!"

And Tamatha took a moment to regroup. Zombies were flesh and earth. So a little earth magic... Focusing on the surrounding graves and the little space of land between them, she called up the earth, which exploded around them in a cloud of darkness.

Ed mixed in his dark smoky magic that seemed to adhere to the earth particles and spark when it hit the zombies. Some cried out; others fought against the substance as if it were flames.

A command from Arius shook the electrified earth from the air and it landed with a thump all around them.

Ed glanced over his shoulder at Tamatha. His eyes glowed red. "I'm feeling a bit unkind right now. Pardon me while I try a different tactic."

Spreading out his arms and tilting back his head, he shifted. Black ravens took to air and coiled above the warlock and her unholy crew of zombies. Commanding a breakoff, a single raven from the unkindness dived toward the warlock and snatched the vial of blood in its beak. The warlock's staff caught the end of a feather, but did not hamper its escape.

The raven circled, dodging a flash of green flame as the warlock shouted at it in defiance. Tamatha saw the thing drop from the raven's beak. She held up her hand and caught the vial.

"Destroy it," Petrina ordered.

Dropping the vial, Tamatha crushed the glass under her boot heel and stomped it furiously. A mist of red smoke sifted around her feet. Salt from the circle crept toward the crushed glass and soaked into the blood.

At that moment the zombies shifted alliance and turned on Arius. The warlock's staff shot out random sparks of green, but she could not control her dead minions. Demonic curses filled the night air, crashing against the protective shield Tamatha and Petrina stood behind.

It was the male zombie Martine who shuffled up to Arius and shoved his hand into her chest. The warlock gasped for breath. Martine pulled out her heart and tossed it aside to his cohorts. The feast that ensued was enough to make anyone go vegetarian.

Ed landed inside the circle and shifted back to human form, coming complete with his arms about Tamatha. "You okay?"

She nodded. "Yes, almost finished."

Petrina's chanting grew louder. She sent out exorcising vibrations while Tamatha recited the exorcism, commanding the dead to return whence they came. The zombies responded. As the warlock's body wilted onto the cobblestones, her hair was tugged out and chunks of flesh were taken as repayment for her vile magic. The zombies began to wither. The metallic material gushed from their mouths and ears and noses, and soon there was nothing but a spreading puddle of the shiny substance.

"It's too awful."

Ed hugged Tamatha tighter. "Don't watch. Your mother has it under control." And he swept his hand before him, sending a black cloud over the massacre, obliterating their view. "Rascon has gone."

Tamatha nodded and hugged him tighter. "He served his part."

Petrina stopped and dropped to her knees, exhausted from the spell.

And when the black smoke cleared, nothing remained but piles of ash, still smoking as if a funeral pyre. The white-boned skull the warlock had wielded rolled to the edge of the salt circle and cracked in half.

"We'll bury them," Ed said. "This time for good."

"I can put a fastening spell on them to ensure that," Tamatha said.

"You can?" He pulled her to him and kissed her soundly. "Did I mention that I love you?"

"Yes, but you can tell me again and again. I'll never tire of hearing it."

"Come on, you lovebirds." Petrina snapped her fingers and three shovels appeared before them. "Save the lovey-dovey stuff for later. Pineapple gelatos for all after we've laid my mother to rest."

Epilogue

It was three in the morning by the time they returned to Tamatha's home. Petrina collapsed on the sofa and fell instantly asleep, while Tamatha led Ed into the bathroom and they showered together.

They made slow, quiet love under the spill of warm water. She didn't want to think about what had happened in the graveyard. And pressing her fingers over Ed's skin, tracing the dark ink and following that path with her tongue was a distraction she needed.

As the two of them came, their mouths together and their gasps muted by the connection, she hugged him tightly about the neck as he pumped inside her. "I love you," she managed through tears.

"You've made me believe in love," he said. "And if that isn't bewitchery, I don't know what is."

"Look," she said, holding up his hand. "The thorns chained about your wrist are gone."

"So they are. I guess I defeated the death curse after all. Your grandmother did good work."

"As did your grandfather."

"I'll give him a pass on his strange disappearance. Maybe we'll talk someday. Hey. I made it to the end of the story!"

"What does that mean?"

"It means my mother's faery tales weren't always correct. Kiss me, lover. Give me some more of that love often."

In the morning, the threesome headed out for the patisserie where Ed treated them to croissants and coffees. But they couldn't pass Amorino without stopping in to buy pineapple gelato.

Petrina hugged Tamatha and then handed her her gelato so she could turn and hug Ed. "You be good to her," she said to him. "You may have dodged the family curse, but I'm pretty sure Lysia put a new one on you."

"She did. And not to worry. I adore your daughter and will spend every moment trying to earn her respect and adoration."

"You won't have to try too hard. You're a good man. Cute, too."

"All right, Mom, enough flirting." She handed her mother her treat.

"I'll be going, then," Petrina announced. "All is well in Paris. And I've a plane ticket to Andalusia. I do love those bullfighters."

"You need a ride to the airport?" Ed asked.

"No, I've Jacques, who is always willing to give me a lift when I need one." She winked and blew a kiss to Tamatha. "Love you, Tam. Love often. I think this one will last longer than all the rest." She turned and strolled off, her long pink skirts dusting the cobblestones and her blue-silver hair pulled up in a messy bun.

"I like your mom," Ed said and sneaked a bite off the top of Tamatha's gelato cone.

"Hey! You should have got some for yourself."

"No sharing?"

Tamatha studied her treat. Seriously?

"So that's the way of things, eh? You'll share your magic with me and risk my very life to save a dead family member, but you won't let me have the sweet stuff?"

"But…it's pineapple."

He tucked his nose against her neck and licked her skin. "Good thing I prefer lemon. Mmm…you saved my life," he said. "The curse is lifted."

"We don't know that for sure."

"I do. I feel great."

"That's what they all say. And then hours later they're plastered to the side of a Mack truck or struggling within a straitjacket."

"Sweetness, have some faith in our love. I know your family curse is broken. It's as simple as that."

"Very well. Simple as that. What about Grandmother's new curse?"

"I will never harm you, so I've no worry about that one. If pineapple is your favorite, I don't know what else we can do to celebrate."

"I can think of a few more things."

"Such as?"

She waggled her eyebrows and slid on a teasing smile. "Sex."

"That's always a celebration. You mentioned a *few* things?"

"Yes. Call me crazy—or wait. Don't call me crazy. Call me impulsive, but…"

"What?"

"Would you be my boyfriend, Edamite Thrash?"

"I will. If you can handle being the evil overlord's woman."

"Why don't you make that 'his gorgeous sidekick, the most powerful witch in all of Paris.'"

"Works for me." He kissed her and spun her in a hug that toppled her gelato to the ground. But it didn't matter. Tamatha loved Ed. He loved her. And together they would make bewitching magic.

* * * * *

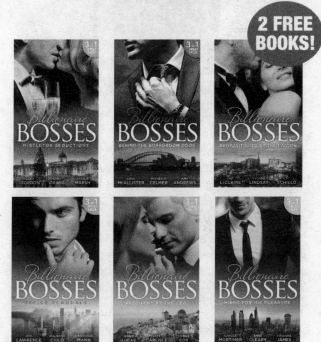

'The perfect Christmas read!' - Julia Williams

Jewellery designer Skylar loves living London, but when a surprise proposal goes wrong, she finds herself fleeing home to remote Puffin Island.

Burned by a terrible divorce, TV historian Alec is dazzled by Sky's beauty and so cynical that he assumes that's a bad thing! Luckily she's on the verge of getting engaged to someone else, so she won't be a constant source of temptation... but this Christmas, can Alec and Sky realise that they are what each other was looking for all along?

Order yours today at
www.millsandboon.co.uk

MILLS & BOON®

Man of the Year

Our winning cover star will be revealed next month!

**Don't miss out on your copy
– order from millsandboon.co.uk**

Read more about Man of the Year 2016 at

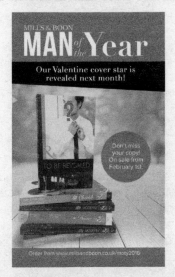

www.millsandboon.co.uk/moty2016

**Have you been following our
Man of the Year 2016 campaign?
🐦 #MOTY2016**